Sisters and Friends in Lavender Bay

The Lavender Bay Chronicles Book 6

Michele Brouder

Part One

Debbie

Chapter One

Present Day

Debbie Melvin stood in the main room of the Lavender Bay Animal Shelter and stared, perplexed, at one of the newer rescues, a beagle named Spotty. The dog had been dumped there the week before, after his elderly owner had passed away and there had been no takers among the deceased's family and friends. When he was dropped off, the relative had said, "He's a little too strange for most." Spotty was now sitting near the bare wall and barking at it.

"Spotty," Debbie called, but the dog did not break his stride or acknowledge her, continuing to bark at the wall, which was painted a cheerful shade of orange, reminding her of a tangerine. He lifted his head, his ears hanging down by his sides, and howled.

She felt sorry for him. She felt sorry for all the animals that ended up there. It was heartbreaking. To not be wanted or worse, to have been abused. She had a soft spot for every animal that came through those front doors. To her, there was no such thing as a bad dog or cat.

As Spotty howled on, she could hear the other dogs back in the kennel join him in commiseration. From the plastic bin by the door, she pulled out a toy—a rubber chicken—and waved it in front of the dog, tempting him.

It worked.

As the dog wrestled with the rubber chicken, Debbie bent down next to him and smiled, stroking and reassuring him.

Sometimes she wanted to pinch herself. She couldn't believe how lucky she was to work there. After her best friend, Angie, had battled breast cancer, Debbie decided to take stock of her own life. She'd been working at the CPA agency for almost eighteen years since graduating from college with an accounting degree, and although she loved numbers, she loved animals more. After many years as a volunteer at the animal shelter, she approached Cyril, who ran the organization, about a more permanent job, and he told her her timing was perfect. He was stepping down to retire, five years later than he'd originally planned, and he put her name forward to the board as a replacement. From there, things happened quickly, and she packed in her accounting job and took the reins at the LBAS. Her appointment coincided with the move to a purpose-built shelter, built with the generous donations of the residents of the small lakeside town of Lavender Bay.

The oddball dog abandoned the toy and as his gaze moved slowly toward the wall, Debbie distracted him again by taking him by the lead. "Come on, you. Time to go back."

He trotted along at her side.

The area that housed the dogs was a space filled with natural light from the large windows that ran the length of one wall. Each individual kennel was made of galvanized steel, and a tiled wall of yellow, white, and mint green separated each occupant from its neighbor. Tiled walls were so much easier to clean. Each kennel had a dog door that led to an outside area.

When they reached Spotty's assigned spot, he hung his head and walked slowly back into his new, but hopefully temporary, accommodation. Her heart tightened. "It's all right, bud, we'll find you a new home."

Spotty curled up in the far corner of the pen. Debbie closed the door, latched it, and looked at the laminated information card attached to the outside of the cage. Beneath the dog's name were a few pieces of information written in black Sharpie: *Beagle mix. Seven years old. Neutered. Vaccinations current.* And finally, trying to play up his weird ways, she'd added, *Loaded with personality.*

She looked around at all the residents. A variety of dogs. The cats were housed on the other side of the building. Currently there were six dogs in residence. She was hopeful they'd find homes for all of them, especially Quint, who'd been there for two years. She glanced at her watch. Time to get back to work. Everyone had been fed and given fresh water. And all had been walked by the volunteers.

She walked through from the kennels to the welcoming lobby, which had a set of skylights that kept the room bright even on the darkest of days. The space was done up in blue, orange, and yellow, with a mix of all those colors in the industrial tile floor. It was an attractive area with vinyl seating, which encouraged visitors to spend time with the animals. An acrylic display was mounted on one wall offering various pamphlets regarding dogs and cats and their care.

Debbie made her way to the office just as her relief was pushing through the front door.

"Hey, Barbara," Debbie said.

"Hi, Debbie. Thanks so much for covering for me this morning." Barbara was sixty-eight, with sharp gray eyes and straight gray hair she wore in a sleek bob. She also had beautiful skin. Her secret: always wear a hat outdoors. She'd been at the animal shelter for eighteen months and was a good and reliable employee.

They spoke for a few more minutes, making small talk and Deb bringing her up to speed about what was going on at the shelter

"I'm going to head off, then," Debbie said.

"Enjoy your Sunday," Barbara said.

"Thanks."

Debbie slipped into the office, which was just off the lobby. It, too, was a large room with a lot of natural light. There were windows everywhere. Although Debbie had been a volunteer when the new building had been designed, she'd campaigned tirelessly for windows in every room. Even the housekeeping closets had skylights.

As she gathered her things off one of the desks, her phone began to ring. Glancing at it, her heart sank when she saw *Mom* flash across the screen. It continued to ring as she debated whether to answer it or not. Was she up for it? Did it make her a terrible daughter if she didn't want to answer a phone call from her mother? This was a question she asked herself on a regular basis. Finally, she caved in and pressed the green phone icon on the screen.

"Hi, Mom," Debbie said with as much cheer as she could muster, which wasn't much.

"It took you long enough to answer the phone," was her mother's greeting.

"I'm at work."

"On a Sunday?"

"Covering for one of the staff."

"You need more backbone, Deborah. Don't let people walk all over you," her mother said.

"All right, Mom."

"Can you stop over?"

"Now?"

"Yes."

"I'm at work," Debbie said again. She didn't want to stop at her mother's. She was actually on her way to Louise Cook's house for the weekly coffee morning, but her mother didn't need to know that. No sense in setting Darlene Melvin's teeth on edge.

"Can you stop after work?" her mother pushed.

Debbie's posture sagged. "Sure."

"What time?"

"After lunch," Debbie told her. The coffee mornings only lasted an hour or two. She'd missed the last few due to previous commitments, so she was determined to go to this one if only for the camaraderie of the Cook clan. The entire experience never failed to buoy her spirits.

"All right, I guess that will have to do," Darlene said, her displeasure evident in her tone.

"See you later, Mom."

She hung up and threw her phone into her purse, then slung her purse over her shoulder and headed out the door, waving goodbye to Barb, eager to get to the coffee morning to relax and see her second family.

CHAPTER TWO

It was a beautiful October day, and the air was crisp. Debbie was glad she'd decided to walk. There was the smell of woodsmoke in the air, and the ground was covered with a blanket of fallen leaves in reds, oranges, yellows, and browns. She loved this time of year: of heavy sweaters, jeans, Halloween, and pumpkin-spiced everything. Some houses already had pumpkins out on their porches. The leaves rustled beneath her feet as she walked over to the Cook house on Heather Lane. She'd been visiting this place for over thirty-five years, ever since she'd met Angie Cook in the second grade. They'd been best friends ever since.

The sun was bright and shone gloriously that Sunday morning. It enhanced the warm fall colors, lending a feeling of vibrancy. She took a deep breath, blew it out, and smiled to herself. Her well-being depended on these small, singular moments of happiness. She'd read somewhere that these moments were called *glimmers*. How she loved that word.

The house on Heather Lane soon came into view. It was a small Victorian done up in olive green, cream, and maroon. A rectangular slate board with the word *Home* on it leaned against the only corner of the small porch. To Debbie, this house and this family were the embodiment of the idea. She smiled to herself again, another glimmer of happiness.

It truly was a beautiful day.

She walked past a few cars parked in the driveway. More were parked out on the street, on both sides. Deb went around to the rear of the house and went through the back door, knocking first before opening it and stepping inside. Immediately, she was hit by an increase in volume of voices and the smell of freshly brewed coffee.

She spotted Louise in the kitchen with her eldest daughter, Maureen.

"Hey, Debs," Maureen called out. "It's great to see you."

"Hi, Maureen."

"There she is!" Louise said, her smile generous. She put down the coffeepot and came over to Deb and wrapped her in a hug. Deb closed her eyes and breathed in the soft signature scent of her best friend's mother: Philosophy's Amazing Grace.

When they pulled apart, Louise studied her face. "We've missed you. I was beginning to wonder what happened."

Debbie laughed. "No, everything is fine. Some family things, that's all."

Louise gave her a sympathetic smile.

Debbie wanted to add that she would rather spend time with *this* family than her own, but felt it would be disloyal.

"Anyway, glad you're here. Take a seat, and grab a mug and a plate," Louise said.

Deb removed her heavy cardigan and looked for a seat around the packed farmhouse table.

"Here, Deb, take my seat." Jim Sloane jumped up from his chair. He and his brother, Tom, had become regulars at the Cook family coffee mornings since Tom had begun dating Angie. Jim operated Lavender Bay's only tattoo parlor, the Ink Stain.

"Oh jeez, I don't want—"

Jim held out his hand toward the now-vacated chair. "Please. I insist."

"Well, all right, if you insist," she said with a laugh.

Esther, cousin to the Cooks, stood and announced, "I'll get some chairs from the spare room."

"Let me give you a hand," said Allan, Maureen's husband.

Jim held the chair out for Deb, and she sat down and looked up at him. "Thanks, Jim." He was always so kind and polite. His brother was the same way. They'd been raised right. She tried to picture her own brother holding a door or pulling out a chair and no matter how hard she tried, she could not get that image into focus.

Esther came over with a folding chair and nudged DeeDee, the youngest of the Cook sisters. "Move over and Jim can sit right here, next to Deb."

"Oh, right," DeeDee said, and she pushed her chair over, resulting in a domino effect of everyone moving their chairs in closer to the table.

Jim took the seat. His cologne was nice. Something spicy but light. He looked at Deb and she gave him a quick smile. Someone handed her a mug full of coffee and an empty plate. To Jim, she said, "Would you pass me the sugar and creamer, please?"

"Sure."

He extended his muscled arm across the table to grab the creamer and the sugar, and she arched an eyebrow. It appeared he didn't miss arm day in the gym.

"Thanks." She poured a liberal amount of creamer and spooned an equally generous amount of sugar into her coffee. She was aware of Jim watching her, and she glanced at his coffee cup. Full of black coffee. With a nod she asked, "Do you not use creamer or sugar?"

He shook his head. "No."

Her almost–milky white coffee made her feel conspicuous. But it was how she liked to drink it.

When she helped herself to a pastry heart from Angie's bakery, Coffee Girl—nobody made them like Ang—she noticed that Jim had no plate in front of him.

"Did you want a pastry heart?"

Jim laughed, and his eyes crinkled in the corners. "No, I'm fine."

She wiped flaky pastry off her lips, aware that he was staring at her mouth. "These are really good. You should try one."

"They look good," he admitted, not removing his gaze from her lips.

She shrugged and took another bite. "It's your loss."

"I suppose it is."

Angie arrived with Tom just then. Angie, all smiles, spotted Deb and waved.

Debbie smiled and waved back, pleased to see her best friend looking so well. Angie seemed to be coming out on the other side of her battle with cancer. Her radiation and chemotherapy treatments were completed, her hair had grown back, and subsequent scans were all clear. Her friend's illness had really worried Deb; she couldn't imagine a world without Angie, who'd been a beautiful anchor for Deb all her life.

Across the table, the last of the Cook sisters, Nadine, moved aside to make room for Angie and Tom. Tom set up two of the folding chairs and held one out for Angie to sit down.

Deb studied her friend. Angie was all loved up. Tom was good for her. He knew how to handle her, softening her sharp, blunt edges. Deb often went over to their house for dinner, and Jim was usually invited to even out the numbers. It was always a lot of fun.

She helped herself to another pastry heart. Beside her, Jim raised an eyebrow.

Debbie grinned. "I didn't have breakfast."

"Breakfast is the most important meal of the day," he said.

"So I've heard."

Across the table, Angie winked at her. Debbie frowned, confused.

Later, full of coffee, pastry, and conversation, she stood and said goodbye to everyone, promising to try and make it the following week.

Jim stood and shifted on his feet. "I better get going too."

They walked out together and paused in the driveway near Maureen's car.

"How's Timmy?" Debbie asked, referring to the rescue cat Jim had adopted after some convincing—some might say strong-arming—from Debbie.

Jim fiddled with his car keys in his hand. He grinned. "He's fine. He's so docile I wish I could take him to work with me every day. The clients would love him."

This brought a smile to Debbie's face. "Probably not the best place to have a cat."

"Probably not," he agreed. "Department of Health and all that."

"You're not working today, are you?"

He shook his head. "Nope. But I've got a lot of yard work to do." Jim had bought a house recently, but Deb couldn't remember the name of the street. His gaze scanned the lawns on Heather Lane. "Mostly raking up the leaves."

"At least you only have to get them out to the curb," she said. The town picked up everyone's leaves. All the residents had to do was blow or rake them out onto the street.

"That's true. But I also need to get the gardens winter ready," he added.

Winter ready? She didn't know that was a thing. She refrained from commenting, not wanting to look stupid, but couldn't help but wonder what that would entail. She had no interest in gardening, and the sorry state of her yard proved it.

"Do you like gardening?" she asked.

He nodded. "I do. I find it relaxing. Being cooped up all week in the shop, I'm always anxious to get outside."

"I like being outside too," she said, realizing it must sound inane. But it was true. The vast open space relaxed her. Joking, she said, "But I'm no gardener. I should see what you could do with my yard. It's a mess."

His expression brightened. "Sure, I could come over and give you some pointers."

Her phone rang. She pulled it from her purse and her eyebrows knitted together when she saw it was her mother.

"I've got to go," she said.

"Can I give you a ride somewhere?" he asked. His truck was parked at the curb.

"No, thanks. It isn't far. And I don't mind the walk." Walking would give her time to prepare for her encounter with her mother. "Take care, Jim."

"Will do."

As she walked away, he called out after her, "Stop by anytime and see how Timmy is doing."

Smiling, she looked over her shoulder and said, "I will."

Chapter Three

Debbie headed east along Heather Lane and turned right on Vine Street, walked two blocks, and then turned left onto her parents' street. Clover Drive sounded nicer than it actually was. In the short ten-minute walk, it amazed her how the landscape changed so drastically. From the tidy, neat Victorians resplendent with three shades of paint to a street populated with small cottages that had been built for the lower middle class. Of all the places in Lavender Bay, it was the only street that boasted a plethora of trees. Dutch Elm disease had swept through the town more than seventy years ago, and it was nothing short of miraculous that the trees on this one street hadn't been affected. It was as if the fungal disease hadn't wanted to settle in on Clover Drive. Now, the oaks and elms were giant and mighty, and in the dead heat of summertime, most of the street was well shaded. However, sometimes Deb found all that shade dark and depressing.

Her childhood home came into view. Number six-teen. It needed a lot of work. Dad was never what you would call handy. It was painted in a shade of mint green, the same color it had always been. And it had been so long since it had received a fresh coat—she'd been a child—that she wondered if they even made that kind of paint anymore. The three boxy shrubs that lined the front of the house were scraggly and had seen better days. There was a slight sag to the porch roof. The porch was bare, devoid of any furniture. Her family had never been the type to sit outside and besides, the view across the street was of the parking lot behind the Dog Days Bar.

She didn't access the house through the front door; she wouldn't have been able to if she'd wanted. Her mother had put a bookcase in front of it despite fam-ily members' protestations that if there were ever a fire . . . But Darlene Melvin had her own ideas about things, and she did what pleased her.

Debbie stepped through the side door and steeled herself.

"Hi, Mom," she called out. The television blared from the living room. It was always on. She didn't know how her mother stood it. Most of the time, her mother barely looked at the screen, which led Debbie to believe that it was merely there for background noise. For a distraction. And she wondered what it was that her mother wanted to be distracted from.

"It's about time, Debbie, you took your sweet time coming over here," her mother said.

"Sorry." Deb didn't explain or defend. To do so would have been pointless. That would have been a treacherous downward spiral. With slumped shoulders, she let her purse slide off her arm until it landed on one of the kitchen chairs.

Her mother was on her perch in the living room. Her perch being her recliner by the front window. Next to her was a table filled with various things, including a bottle of Tylenol and a glass ashtray the color of smoke.

On the other side of the table was another recliner, Deb's father's, which he rarely used as he preferred to stretch out on the couch on the rare occasions when her mother allowed him into the living room. Debbie sat in the vacant recliner and turned to face her mother.

"You never come right over when I call." A cigarette bobbed from Darlene's mouth as she spoke. Her voice was rich with disappointment.

"I'm sorry, Mom," Debbie said, noting it was the second apology within the span of five minutes.

Darlene Melvin was not an unattractive woman. Like Debbie, she'd once been blessed with an abundance of red hair. It was now white and pulled up into a messy bun on top of her head. Often, Debbie thought her mother must have been really pretty when she was young. She was slim—smoking had killed her appetite, and when she did eat, she picked at her food, never fully finishing her meal. Currently, she was padded with a turtleneck, a sweatshirt, and a cardigan. In front of her, some crime documentary played out on the television.

"Where's Dad?"

Darlene shrugged, picked up the remote control, pointed it at the television, and turned down the volume. "Who knows where he goes."

Debbie had an idea, and she was sure her mother did too. Her father had probably walked across the street, cut across the gravel parking lot behind Dog Days, and found himself a stool in the far corner of the bar, where he was a fixture. It was something he'd been doing all his life, from this house, as it had previously been his parents' home.

Jerry Melvin was quite a bit older than his wife. How they ever connected was beyond Debbie. Seized by a moment of not thinking, she asked, "How did you meet Dad?"

Her mother turned her head slowly and frowned. "I don't know. He used to work with my father. He was always around, you know?"

Debbie did not know. "Did he ask you out?" She wondered how that had gone down with her mother's parents, with him being so much older.

Her mother tapped the ash off her cigarette and then folded her arms over her chest. "What is this? Twenty questions?"

Debbie laughed nervously. "No, Mom, I'm just curious. Everyone wants to know how their parents met."

Skeptical, Darlene asked, "Do they? I don't see why."

The television continued to play in the background, and Debbie was briefly pulled out of the moment by the graphic picture of a crime scene, a large scarlet pool of blood on a linoleum floor surrounded by numbered yellow markers resembling tiny sandwich boards.

She turned her attention back to her mother. "I don't know, it's kind of romantic."

Darlene snorted. "Trust me, our beginning had nothing to do with romance."

"That's mysterious."

Her mother pulled a puzzle book off the table and began to flip through it. "Is it?"

"What *did* it have to do with?" Deb asked, thinking if it didn't have to do with romance, what had been the impetus?

Her mother heaved out a large sigh. "Come on, change the subject." She chose a word search puzzle, flattened the crease of the binding, and picked up her pencil.

Obedient, Debbie changed the subject, wondering if there had ever been any romance in her parents' marriage. Although she'd never witnessed it, she assumed there must have been at the beginning. But then again, her father signed all of her mother's birthday, anniversary, and Christmas cards with the words *From Jerry Melvin*.

"What's new with Dawn and Darren?" Debbie asked, referring to her older sister and brother.

"I don't know, I haven't heard from them."

"How are the kids?" she asked of her nieces and nephews.

"Haven't heard from them either."

They weren't the type of family that stayed in touch. Deb's communication with her siblings was spotty at best. She wished they could be more like the Cook family. But wishing and hoping didn't make it so.

"You know what we should do?" Debbie said.

"No, what?" her mother replied, not lifting her gaze from her word search, circling letters on a diagonal with her pencil.

"We should get together once in a while." She'd almost said *weekly* but thought, *Baby steps*.

Her mother looked up. "Who?"

Debbie plowed on. "Us. You, me, Dad, Darren, and Dawn, and the kids if they want to."

"For what?"

Debbie shrugged, frustrated her mother didn't get it. "To stay in touch. To spend time together."

Darlene looked at her daughter like she was speaking a foreign language, and she didn't understand one word of it.

Debbie forged on. "You know, we could have coffee—"

"I don't drink coffee," her mother said.

"Or tea. Or Pepsi," Debbie said. "And we could have something to eat. Donuts. Pastries."

"And where would we do this?"

"Right here," Debbie replied with a glance over to the dining room table, which was never used. It was covered in *stuff*. Mostly items purchased from late-night infomercials, with the red sticker that screamed *AS SEEN ON TV*. There were all sorts of items: copper socks, a pillow pad, a tub of universal cleaner, a portable air conditioner, a miracle bra. The chairs were similarly burdened.

"And who would do all the cleanup?" her mother asked.

"I could do that," Debbie replied. But the more the idea floated out there around them, the less enthusiastic she became. Reality set in as she realized she wanted her family to be something they couldn't be.

"That wouldn't work," her mother finally pronounced. Her answer was expected, but it took a moment to get to it, as if she might have considered it, however briefly.

Debbie remained silent, her energy depleted.

"There is a reason I wanted you to come over," Darlene said.

Debbie waited.

Her mother pulled out her wallet from her purse, which she kept on the floor next to her chair. "I was hoping you could do some shopping for me. I've got nothing here for dinner."

"Sure, Mom."

"There's only a few things on the list." Darlene unfolded a piece of notepaper and looked it over before handing it over to Debbie along with a few bills.

Debbie glanced at the list. It was more than a few things. It looked like the weekly grocery shopping.

"Oh, and get me some liver from the butcher."

"Mom, the butcher is closed on Sundays."

Her mother swore under her breath. "All right. Look at the pork chops. But make sure they're nice looking. Nothing scraggly."

"Okay." Deb stood. The visit was over. The task to be completed handed over. There was no further reason to stay or hang out.

Darlene looked up at her. "Now, you're not going to get lost, are you? You'll come right back?"

Debbie nodded and put the grocery list and the money in her purse.

As she walked out, her mother called after her, "And don't forget to bring me the receipt and the change."

Debbie closed the door behind her and stepped outside, feeling both anxious and relieved. Anxious as she always was after visiting her mother, and relieved to be outside in the fresh air and sunshine.

CHAPTER FOUR

The following week, Debbie was at work, putting up Halloween decorations throughout the lobby and in the front window. It was after lunch, and all the dogs had been walked and fed by the volunteers. Barbara was in the back, tending to the cats. A box of kittens had been dumped on the highway over the weekend, and a Good Samaritan had brought them to the shelter. Of the three, one had already passed away. This upset Debbie. She also worried and wondered about the fate of the mother. She'd seen mother cats who'd lost their litters through death or misadventure, and they could become very depressed. It was difficult to watch.

They'd put the kittens in a small room off the cat section, in a plastic tub lined with a heating pad set on low. Anxiety drove Debbie to keep checking the heating pad and reminding staff to do the same. The priority with orphaned newborn kittens was feeding, warmth, and getting their elimination systems going, and currently, Barb was bottle-feeding the remaining two kittens and keeping them warm. Volunteers were in and out throughout the day, and feeding the newborn kittens every two to four hours was always a favorite task. They were waiting for the vet to arrive to assess them medically.

Debbie placed a ceramic pumpkin vase on the reception counter and filled it with sample-size candy for visitors to help themselves. She had to be careful about what she used for decorations and where she put them. The dogs tended to be curious and last year, a mild-mannered golden retriever went after a stuffed witch whose legs hung over the counter. Debbie had been partial to the witch's black-and-white striped legs. And so had Lexie, for she'd grabbed one leg, pulled it down from the counter, and shredded it to pieces.

As Debbie taped up a large cardboard pumpkin with arms and legs and wearing a purple suit to the front window, she saw the vet arrive in his 4x4 and pull into a parking space in front of the building. She taped up one arm up in a wave, causing the vet to laugh as he walked into the shelter.

She jumped down from the chair and greeted him at the door.

"Good afternoon, Deb." Dr. Brett Jovanovic was handsome in a classic way: tall and fit, with short blond hair. "What do you have for me today?"

"I've got two orphaned newborn kittens and one dog who I suspect is newly diabetic."

"Let's take a look. Let me see the dog first."

As they walked back to the kennels, she asked, "Have you done any neutering this past week?" They ran a TNR program for the strays of Lavender Bay: Trap. Neuter. Release. From time to time, Deb ran an ad in *The Lavender Bay Chronicles* reminding residents of the importance of neutering their pets. If she knew a family who couldn't afford to neuter, she had them run it through the shelter. It was too important not to. Local residents were encouraged to catch strays and bring them in under the shelter's business. She also provided cages for capture.

"I only neutered two female cats last week," he said.

"Make sure you bill us," she said. Sometimes, he *forgot* to send them an invoice. And when she'd question him, he'd shrug and say it was a donation to the shelter. But she was on top of it. She didn't want to take advantage of him. He was already coming out to the shelter once a week on his own time to help with vaccinations and health checks of newly brought-in animals.

As soon as she opened the door to the dog kennels and the animals heard her voice, they came alive, barking and jumping around.

Brett laughed. "You're like a celebrity."

Debbie brushed off the compliment. "No, they're like that with everyone."

They approached Bailey's cage. The dog was an eight-year-old labradoodle whose owners had moved out of state and decided not to take her with them.

Bailey was on the cool concrete floor of her kennel, panting. Her water dish was empty, even though Deb had filled it half an hour ago.

"She's not eating and she's drinking water nonstop," Debbie said. She opened the cage and stepped in. The dog did not get up. Deb sank to the ground next to her and stroked her head. "What's the matter, pet?"

Brett knelt down on the other side of the animal. "Deb, do we know how much she weighs?"

Having anticipated this question, she said, "I got a weight this morning. She's sixty-two pounds."

"Let me get a quick blood sugar, but I'm going to need a fasting blood sugar too."

"She hasn't eaten since last night."

"Okay."

Deb restrained the dog so Brett could take a quick blood sample from the ear flap.

"I'll take a panel to see if the pancreas is damaged," he said. He examined the dog, listened to her lungs, and took a temperature.

"Blood sugar is high. I'd like to confirm it with blood work, though."

Deb nodded. She continued to stroke the dog, who seemed restless.

"You know the drill, Deb," he said with a smile.

She nodded again. "I do. See if I can get her to eat, and if not, she'll need some IV hydration." She'd had success in the past with hand-feeding dogs who were very ill, and she'd see if she could get that going with this dog.

"If Bailey doesn't eat by the end of the day, call me—you have my cell number—and I'll bring out the IV stuff and we'll run a line and hydrate her."

Deb nodded.

He further examined the animal and once finished, he ran his hand over her soft fur. "She's a fine-looking dog."

"She is. Sweet-tempered, but lost since she arrived. She doesn't know what's going on."

"Sure. Who's next?"

"The kittens," Deb said.

Barb was just finishing with the second kitten's feeding when they walked in. She looked up, smiled, and tucked the kitten into the small bed with its sibling.

"Hello, Barb," Brett said heartily. "I see you're on bottle-feeding duty."

"And I couldn't be happier," Barb said. "There are a lot of perks to the job."

"Let's hear it for the animals," Brett said.

Deb smiled. He was such a nice man. She'd been glad to see that he had paired up with DeeDee Cook. They were both kind, gentle souls and were perfect for one another.

Deb lifted the small tub that held the kittens onto the stainless steel table so Brett could examine them. Gently, he removed one kitten at a time. He observed each one, inspecting the eyes, ears, throat, and coat, declaring everything within normal limits and no parasites or fleas, which was music to Deb's ears.

"Keep doing what you're doing with the bottle-feeding. Do you think you can track their weights every day?" he asked.

"Sure," Deb said.

He grinned. "Or have you already started doing that?"

Barb's laugh gave the secret away.

"I'll pop in tomorrow and see how they're doing," he said.

"That would be great," Deb said. She walked him out. "Can I get you something to drink before you go? Coffee or tea?"

He shook his head. "No thanks. I've got to get back to the clinic. My afternoon is booked."

"Of course."

She waved goodbye and headed back to the dog kennels to clean them out.

CHAPTER FIVE

On a rare day off, Deb knelt on her kitchen floor, washing it up with a sponge. Her home on Peach Street smelled of lemon-scented floor cleaner. She'd read somewhere that if you were suffering with anxiety, to cut a lemon in half and sniff it. Whether that was true or not she didn't know, but it certainly couldn't hurt. With the dogs and cats, hair was a never-ending problem and therefore, vacuuming and washing the floors on a regular basis was a requirement. The floors got a weekly wash and her goal was to vacuum every day, although sometimes she fell short of that goal.

She'd put up a baby gate between the living room and kitchen to keep the dogs and cats out until the floor dried. She swung her leg over the gate, leaving the bucket on the kitchen floor to be emptied later when she was able to walk on it. She dressed quickly, pulled on a heavy fleece, and slipped her feet into her sneakers. The dogs, Oscar and Bella, watched her, and as soon as she took the leads down from the hook by the front door, they ran toward her, barking and wagging their tails. True to form, the two had been rescues and were of indeterminate breed. Oscar, a short-hair mix of white, black, and brown, was the bigger of the two at seventy pounds. Bella, meanwhile, could hold her own at forty pounds, and was a long-haired black dog with a wide snout.

Before closing the front door behind her, she eyed the two cats, one sitting on the coffee table and the other on the arm of the sofa, and said, "Do not walk on the kitchen floor, please." They regarded her with disinterest.

Both dogs pulled on their leads, one veering right and the other left. She practically had to trot to keep up with them. The morning was dull and damp, and the fog that had rolled in the previous evening refused to disperse. The weather made her feel sleepy, and she was glad it was her day off.

Although technically she wasn't required to go into the shelter on her days off, she almost always managed to pop in for a quick visit. But today, she decided she was having a pajama day at home with her family: her dogs and cats. She hadn't slept well the previous night and thought a lazy day might be in order. She might even get takeout for dinner. She didn't mind cooking but she didn't do a lot of it, choosing instead to focus on other things. Sometimes, she'd get the itch to cook or bake something, but once that was done, she was good for a while. She expected a text from Barbara by four o'clock asking whether she was all right. Her not showing up was bound to raise concerns with the rest of the staff.

After fifteen minutes, when the dogs appeared to slow down, their excess energy spent, she turned around and headed in the direction of home, accommodating Oscar and Bella every time they stopped to sniff something.

Once home, she wiped their paws with a towel she kept folded by the front door and removed the leads and hung them on their hook. Both dogs sauntered over to the sofa, jumped up to their favorite spots, and settled in. The kitchen floor was dry, so she removed the baby gate and went to empty the bucket of water but spied a set of paw prints across the floor. She huffed and looked around for the guilty party but saw neither cat. She decided to leave the paw prints until next time. After she changed back into her pajamas, she plopped down onto the sofa, where she was immediately set upon by the dogs and cats, all vying for space next to her or on her lap. Once they got settled, she reached for her coffee, which was now lukewarm, and sipped it. She indulged in her guilty pleasure of watching cat videos on her phone, laughing from time to time.

Her phone rang and she picked it up on the first ring when she saw that it was Angie.

"Hey bestie," Angie started.

This made Debbie smile. "Hey, you," she replied.

"Are you at home?"

Debbie nodded even though Angie couldn't see her. "Yes, I'm having a pajama day today."

"Good for you!" This coming from Angie was incredible. Ang used to be a workaholic, working all the hours God gave her, but had done a complete one-eighty with her recent cancer diagnosis. Now, she stopped to smell the roses. She had what Debbie liked to say was balance in her life.

"Can you get out of your pajamas later and come over for dinner?" Angie asked.

Debbie didn't have to think about it. "Sure, love to. What time?"

"The usual, sevenish," Angie said.

"I'll be there. Can I bring anything?"

"Just bring yourself. All right, I'll see you later. Enjoy your day off."

She no sooner hung up with Ang than her phone rang again. She answered the call. "Hi, Mom."

"It's me, Mom."

"I know."

"Look, why don't we get together for brunch on Sunday," Darlene said.

Debbie almost fell off her sofa. Almost. "Really?"

"Yes, really. You sound surprised but it was your idea, wasn't it?"

"Yes, it was." After a small pause, Debbie asked, "What can I bring?"

"Everything. It was your idea. I'll provide the venue."

"So brunch items."

"I did say brunch, didn't I?" Darlene challenged.

"How many people?"

"Well, me and Dad and you, and I invited Dawn and the kids and your brother."

"Is he bringing his girlfriend?"

"I think they broke up."

"Oh, okay. What time?"

"Eleven. Not too early. I'm not a morning person."

Debbie wanted to say *And not an afternoon or evening person either*, but said instead, "I know. Will Dad be there?"

"Who knows. I told him." Her mother's voice had a sharp edge to it.

Debbie decided to end the call before her mother's mood deteriorated any further. Any mention of her father tended to be a trigger.

Plans made, she relaxed with the drapes wide open, watching old movies. First was *Sorry, Wrong Number* with Barbara Stanwyck, a movie she'd seen a million times. Although a black-and-white movie addict, she opted for a color movie for the second feature. After a break to let the dogs out and give the pets a treat, she settled in for the panoramic splendor of *Giant*. When the afternoon was over and the movies watched, she stood to change and take the dogs out for a walk one more time and then get ready for dinner.

There was no sense in stopping at a bakery to pick up a dessert or cake when Angie was the queen of baked goods. Anything Debbie could buy would fall short of her friend's expertise. So she made a dump cake. It was super easy: one box of yellow cake mix and a can of fruit cocktail, then into the oven to bake. And done.

She bumped into Jim Sloane walking up Angie and Tom's driveway. She was no longer surprised to see him there as he was always the other guest at these dinners.

"Fancy meeting you here," she teased.

He grinned and with a nod toward the cake pan, asked, "Can I carry that for you?"

"No, thank you, that's all right," she said. They approached the side door of the house. "You and I are like spare parts or something."

Behind her, he laughed. He held open the door for her so they could make their way in.

"Surprise, surprise," Debbie called out.

Tom poked his head around the doorframe of the kitchen. "Right on time. Dinner's almost ready."

"Great, I'm hungry," Jim said.

"You're always hungry," Tom said, and then to Debbie, "Here, let me take that from you."

"Thanks, Tom," she said, and handed him the cake pan.

Debbie removed her coatigan and laid it over the back of one of the kitchen chairs. Jim did the same.

Angie appeared in the doorway and immediately went in for a hug.

"Always good to see you," she whispered in Deb's ear.

"Are we supposed to hug?" Jim asked his brother.

"I'm not sure," Tom said. "Hold on. Angie will tell me what to do."

Laughing, Angie grabbed the kitchen towel from the hook and snapped it playfully against Tom's thigh. "Okay, smarty," she said with a laugh.

Tom and Angie herded them into the cozy dining room off the kitchen. It was big enough to hold a square table custom-made of black walnut and a matching sideboard. Debbie took the chair in front of the window, like she did every time she came over. They all humored her avoidance of windowless rooms.

Jim took the chair to her right, like he always did. "You're like my right-hand man," she cracked.

Grinning, he said, "I don't mind that at all."

On the menu that evening was deconstructed fish tacos: all the ingredients of a fish taco over a bed of basmati rice with mahimahi and a mango sauce. They were delicious, and Jim was already into his third helping while everyone else was on their second.

"Your grocery bill must be high," Debbie noted.

Sheepishly, he said, "A little bit." Changing the subject, he said, "I had an elderly couple come into the shop to get matching tattoos."

"Really? How old were they?" Angie asked between mouthfuls of dinner.

"That's the funny thing. They were high school sweethearts back in 1961, and somehow got separated, married other people, lived in other states, raised children. And it was at their sixtieth high school reunion that they reconnected, both being widowed by this time."

"That's wonderful," Debbie said. Although she didn't believe in true love for herself, she believed in it for other people, like Angie and Tom. And this couple that Jim spoke about.

Jim looked at her and appeared thoughtful. "I thought that too. That after all that time, they could reconnect and still feel the same way about each other."

"Lovely."

"How are things at the rescue, Deb?" Tom asked.

"Good. Busy." She went on to tell them about the kittens.

"We went out to dinner the other night with DeeDee and Brett," Angie said. "Brett said he thinks you could go back to school to become a vet tech. He said, and I quote, 'She's practically a vet already, for Pete's sake.'"

Aware that all eyes were on her, Debbie blushed, pretty sure that it evened all her freckles out. She squirmed beneath the scrutiny. "That was nice of him to say."

"He only spoke the truth," Angie said enthusiastically.

Debbie didn't know about that. She'd already been to college and had no plans to return.

"I think it's time for dessert," Angie announced. She and Tom stood and cleared the plates. Angie returned carrying the cake pan, and Tom held a stack of dessert plates and forks.

Debbie was glad the subject was off of her.

"Anyone care for a piece of dump cake?" Angie asked.

Jim and Debbie both raised their hands, looked at each other, and burst out laughing.

When Debbie left at the end of the evening, she was content, feeling pretty good about things.

CHAPTER SIX

Sunday morning rolled around, and Debbie loaded all the brunch items into the trunk of her car. It would have been easier to cook and bake everything at her mother's house, but that would have been an exercise in frustration and aggravation as her mother was territorial about her kitchen.

At her own house, she'd planned the menu and prepared everything earlier that morning. For a split second, she'd thought about making mimosas, but just as quickly nixed the idea. Alcohol and her family did not mix. For the gathering, she made two pans of egg strata, one with ham and cheese, the other with bacon, cream cheese, and tomato. Angie had given her a recipe for blueberry french toast bake, and that rounded out the offerings. The only things she didn't make were the coffee cake and the dozen donuts she picked up on her way to the house on Clover Drive.

Humming a happy tune, she carried in the first armload of items and set them on the counter in the kitchen. Her mother sat at the kitchen table, smoking a cigarette and reading the Sunday paper.

Darlene looked up at her. "You're here," she said, her tone unreadable.

Debbie steeled herself for her mother to tell her to take everything home, that she'd changed her mind and didn't want to do brunch. With her mother, anything was possible because she was so impossible. But Darlene Melvin said nothing further, returning her attention to the front section of *The Lavender Bay Chronicles*.

Debbie spotted the dining room table, still full of stuff. Her heart sank. Couldn't her mother make the effort? Where were they supposed to sit? In the cramped kitchen, where one side of the table was pushed up against the wall to make room to get through?

Carefully, she asked, "Are we not eating at the dining room table?"

Her mother scowled. "No. Everyone can grab a paper plate and find a seat."

"I thought it might be nice for us all to sit down together at the table," Debbie pushed.

"Too late."

"I can clear it off."

"No, leave it," her mother said sharply. "I know where everything is. You'll mix it all up and I won't be able to find anything."

With the amount of dust covering the boxes on the table, Debbie doubted her mother ever needed to find or use anything from all that clutter.

"All right, Mom." There was no sense in things devolving before they even had a chance to eat. She took a deep breath and forced herself to relax, determined they would have a lovely meal.

"Mom, where are the paper plates?" Debbie asked. She knew better than to campaign for the use of dinnerware. It would have to be washed.

"Bottom cupboard to the left of the stove," her mother said without looking up.

Deb's father appeared in the doorway, a smudge of shaving cream on his cheek.

"Something smells good," Jerry Melvin said. For eighty-five years old, he was in pretty good shape despite the constant onslaught of alcohol and cigarettes down through the years. Short and wiry, there was something about him that was tough.

Darlene didn't acknowledge her husband. An image of a train compartment from one of the old movies Debbie had watched came to mind. Her parents were like strangers forced to share an intimate space but where no conversation or even acknowledgement was necessary.

"Hi, Dad," Debbie said, looking around the kitchen. "Mom, where should I set things up?"

Her mother sighed. "I guess along the countertops. Do you have a lot?" She looked over and saw the three pans. "Oh, you do."

"It looks like you went to a lot of trouble, Deb," Jerry said.

"I don't mind."

"Try to make space along the counter so some of us can sit at the table," her mother suggested.

"I could put the donuts and the coffee cake in the center of the table," Debbie mused out loud.

Her mother went to say something but thought better of it and closed her mouth.

Debbie brought in the rest of the items from her car and as she set up the table, bundling silverware next to a stack of paper plates, her brother Darren walked in. He was the eldest and six years older than Debbie. Divorced with children he didn't see, he worked for Lavender Bay's highway department and lived on the other side of town. Like her, he resembled their mother, with the same red hair and freckles. He was quiet, had a slumped posture, and she didn't see him that much.

"Hey, Debs, how are you?" he said. "I got a strange call from Mom, saying we were having brunch together."

"I'm right here in the room with you," Darlene said, offended.

"Oh, sorry, Mom," he said.

"I thought it might be nice for us all to get together once in a while," Darlene explained. "When I was growing up, we went out for breakfast every Sunday morning."

"All right." He sounded unconvinced. He'd always reminded Debbie of Eeyore from the Winnie the Pooh movies. He sat down at the opposite end of the table, pulled out his phone from his back pocket, and gave it his undivided attention.

Debbie did not know this about her mother. She used to go out to breakfast every Sunday? With whom, she wondered? Her parents, possibly? She'd had no brothers or sisters. There were so many questions ping-ponging around inside Debbie's head, she didn't know what to ask first. But before she could voice anything, her older sister arrived.

Dawn would best be described as the perfect amalgamation of Jerry and Darlene. She possessed a short and wiry build with sloped shoulders like her father and the bright red hair and freckles her mother's side was noted for.

"Yeah," she said when she entered.

Darlene, Jerry, and Darren looked at her and said nothing. Debbie thought of the Cook household, where hugs, laughter, and conversation were abundant. She decided she shouldn't compare her own family to the Cooks. It wasn't the Melvins' fault that they didn't know any better. But she did now, thanks to her exposure to Angie's family. Maybe she could transfer some of that to the Melvin clan.

"Where are the kids?" Debbie asked. Her sister had a son and a daughter who were in their early twenties. Darren had gotten the boy a job at the highway department, and Debbie's niece worked as a teacher's aide at the elementary school. She was disappointed not to see them.

Dawn snorted. "They were out late last night. They won't be showing their faces until late afternoon."

"Oh."

Debbie removed the tin foil from the pans and invited everyone to dig in.

"If I bring in one of the dining room chairs, we could all sit together at the kitchen table," she suggested.

Darlene stood, picked up a paper plate, and began to help herself. "You can all sit where you want, but I'm going to sit in my recliner."

Once the plates were filled, Darlene and Dawn sat in the living room, and Jerry and Darren sat in the kitchen.

They were so difficult.

Deciding her father would be more amenable to her suggestion than her mother, Debbie said to Jerry, "Dad, why don't we all go sit together in the living room."

Darren scrolled through his phone, his eyes glued to the screen as he forked strata into his mouth.

Jerry appeared to weigh his options.

"Dad?" Although her father was imperfect, he was prone to moments of reasonableness.

Without a word, he stood and carried his plate into the living room.

"Come on, Darren," she said.

"I'm fine here."

"Please."

He looked up at her. Finally, he stood, put more strata on his plate, and grumbled, "I don't know what the big deal is," before making his way to the front room.

Carrying her own plate, Debbie followed her brother. Her mother and father were in their recliners, while Dawn sat in one corner of the sofa. Darren made a bee-line for the other corner. That left Debbie with a chair that was currently laden with boxes. She set her plate down on the coffee table and cleared the chair, piling the boxes carefully next to it under the watchful eye of her mother.

Once seated, she took a forkful of french toast bake and asked, "How's the food?"

"Mine's a little cold," said her mother.

"I can heat it up in the microwave," Debbie offered.

Darlene waved her away with her fork. "Not necessary."

"What's new with everyone?" Deb asked.

They all stopped eating and stared at her as if she'd asked them what their opinion was about the planet Pluto being demoted.

"Nothing," Darren said. And apparently he was the group's spokesman because no one added anything after that.

Debbie tried not to allow herself to feel let down by her family. *Couldn't they even try?*

Dawn scraped her fork along her paper plate, gathering up the blueberry juice from the french toast bake. She frowned and asked, "What's going on? What's the reason for this get-together?" She directed her gaze to her parents. "Are one of you sick or something?"

"No, I'm fine," Darlene said. She looked over at Jerry. "Are you sick?"

"Not that I know of," he said, scratching the back of his head.

Debbie swallowed her mouthful and said, "There is no reason. I thought it might be nice to get together and . . ." Her voice trailed off, unable to fill in the blanks.

"Why?" Dawn asked.

Darren stood, went to the kitchen to fill his plate again, and returned to his spot on the couch.

"Do we need a reason?" Debbie asked.

By the looks on their faces, apparently they did.

She continued to talk, looking around at each one of them. "I mean, we're family. We should spend more time together."

"Will there be beer?" her father cracked.

"That's not funny, Jerry," Darlene said. And again, in a sterner tone, "Not even remotely funny."

To Debbie's dismay, her brother set his empty plate on the coffee table, pulled out his phone, and leaned back on the sofa. Obviously, he was not going to fully engage.

But she wasn't having it. "What do you think, Darren?"

At the mention of his name, he looked up at them all, appearing sheepish, as if he'd just been asked a question in class but wasn't paying attention to the subject. "Yeah, sure, whatever."

Debbie didn't bother rolling her eyes, it would require too much energy.

Dawn narrowed her eyes at her and smirked. "Oh, I know what this is about. Happy families. You've been spending a lot of time over at the Waltons' and they've brainwashed you."

It set Debbie's teeth on edge when her sister referred to Angie's family as the Waltons.

"They're not all they're cracked up to be," her mother added.

"You always say that," Debbie said, trying to tamp down the anger rising within her. "But you never give a reason why."

Darlene placed her plate of half-eaten food on the table between the recliners. "I don't need to give a reason, I just *know*."

Debbie shrank in her chair. It was wrong to think they could have a nice meal together. Spend some time together. It was disheartening. This was the family she'd been born into, for better or for worse. And it was a whole lot of worse.

"What's new with you, Debbie?" her father asked.

She smiled at him. Her father had his own issues, but at least he tried.

"Not too much," she said. "I'm loving my new job at the animal shelter."

As soon as she said it, she regretted it. You couldn't tell people like this about any happiness you might have in your life. There were some people in the world whose sole purpose in life was to ruin your joy, and she had a family full of them.

Dawn shuddered and her face contorted in a grimace. "All those dogs and cats. No thanks."

Her mother shook her head. "Why you gave up that perfectly good job at the accounting agency, I'll never know. Not one of your smarter moves."

"But I'm happy at the shelter," Debbie replied. She'd made the mistake of telling her parents that it was a slight pay cut, which it was, but one she could live with. Sometimes a job was about something more than the money.

Her mother snorted. "Happy? What does that have to do with anything?"

"I love working with animals, and I know a lot about them," Debbie replied.

"How that happened, I don't know," Darlene said with a sour expression. "We never had dogs and cats here."

"More's the pity," Debbie said.

Dawn shuddered again. "Not me. I don't want any dogs and cats in my house. You can always tell a house that has dogs and cats. It stinks."

Quietly, Debbie said, "My house does not smell."

Dawn leveled a glare at her. "That's what you think."

That was enough. Deb stood and walked around, gathering the paper plates. "I'll do the cleanup, Mom."

"Make sure you put everything back where it belongs."

Debbie nodded.

She hurried to clean up, anxious to get out of there. She put everything back where it belonged. After she emptied the paper plates into the garbage, she stored the leftovers in Tupperware and placed them in the fridge. She washed out her pans and gathered them up.

She poked her head into the living room. "I'm going. Talk to you later."

"Bye, Debbie," Jerry said.

And she left, disappointed and disheartened. It had been an exercise in futility. As she loaded up her trunk, she thought, *Lesson learned. Never again.*

Chapter Seven

Debbie pushed the disastrous brunch to the outer recesses of her mind, hoping that eventually, the memory would drop altogether from her radar. She should have known better. Days later, she was walking by the Ink Stain, having just enjoyed coffee and a cinnamon bun at Coffee Girl, when Jim poked his head out the door and called after her.

"Debbie."

She stopped, pivoted, and walked in his direction. He was wearing his usual uniform of a T-shirt and a pair of jeans. The T-shirt bore the name and logo of some obscure rock band she had never heard of.

The autumnal sunshine highlighted Jim's blond hair and beard, and she observed that he was handsome in an athletic way: tall and broad shouldered, with eyes that belied a sharp intelligence. There was evidence of a recent trip to the barber.

"Hey, Jim. I see you've had your ears lowered," she said.

He responded with a quizzical look.

She laughed. "Sorry. It means you've had your hair cut."

Self-consciously, he rubbed the back of his head. "Yeah, it was starting to get out of control."

Debbie burst out laughing.

Grinning, he asked, "What's so funny?"

"Your hair is always short. I can't imagine it getting out of control." She paused and pointed to the top of her head, where her mass of red curls was piled loosely. "This is out of control."

Now he was laughing. "Maybe. But out of control looks better on you than me."

"I don't know."

"Come on in for a second, my next client isn't due for ten minutes."

"Sure."

She followed him into his shop. She'd been there before. The overall smell was a combination of fresh ink, the medical-grade soap he used to disinfect the skin of his clients, and a hint of his cologne. It was oddly relaxing. It was a small space with a large front window that faced Main Street. On the glass had been painted *The Ink Stain*. The floors were refinished hardwood and the walls were painted a deep scarlet with white trim work.

There were two small rooms off the main room and by the looks of the dark shadows, Deb assumed they were windowless, and therefore she would avoid going into them at all costs.

"How's it going with Timmy?" she asked.

Jim nodded. "Good. I've never had a cat before, so I didn't know what to expect."

"And?"

"It's been a pleasant surprise. He's pretty low maintenance."

"For the most part, cats are. As compared to dogs. But sometimes you do get an oddball."

"I can imagine."

Debbie took half a step away to look at the framed black-and-white photos of tattoos he'd created. She studied them for a moment; it was an impressive gallery.

"You did all these?" she asked, narrowing her eyes to study the amazing detail.

"Yep."

"Do you do your own?" she asked, with a quick glance to his tattoo-covered arms. She moved on to the next wall photo.

He shook his head. "No. I've got a guy up in Toronto."

Deb raised her eyebrows. "That's not around the block."

"No, but he's worth the drive."

Eyeing his arms again, Deb had to agree.

At a loss for where to take the conversation next, she asked, "Did you get all your yard work done?"

He narrowed his eyes in confusion. "I'm sorry?"

"You said you like to do yard work and gardening, and I wondered if you managed to get all those leaves raked up."

With enlightenment, a grin emerged, and he nodded. "I did. All done. What about you?"

She scrunched up her face. "Uh, no." The state of her garden left a lot to be desired.

They made small talk for a few more minutes until Deb announced, "I better get back to work."

"It was good seeing you, Deb."

She smiled and waved goodbye.

The following weekend, she arrived home from grocery shopping to find Jim standing next to her driveway, leaning on a rake. A smile slowly formed on her face.

What's this?

She pulled into her driveway, noting his truck parked on the street in front of her house. Before she stepped out of the car, she did the reverse of her getting-into-the-car ritual: she undid the seatbelt and pulled it back and forth three times, and touched the rearview mirror as if she'd need to adjust it, although she never did as she was the only one who ever drove her car.

When she stepped out, she became aware of her dogs in the front window, paws on the back of the sofa, barking their heads off.

"Hey," Jim said.

"Hey yourself." She smiled.

He lifted the rake. "Thought I'd stop by and give you a hand."

She was about to protest and say that it wasn't necessary, but she could really use his help. She wondered if she gave off a helpless vibe. She hoped not.

"Were you waiting long?" she said instead.

He shook his head. "Actually, I pulled up just before you did."

"Perfect timing."

He looked around at her front yard. "Doesn't look too bad."

"That's because there's no trees," she explained. "Wait until you see the backyard."

With a grin, he said, "Bring it on."

Debbie pulled a couple of canvas bags of groceries out of the backseat, thinking Jim Sloane was very kind. So refreshing!

"Here, let me take those," he said, and relieved her of the bags, carrying them in one hand and the rake in the other.

They walked alongside one another until they reached the side entrance. She opened the storm door, held it with her shoulder, and turned the key in the lock. Before she opened the door, she said, "Do you like dogs?" When he nodded, she said, "Good, because they love company."

She opened the door to Oscar and Bella clamoring to get out, barking, tails wagging. The two of them circled Jim and whined. He set the bags down and lowered himself on his haunches to pet each dog in turn. In general, Debbie didn't trust people, but she trusted dogs. And her dogs liked Jim. That was good enough for her.

She gave a few commands, and Oscar and Bella settled down. Jim carried the groceries inside and then the two of them stepped out back. Her backyard was long and narrow and surrounded by a white vinyl fence. Although she had no trees, her neighbors did, and the grass was covered in wet leaves. She was so grateful that she was vigilant in regard to poop patrol. How embarrassing would that have been?

"You know you don't have to do this," she said.

He shrugged. "I don't mind, really. At least it's not raining." His gaze swept over the area. "It won't take long."

And it didn't. He had the whole yard raked up in no time. Debbie went around with a small garbage bag, picking up litter and debris that had blown in.

After an hour, he leaned the rake against the fence. He'd dumped all the leaves in a wheelbarrow he borrowed from a neighbor and taken them out to the street, where the town would eventually pick them up.

She invited him in for coffee and a bagel and cream cheese, but he declined. "No thanks, Deb. I've got to meet Tom."

"Another time."

He hesitated before finally saying, "Look, I was wondering if you'd like to come over for dinner sometime."

Caught off guard, all she could manage was an *oh*.

"Maybe you'd like to see how Timmy is coming along," he suggested. The fingers of his right hand played with his beard as he studied her face. "And I like to cook."

"That's good. I hate cooking, but I love to eat," she said. "Sure, I'll come for dinner."

"What's good for you?"

As she was thinking, he said, "What about Tuesday night?"

She thought for a moment. "I could do that."

"Seven all right?"

"That's perfect." It would give her time to go home after work and feed the pets and let the dogs out. "All right, I'll see you then."

She walked him to his truck, where he threw the rake into the bed.

"I don't know where you live," she said.

Once she had retrieved that piece of information, she waved goodbye and didn't go back inside until his truck disappeared. She thought it was nice that Jim would host dinner for a change; it would give Tom and Angie a break. She supposed she should have them over for dinner one night too but immediately dismissed the idea. She'd take them all out for a meal at the Annacotty Room. That was the easiest way.

CHAPTER EIGHT

Jim didn't live that far from Debbie's house. In fact, although the evening was chilly, it was dry, and she decided to walk over. She'd bought a bottle of wine to take to dinner and that way, if she decided to have a glass, she wouldn't have to worry about driving.

She was late coming home from the rescue and immediately fed the cats, who meowed their displeasure at her tardiness with their dinner. Once the dogs were fed, she let them out into the fenced-in backyard. While they were outside, sniffing at everything and doing their business, she went to freshen up and get changed. As much as she loved working with animals, at the end of the day, her clothes ended up smelling like them, so a costume change was in order. Last, she spritzed herself lightly with perfume.

Autumn meant early evenings, and Debbie stepped outside into a night as dark as pitch. As she walked along, she was mindful of the sidewalks covered with leaves. Some were wet, which made them slippery, and she wondered more than once if she should have just driven and brought a cake instead of a bottle of wine. Or had Angie and Tom pick her up. Maybe she could bother them for a ride home later.

Jim Sloane lived in a modest cottage-style home, not dissimilar to her own. In the darkness, she could barely make out the color of the house but decided it was brown with cream trim. The porch light was on, illuminating the entire entrance and the steps that led up to it.

There were no vehicles parked in the asphalt driveway that stretched all the way to the single-car garage at the back of the property. A quick glance along the street showed no sign of Angie's car or Tom's truck. They must be running late, she thought as she climbed the porch steps. She pressed the bell and waited.

Jim opened the door and smiled. "Hey, Debbie, come on in." He sported a dark T-shirt and a pair of jeans, and he had a freshly showered look about him.

As she crossed the threshold, she handed him the bottle of wine.

"Not necessary to bring anything, but thanks anyway," he said.

Something smelled good. Her stomach growled loudly in response, and she felt her face redden.

Jim laughed. "That's a good sign!"

"It smells wonderful in here."

"Hopefully, it will taste as good as it smells," he said, holding out his hand for her coat.

"I'm sure it will," she said as she shrugged out of it and handed it to him.

"I'll hang up your coat and open the wine."

"Great."

Jim disappeared into the kitchen, and Debbie took the opportunity to look around his home to get a better sense of him. The interior, though small, was well lit, and the overall feel was cozy. He'd furnished the living room with an overstuffed sofa and matching chair, and a large-screen television mounted over the fireplace dominated the space. But the surprise was the number of books. They were everywhere. Black shelves lined one wall, and they were crammed with books. She approached them, tilting her head slightly to read the spines. Dashiell Hammett, Raymond Chandler, Elmore Leonard, Robert Galbraith, Ann Cleeves, Val McDermid, Abir Mukherjee, Ian Rankin, Jo Nesbo, Jussi Adler-Olsen. It appeared to be an international roundup of crime writers.

Jim reappeared.

"So, I guess you like reading," Debbie said with a smile.

"You could say that."

It was easy to imagine him sitting here in the evenings in the corner of his sofa, with the reading lamp turned on overhead and a beer on the coaster on the end table next to the couch.

"Do you read?" he asked. He shook his head and started again. "Of course you know how to read. But do you like it as a hobby?"

"I'm sorry, I don't."

"What do you like to do in your spare time?"

"Although my life tends to revolve around cats and dogs, I have an affinity for old black-and-white movies."

On cue, Jim's rescue cat, a handsome tuxedo named Timmy, strolled into the room, acting as if he owned the place. She'd always loved the confidence of cats and more than once, had wished it were contagious. He paused, stood next to Jim, and regarded Debbie.

Debbie bent down and said, "Hello, Timmy, do you remember me?"

With a meow, he stepped closer to her, allowing her to pet him. It wasn't long before he was purring and rubbing himself against her legs.

"Why does he do that?" Jim asked.

"A couple of reasons. Affection, a greeting, and marking his territory." She continued to stroke the cat. "He looks well, Jim."

"Thanks. Like I said, he's pretty low maintenance."

"What about the window blinds?" she asked. While she had been fostering Timmy at her house, she'd discovered he had a thing for closing the venetian blinds, and they went round and round opening and closing them. It had been a battle of wills. "I don't see you have any blinds, so you dodged that bullet."

He grinned. "Not exactly." He disappeared from the room and returned with a large wooden board that had a venetian blind attached to it. He set it down against the wall and pulled the cord at the end, opening the blinds to reveal an image of a garden replete with a bumblebee and two finches. Debbie's eyebrows lifted. Timmy abandoned her, ran over to the board, sat in front of it, and used his paw to swipe the blinds closed.

Debbie was speechless. She covered her mouth with her hands and laughed. "Did you make that?" He certainly didn't do things by half measures.

"I did. As a toy. I ordered a custom-made blind for it. The blind company thought I was nuts."

"But in a good way."

He appeared sheepish. "Hopefully."

Debbie bent and opened the blind. The cat immediately closed it with his paw. She looked at Jim and smiled. "I love it, I absolutely love it."

Jim was a perfect match for Timmy. Debbie loved a happy ending.

"Dinner's ready," Jim said. "Come on and sit down."

"What about Angie and Tom?" she asked. They were really late. It was so unlike them.

Confusion rolled over Jim's face. "What about them?"

"Aren't they coming?"

He hesitated before saying, "No, I didn't invite them."

Her mind went blank. Jim shifted on his feet, his gaze firmly fixed on Debbie's face.

Raising one eyebrow slightly, she said, "Oh." Then as the meaning of it dawned on her, she let out a long, drawn-out "ohhhhh."

Finally, he asked, "Did you want to take your dinner to go?"

She burst out laughing. "No, of course not. Come on, let's eat. I'm starving."

Normally, she would have made excuses and exited. She wasn't looking for a relationship. An early marriage that had not ended well had put her off any kind of long-term commitment. But there were two things working in Jim's favor. First, he was a nice person, and she didn't want to hurt his feelings. Second, she was really hungry.

His posture relaxed and he led her to the kitchen, where a table was set for two. The room was done up in black and stainless steel. It could have been severe and cold except for the turquoise accents.

She picked up a ceramic vase and said, "Someone has a nice touch."

"Not me," he told her. "My sister. She said the splash of color would lighten it up a bit."

"Tell her she was right. It works."

Debbie approached the table. In the center was a shallow casserole with chicken in a cream sauce with spinach and sundried tomatoes.

"That does smell wonderful. Does it matter where I sit?"

"Not at all."

She moved one of the place settings around the table until she was seated with her back to the window, which was her preference. This placed her kitty corner to Jim instead of across from him. He watched her with interest.

"Sorry," she said. "I like to sit in front of a window."

"Don't apologize. I'd hope you'd make yourself comfortable."

She sat, her stomach now rumbling aggressively. "I'm comfortable now."

"Let's serve it up."

Jim carried over a pot of rice and scooped out generous portions of it onto their plates. Then, using a large serving spoon, he dished out chicken and cream sauce over the rice. Finished serving, he took his seat and said, "Let's eat."

Debbie happily picked up her cutlery, cut off a piece of the chicken, and forked it up with a little bit of rice and some of the creamy sauce. She closed her eyes. It was simply delicious.

"Jim, this is amazing."

"I'm glad you like it," he said. He jumped up. "I forgot the wine."

He poured a generous amount into each of their glasses.

Debbie took a sip and returned her attention to her meal. "Who knew chicken could be so extraordinary."

"It's amazing what you can do with chicken."

"I'm already amazed."

They made small talk and somehow the topic settled on grandmothers. Jim spoke fondly of his, who babysat them while their parents worked and not only taught him how to cook but encouraged him as well. Debbie admitted that she never knew her grandparents as they'd died before she was born, but that Angie's grandmother, Diana Sturges, had had a strong influence on her.

"Remember how I told you that I loved black-and-white movies? That's because of Angie's grandmother, Grammie. She and I would watch old movies together. And I guess I was hooked," she said. Truthfully, she didn't know if it was because she associated those types of movies with Diana Sturges and how she made her feel or if she truly loved them. It was most likely a combination of the two.

"Grandmothers are great, aren't they?" he said.

"They sure are," she agreed. She liked to think of Diana as her honorary grandmother.

Jim looked at her empty plate. "Would you like another helping?"

"Please."

He served up another round of chicken and rice, and Debbie immediately dug in. "Have you always wanted to be a tattoo artist?"

"No. I actually started out in finance," he said.

Her fork paused mid-air. "Really? My, you are a dark horse."

He laughed. "I worked for years on Wall Street. It was intense, it was fast-paced, and I made a ton of money. It was also soulless. By the end of ten years, I was burned out and I knew there was no way I could do it for the rest of my life."

She'd not imagined this other side of Jim. Dinner was worth it if only to learn something more about him. Even if he'd had other ideas.

"I wasn't sure what I wanted to do," he continued. "All I knew was I wanted to do something creative, and Tom had moved to Lavender Bay and liked it and suggested I give it a try."

"How did you end up becoming a tattoo artist?"

"I already had a couple of tattoos and was getting another one, and I looked around and thought, yeah, I could do this. This was something I'd be interested in. Using the human body as a canvas."

"So you came to Lavender Bay," she said.

"I did. As soon as I was ready to set up my own shop, I left New York City and never looked back. I've been here a little more than ten years."

"And you're happy?"

He didn't have to think about it. "I am."

"Good for you," she said. "What is it about your work that makes you happy?"

"A satisfied client, first of all. The ability to create a meaningful piece of art for someone that becomes a part of them."

The silence was companionable as they finished their meals. Debbie was beginning to feel full, and truth be told, she was sorry to see the meal end, it had been that delicious.

"Was this dinner intended to be a date?" she asked with a grin.

He laughed. "Maybe more like a get-to-know-you-better dinner?"

"Okay," she said, nodding her head. She lifted her wine glass to her lips. "What is the name of this dish you made?" The chance that she would actually go online to get the recipe was slim to none, but she could tell other people about this amazing meal.

He hesitated, looked at his plate, and finally lifted his head, wearing a sheepish grin.

"It's called *Marry Me Chicken*."

And with that, she burst out laughing.

Chapter Nine

Debbie hurried down the windowless corridor at the back of Coffee Girl. As she'd done a thousand times before, she propped open the back door and then knocked on the doorframe of Angie's office. "Knock, knock." From the front of the café came the muted sounds of cutlery, the din of conversation, and the music playing through the sound system. There was the smell of freshly brewed coffee throughout the place.

Angie looked up from her desk, and a big smile broke out on her face. "Hey, there!" She did not invite her friend in to sit down. Her office was a windowless room and therefore, Debbie remained outside of it.

Deb leaned against the doorframe and folded her arms against her chest. "Did you know that Jim invited me over to his house for dinner?"

Angie nodded. "He mentioned it to us."

"I went over there thinking it was going to be the four of us."

"Oh no." Angie laughed. "What happened?"

"Let's just say there might have been an awkward moment."

Angie winced. "Debs, you didn't know that he's been crushing on you for a long time?"

"No! Did you know?" Debbie asked.

"Of course, everyone knows. He can't hide it. It's written all over his face every time the two of you are in the same room."

"It is?"

"He's what you would call *smitten*, as Grammie used to say."

"Smitten, huh?"

"Definitely. It's one of the biggest open secrets in Lavender Bay," Angie said.

"And I was the only one who didn't know," Debbie said. Boy, she felt clueless. How had she missed that? Maybe because she hadn't been looking for it.

"Anyway, how did it go?"

"It was nice, we had a good time," Debbie admitted. "But I'm not sure I even want to be seeing anyone much less enter a relationship."

Angie's smile disappeared. "Why not? You couldn't do better than Jim."

Debbie didn't point out that her friend was biased. "I know that. He's a great guy. But my life is pretty crowded right now."

"With animals, yes, but humans are low on the ground in your life," Angie pointed out. She went on to expound all the great things about being in a stable, happy relationship.

Debbie smirked. "You know, Ang, I remember a time not too long ago when you'd sworn off men and Tom was your mortal enemy for opening his café directly across the street from yours."

Angie dismissed this with a wave of her hand. "Yes, but I was young and foolish back then."

Debbie laughed.

"All I'm saying is, don't rule it out. Expand your horizons."

"We'll see," Debbie said. She wasn't committing to anything. Not yet. A failed early marriage had made her uninterested in getting involved with anyone else. Debbie's singleness had never bothered her. From a young age she'd known she would never have children. She'd been too afraid that she'd unintentionally bring her own background and rearing into it, and she'd decided she definitely didn't want to do that. She wouldn't wish that on any kid. It was time to break that generational curse. She was happy with her family of dogs and cats.

"I'll let you get back to work," Debbie said. She'd only stopped to get a coffee before she headed back to the rescue after her lunch hour.

"Are you coming over to Mom's house on Sunday?" Angie asked.

Debbie had missed the previous Sunday because of the brunch at her parents' house. She hadn't told anyone about it, not even Angie, afraid they'd see right through it and label it a Cook coffee morning knockoff.

"I can't," she lied. She offered no explanation and her friend demanded none, knowing that Debbie had her reasons and her quirks.

The truth was, she wouldn't be up for it, not so soon after her own family gathering. The closeness and the camaraderie would only serve as a painful reminder of how very different and lacking her own family was. No, she'd give the coffee mornings a miss for a while.

Debbie walked toward the shelter, humming a little tune. She couldn't account for her good mood, only that she was in one. Maybe it had to do with Jim Sloane, which had turned out to be a pleasant surprise. *One day at a time*, she told herself. As she entered the bright, airy space, she was greeted by the incessant sound of barking. A bark she recognized: Spotty, the beagle.

I must be hearing things, she thought. Spotty had recently been adopted by a family of four with two pre-teen girls who were shrill, loud and screechy. At the time, they seemed excited about the prospect of the dog. And she'd thought with their screechiness and his barking, they'd be a perfect match.

Barbara stood behind the counter, her nose scrunched up. "Guess who's back."

"Spotty?" Deb's heart sank.

The oldies station played a Barry Manilow song, "I Write the Songs." In the back, Spotty continued to bark.

Debbie tilted her head. "Why is he barking now? I thought he only barked at this wall in the reception area." She indicated the one side wall he seemed to gravitate toward.

"You know, I think it's Barry Manilow."

Deb frowned. "What?"

Barb laughed. "Listen. This happened twice before. A Barry Manilow song comes on and he starts barking."

Sure enough, as soon as the song ended, the barking ceased.

"What happened with the family?" Debbie asked.

"They brought him back while you were out at lunch," Barbara explained. "Although they initially thought his behavior was cute, by the fourth day it was freaking the younger daughter out. She insisted that either Spotty was possessed or they had a ghost in the house, which was why the dog kept staring at the wall and barking at it."

"Did you explain to them that he does the same thing here? At the shelter?"

Barbara nodded. "I did. But the younger daughter wants nothing to do with him."

Debbie sighed. That was it then. There was no way a dog could remain in a home where one of the residents was spooked by him. "Poor Spotty."

"Don't feel too bad, he seemed happy to be back."

Deb shook her head. He was one strange dog. "Perhaps they weren't the family for him, then."

"They couldn't appreciate his uniqueness," Barbara said kindly.

Deb agreed with that sentiment. But it was still a kick in the shin. She hated failing an animal. And this was on her. "Did we throw out his card?" she asked.

Barb shook her head. "No, I put it in his file."

"Good. Just post it back up on his cage." She thought to herself, *Fingers crossed, Spotty.*

"Already done."

"Thanks, Barb."

Her phone rang, and she frowned when she saw her father's name flash across her screen. Her father almost never called her. She tried to think of the last time it had happened. It had to be about five years ago, when he was stuck at the Dog Days Bar. A blizzard had landed and raged in the middle of the afternoon, and he couldn't see across the parking lot to get home. Why he hadn't stayed put was beyond Debbie.

Barb cleared her throat. "Um, Debs, are you going to answer that?"

Prompted, she touched the green phone icon on the screen. "Hello?"

"It's me. Jerry Melvin."

Deb rolled her eyes. "Hi, Dad. What's up?"

"It's your mother."

Deb's senses went on high alert. "Is she all right?"

He hesitated. "Uh, no, not really. She's in the hospital."

"In the hospital? Why? What happened?"

"She fell off the last step of the staircase and broke her leg," Jerry said.

"You're kidding."

"Debbie, I wouldn't joke about a thing like that," he said seriously.

"Where is she? Lavender Bay Medical Center?"

"That's the place."

"Did you drive her over?"

"Goodness no. She wouldn't let me near her. I had to call an ambulance."

Debbie looked heavenward, thanking the powers that be that her father was home when the accident happened. "I'll try to get out of work and go over there," she told him. "Do you want me to pick you up?"

"No, that's all right. I'll stay home. Your mother gave me strict instructions that she doesn't want me anywhere near the hospital." And then he added, "Or her."

"All right, Dad. I'll talk to you later. Have you called Dawn and Darren?"

"Not yet. But I will."

She hung up and drew a deep breath.

"That didn't sound good," Barbara said behind her.

"It's my mother, she fell and broke her leg and has gone to the hospital." Debbie appeared to be wrestling with some internal issue.

Barbara shooed her away with her hands. "Go, go. I'll take care of everything here."

"Are you sure?"

Barbara nodded. "I am. I know what to do."

"I really appreciate it," Debbie said. "Is there anyone else coming in today?"

"I don't think so. I think it's only going to be you and me."

"Try calling around and see if any of the volunteers would be willing to come in for a few hours. I have no idea how long I'll be."

"I'll take care of it."

Debbie thanked her, grabbed her coatigan and her purse, and headed out the door.

CHAPTER TEN

Debbie had no idea what kind of state she'd find her mother in when she arrived at the hospital. Her mother was a funny creature; the woman had major trust issues, and Deb wasn't even sure if she had a family physician. She couldn't remember her mother ever being in the hospital or going to the doctor. In fact, she couldn't even remember her mother ever being sick. The woman must have the genes of a cockroach: indestructible, and she meant that in a good way.

After parking her car, she hoofed it into the emergency room, and reception told her where she could find her mother. The waiting room was half full, and there appeared to be a lot of coughers and hackers. Eventually, she found Darlene in a curtained cubicle in the emergency room, and she was not happy about it.

The ER was a large space with a nurses' station in the center, flanked on all sides by curtained cubicles. Not one window in sight. Deb's mouth went dry.

"Mom, how are you?" she asked, pushing through her discomfort.

Her mother's head snapped up. "How do you think I am? My leg is going in two different directions, and they're waiting for the surgeon to show up. He's probably out golfing," she grumbled.

Debbie decided it was best not to contradict her mother. Darlene was laid out on a gurney, and the misshapenness of her leg was visible even beneath the hospital-issued blanket. There was no chair, so Debbie leaned against the wall.

The room was dim, and she pulled open the blue curtain to let some light in.

"Close that. I don't want that open," Darlene barked.

Debbie felt her heart rate accelerate, and she drew in a deep breath in a futile effort to get it back to normal.

"Can I get something for pain, please!" her mother bellowed, startling Debbie.

"Mom, you can't yell like that. Not in here."

"But I'm in pain."

"I'm sure you are. Let me see if I can find a nurse," Debbie suggested. This seemed to assuage her mother, and she was grateful for an excuse to leave the small cubicle.

There was a lot of activity at the nurses' station. Every seat behind it was occupied. Phones rang, and people were put on hold. There were small groups of medical professionals consulting over x-rays, scans, and blood results. Paperwork littered the counters, and every desktop was up and running.

Debbie leaned on the counter that separated the medical staff from the rest of the emergency room.

"Excuse me," she started. The nurse in front of her, head bent over a chart, did not look up.

Debbie spoke louder. "Excuse me."

The nurse, whose name tag dangling around her neck read *Pamela, RN*, looked up but did not smile. There were dark purple circles beneath her eyes.

"Um, hi. I'm Debbie Melvin. My mom, Darlene Melvin, is here with a broken leg and was looking for something for pain."

The nurse looked hassled. "I just gave her something fifteen minutes ago."

"Oh."

"And the patient transporter is on the way up to transfer her to the operating room."

"That soon?" Deb asked, for lack of anything better to say. She tapped on the counter with her finger. "Thanks."

As she arrived back in her mother's cubicle, she said, "The nurse said she gave you something for pain fifteen minutes ago."

"I don't think it's strong enough," her mother said with a frown, her forehead deeply creased.

"Hang in there, Mom," was all Debbie could offer.

"Can you get me a cigarette?"

Debbie couldn't help but laugh, but when she saw that her mother was serious, she added, "Smoking's not allowed in hospitals."

"It isn't? Boy, they really know how to take the joy out of everything."

"When was the last time you were in the hospital?" Debbie asked.

"When I had you, that was the last time. You could smoke then," Darlene replied.

More than forty years ago. Kudos to her mother for managing to stay out of hospital for that long, despite a lifelong pack-a-day habit. Deb peeked around the curtain, hoping to get a glimpse of someone coming to take her mother to surgery. Her need to get outside and away from this windowless space was growing exponentially. Her hands had gone clammy, and she felt uncomfortable in her skin.

"I don't like them. Hospitals. They're too full of death," Darlene said.

"Not everybody who comes into the hospital dies," Debbie pointed out.

"Think what you like, but you won't change my mind," her mother said firmly.

"Okay, Mom."

The transporter arrived to take Darlene to the OR. First he made sure all her belongings were safely secured beneath the trolley. "Ready, Mrs. Melvin?"

"Yep. Let's get this over with," Darlene said, her tone abrupt.

"Good luck, Mom," Debbie said.

Darlene nodded. "Okay."

"Should I wait here?" Debbie asked the transporter, a tall, rangy fella dressed in blue scrubs.

"No, come with me. I'll show you where the surgical waiting room is," he said.

She followed him as he pushed the gurney forward. When he arrived at a set of gray double doors, he stopped and pointed to the left, down the hospital corridor. "The waiting room is down there, on your left."

"Thank you."

He swiped his badge across the pad, the doors popped open, and he pushed the gurney through.

Even though her relationship with her mother was complex and difficult, she choked up a little bit. She didn't want her to be afraid.

Before she parked herself in the waiting room, she quickly followed the exit signs out of the hospital, making a mental note of the return route. As soon as she got outside, she bent over, hands on her thighs, and drew in some deep breaths. Her chest had constricted, and she knew she needed to focus on her breathing. After ten minutes, she straightened up, drew in one last lungful of fresh air, and turned and walked back inside, somehow managing to find her way back to the surgical area.

The waiting room was fancier than she'd expected for a hospital. The plus was the long bank of windows on one wall that overlooked the grounds and the highway. The room was done up in hues of gold, amber, and scarlet, with dark, glossy furniture. There were restrooms off to one side and a coffee station set up at the other. She headed to the ladies' room first and then got herself a cup of coffee before finding a seat by the windows. There were quite a few people present, all in the same position as herself: waiting for word on a family member or friend.

As she sipped her coffee, she glanced at the pile of magazines stacked on the small table beside her, but decided she'd better update her sister and brother first. She created a group text and sent off a quick message:

Mom off to surgery. Keep you posted.

Dawn was the first to respond. *What? What's going on?*

Deb mumbled to herself, "Oh, Dad. You had one job."

Fell and broke her leg. In surgery. I'm at the hospital.

There was no immediate response from her sister, so after a few minutes, Debbie added, *You're welcome to join me.*

Dawn's reply came quickly. *No sense in the two of us hanging around there. Keep me posted.* Deb hadn't expected her older sister to accept her invitation, but she put it out there. Dawn didn't like to be inconvenienced. She didn't like any disruptions to her routine or schedule. It was just as well that she didn't come, as Debbie could only take her older sister in small doses. She was small and blunt and sharp. Debbie's secret nickname for her was Captain Blunt Force Trauma.

She figured she had better call her father. The landline rang and rang with no pickup. She tried his cell phone, but there was no answer. Annoyed, she scrolled through her contact list until she found the number for the Dog Days Bar.

It was picked up on the third ring. "Dog Days Bar."

"Kenny?"

"Yo!"

"It's Debbie Melvin, is my dad there?"

"Yes, in his usual spot."

"Can you tell him Mom went into surgery?"

"Sure thing, doll." Debbie liked Kenny. He was harmless and spoke like he was in a gangster flick from the 1930s. And he kept an eye on her father. It took a village to look after an alcoholic.

She heard the muffled message on the other end of the line as Kenny relayed the message to her father. The bartender came back on the line. "He wants to know if she'll be home in time for dinner."

Debbie made a *tsk-tsk* sound. "There's no way that is going to happen. Is the kitchen open today, Kenny?"

"It sure is."

"Can you make sure he gets a dinner? Meatloaf or a roast beef dinner will do," she said. "But make sure he eats something."

"Sure."

"Can you put it on his tab?"

"Speaking of his tab . . ."

Debbie let out a frustrated sigh. Her family certainly didn't put the fun in dysfunctional. "I'll stop in tomorrow on my way home from work and settle his bill."

"That would be great, Deb," Kenny said, and he was gone.

When she hung up, she saw she'd missed a call from her brother. Quickly, she called him back.

"Mom's in the hospital?" Darren asked.

"Yes. Broke her leg. She's in surgery right now," Debbie informed him.

"How bad is it?"

"It's a broken leg," she repeated. She wasn't sure what kind of answer he wanted.

"All right. I'll stop by the hospital on my way home from work," he told her.

She was about to dash off a couple more texts when she spotted a tall man in blue scrubs and a cap with a mask hanging off one ear, approaching the waiting room. Reflexively, she leaned forward, although knowing it was too soon to be about her mother as she'd only just gone in.

The surgeon spotted the intended family with a nod and two women, one elderly and one around Debbie's age, immediately stood up. The three of them huddled close, and he spoke to them in hushed tones. The younger woman let out a yelp and put her hand to her mouth. The elderly woman was shaking as he led them away. Debbie's mouth went dry. Apparently the news hadn't been good. How would she feel if something bad happened to her mother? The first thought that popped into her head was *relief*. Or would it be more complicated than that? Would she grieve the relationship they *didn't* have?

To distract herself from such intrusive, uncomfortable thoughts, she quickly wrote two texts, one to Barbara, and then one to Angie to keep them up to date.

Barb's reply came first: *Will pray for your mother. Everything is fine here.* The next text, from Angie, read *Want some company at the hospital while you wait?*

She smiled and declined. Angie was working, and there was nothing to do here but sit and wait.

Another reply. *Okay. But if you change your mind, let me know. Do you need anything?*

Smiling again, she sent a final text. *I'm good. Tx.* She added a smiley face emoji.

Notifications complete, Debbie sat back and waited.

She had the inside of her cheek bitten raw when finally someone called out, "Family of Darlene Melvin?"

Debbie stood and walked toward the doctor. She realized that other families were more than one. That no one, other than she, had waited alone. There was nothing that could be done about that. You couldn't force other family members to be there with you if they didn't want to.

The surgeon explained that her mother had gone to recovery. They'd ended up putting a screw in her leg and once she was out of recovery, she'd be going to a room. From there, she'd eventually be transferred to rehab if everything went well.

Debbie tried to imagine her mother in the hospital for any length of time and then moving on to a rehabilitation facility. She decided to stay in the present and not worry too much about the future. Because one thing Debbie was sure of was that her mother was a wild card: unpredictable.

Chapter Eleven

"Look at this." Darlene pointed to her breakfast tray. "I can't eat any of that. I don't even like oatmeal. It's like wallpaper paste."

"Try the toast. You have to eat something, Mom," Debbie said. She'd arrived early, wanting to stop in before she headed to work. Her mother was two days post-op and Debbie had arrived to find her in a foul mood. She'd had a restless night.

"The toast is cold." Her mother pushed the over-the-bed table away with a look of disgust.

"Whoa, hold on a minute," Debbie said. She supposed it was a big ask to get the toast from the kitchen—wherever that was—to a patient's room and still have it warm. Forget about hot. But she also knew her mother was particular about what she ate. Not that she ate a healthy diet, but she was fussy.

"Why don't I run over to Burger King and get you a Croissan'wich?" she suggested.

Her mother sighed. "I'd eat that."

"All right, I'll be right back." Debbie grabbed her purse and as she walked out the door, her mother called after her, "Egg, ham, and cheese."

"Got it."

There was a Burger King down on the highway, not far from the hospital. It was a straight run. She sailed through the drive-through, and it took no more than twenty minutes to go and come back.

"Where did you go for it? Ohio?" her mother asked on her return.

Debbie opened her mouth to say she hadn't been gone that long and then thought better of it. She tore open the bag and removed two breakfast sandwiches, handing one to her mother. She took the only chair in the room and placed it sideways so she could look out the window. From here, you could see the town of Lavender Bay and the lake beyond it.

"It's a nice view," she said, taking a bite of her sandwich.

"They tell me my blood pressure is high," her mother said. She removed the top of her Croissan'wich, inspected it, and replaced it before taking a bite.

"Probably from all the stress of the surgery and the fracture," Debbie posited.

"They've been giving me a blood pressure pill."

Debbie nodded, unsure of what to say. Her mother hadn't been to the doctor in just about forever, so she couldn't help but wonder what else might be medically wrong with her.

"Have they said when you're going to rehab?" she asked.

"I'm not going," her mother said casually.

"What? You have to go to rehab," Debbie said. "It's so important."

Scowling, her mother waved her hand several times as if swatting away a fly. "I already told them that whatever they could do at rehab they can do at my house."

"Mom!" Debbie couldn't help it that she raised her voice.

"Please watch your tone, Deborah Ann," her mother warned.

Debbie lowered her voice and hissed, "How are you going to get around at home? You're not going to be able to get up the stairs to go to bed."

Her mother shrugged, refusing to acknowledge the myriad of problems returning home with a broken leg presented. "I'll sleep in the recliner."

"That'll be comfortable," Debbie huffed. Trying to reason with the unreasonable was so frustrating.

"It doesn't matter what it is," Darlene said firmly. "I'm not going to rehab. As it is, I can't stand this place. I'm dying for a cigarette."

"Didn't they put you on a nicotine patch?"

Darlene's sigh was one of impatience. "Of course they did. But I can't smoke a patch, now, can I?"

Debbie returned her attention to her breakfast sandwich, thinking it was safer. She really needed to get to work, and as she crumpled up the wrapper and threw it into the garbage can beneath the television, a woman walked into the room. She was dressed in business casual, but the badge hanging on a lanyard around her neck indicated she was a hospital worker. She had thick black hair the enviable shade of midnight.

"Mrs. Melvin?"

"That's me," Darlene said, finishing her breakfast.

"I'm Kelly, the discharge planner."

Darlene stiffened in the bed. She tried to lift herself up straighter, but the cast on her leg was an impediment.

"Do you want some help, Mom?" Debbie asked.

"Nope."

"Mrs. Melvin, I'm here to start the ball rolling in relation to you going to rehab," Kelly said.

"I'm not going to rehab, I'm going home, and I told the doctor that yesterday," Darlene said sharply.

"Mom, maybe rehab would be the better place," Debbie said gently.

Darlene leveled her with a glare. "I'm going home."

"That is perfectly within your rights," Kelly said. "But we'll need to get supports into place for you at home. Do you live alone?"

"You could say that," Darlene said.

"Mom!" Debbie turned to Kelly. "My dad is there too, but he's eighty-five."

Kelly nodded. "Maybe some home care to help with activities of daily living. And of course, a physical therapist for rehab."

"Would a physical therapist come to the house?" Darlene asked. She seemed surprised by this.

"Yes."

"And what does home care do?"

"Help you with your shower, that sort of thing," Kelly explained. "It would only be for an hour a day."

Darlene waved her hand in a dismissive motion. "No, I won't need that."

"Mom, try it out first before you say no," Debbie advised. "You're going to need help in the shower."

"I'll wash up at the sink. Can't get the cast wet."

"Do you have family to help and support?" Kelly asked.

Darlene nodded toward Debbie. "I've got my daughter. She can help me."

Debbie stared at her mother, incredulous. She'd just been volunteered for a task she dreaded: taking care of her. Prior to her mother's hospitalization, it was always at the back of her mind that someday her parents were going to need some help. It appeared that that day had galloped in and trampled all over her.

Her mother looked at her and kept talking, "Maybe you could move in with me for a few weeks."

"What?" That slipped out before Debbie had a chance to think about how her reaction might sound.

"It would be easiest. Then you'd be there if I needed anything."

Kelly jumped in, and Debbie wished she hadn't. "Is this something that's doable?"

"Not really," Debbie said honestly. "I've got a house full of dogs and cats that need to be looked after."

Her mother scoffed. "This one, always putting animals ahead of people."

Kelly took the criticism in her stride; no doubt she'd seen her share of awkward family dynamics.

"And I have another daughter, Dawn," Darlene said.

Debbie couldn't picture her sister as a caregiver. She might be fine to do a welfare check via phone, but heavy lifting? Debbie didn't think so.

"What about Darren?" Debbie asked.

Her mother scowled. "Darren's a man, he can't do anything like this."

"How do we know?" Debbie asked. She hated when men and women were automatically put into traditional roles without being asked what they'd like to do. And honestly, she thought Darren was a better option than her sister. She'd ask him what he could do to help out.

"Remember, Mom, I work a full-time job," Debbie said.

"But that's volunteer work."

"No, it's a paid job. It's my job that I work to pay my bills."

To Kelly, Darlene said, "She had a perfectly good job as an accountant with a CPA agency. And quit it to work at the shelter." Her tone was a combination of incredulousness and disdain.

"We all have to do what's best for us," Kelly said diplomatically.

"That may be so, but I think it was a stupid move. She had a good job with great pay and benefits," Darlene said sourly.

"Mom, we've been over this before," Debbie said. "Besides, I'm sure Kelly isn't interested."

"All right, then," Kelly said, "I'll talk to the doctor about you going home."

"When will that be?" Darlene asked.

"Hopefully tomorrow if we can get everything in place."

"That soon?" Debbie asked.

Kelly nodded. She left some paperwork on Darlene's bed table and bid them goodbye.

After she was gone, Darlene said, "I suppose you can't take time off to come and stay with me."

"No, I have no time to take off," Debbie lied. She was not using her vacation time to take care of her mother.

"That figures. What am I supposed to do?"

"You should have gone to rehab," Debbie said. "Look, I've got to get to work. I'll see you at some point tomorrow. Darren said he'd stop in again after work."

"All right."

She hesitated before asking the next question: "Did you want me to run Dad up for a visit?"

"Why would I want that kind of aggravation? He called me yesterday from the bar, talking utter nonsense. He was three sheets to the wind, and I have no patience for that."

Debbie wanted to add that her mother had no patience for anything, but kept it to herself. "Okay, Mom, I'll talk to you later," she said instead.

Her mother nodded.

As soon as she walked out of her mother's hospital room, relief washed over her.

CHAPTER TWELVE

Darlene Melvin went home with equipment: crutches, a shower bench for the tub, and a hospital bed. She refused to use the bed, opting instead for the recliner or the sofa, with her leg up on pillows. And she used the shower bench in front of the bathroom sink to wash up. There was a personal care assistant who came every day at ten for one hour, but Darlene wouldn't let her into the bathroom. So the girl—she couldn't have been more than twenty-one—stood outside the bathroom door, waiting for Darlene's instructions. A physical therapist visited the house to do some gentle exercises with Darlene, but the actual therapy wouldn't start for another four to six weeks, after the leg was healed.

She had been home for three days when Debbie discovered a bunch of medications in blister packs at the bottom of the plastic bag her mother had brought home from the hospital. It was Saturday, and Debbie had come over early in the morning to give her mother a hand and to make her breakfast, as the personal care aides didn't come to the house on the weekends. She placed the incentive spirometer on the table next to her mother's chair.

"Don't forget to use this, Mom. It's for your lungs."

"I know what it's for. Leave it there and I'll get around to it."

Debbie was doubtful, but she moved on to the next item on her list. She held up the bag of medications. "What's this?"

Her mother looked up briefly, frowned, and returned to the word search puzzle in her lap. "Oh, those are meds the hospital said I have to take."

"What are they for?"

Her mother shrugged, circling letters in her word search with a stubby pencil. "This and that. They keep saying I have high blood pressure. And there's an inhaler for my lungs. And something for my stomach."

"And have you been taking them?"

Darlene shook her head. "I forgot about them."

"All right. Listen, I'll get a pill box. You can keep it right there on the table."

"I'm not taking any of those meds. I've done fine all along without any medication."

"You can't be walking around with uncontrolled high blood pressure!"

"As you can see, I'm not walking around!" Darlene countered.

Debbie squeezed her eyes shut and pinched the bridge of her nose. "Mom, come on. Do you want to have a stroke? Be paralyzed on one side with a droopy face? Lose your ability to speak? Would you like that?"

Her mother never looked up from her puzzle. "No, I would not like to lose my ability to speak, but I'm sure there are some people who'd love it."

Debbie changed the subject. "I'm going to make us some lunch. I picked up salami and baloney. What kind of sandwich would you like?"

"Salami. Weber's mustard. Not the French's. And butter on the bread," Darlene said.

"Coming right up."

At two o'clock, Debbie looked at her phone, expecting Dawn to arrive at any moment to relieve her. She needed to get home and let the dogs out. She also wanted to get started on her weekend cleaning. Her father was out, probably across the street at the bar. He'd left without a word right after his breakfast. She wondered how her parents stood it, living together under the same roof and not one word of conversation between them.

By two thirty when her sister hadn't shown up, she texted her and asked, *Are you coming over?*

It took Dawn fifteen minutes to reply. *Not today.*

Debbie saw red and quickly texted back. *I need to go home and let the dogs out.*

Then go.

Her sense of exasperation made her want to cry.

"Dawn's not coming," Darlene said matter-of-factly.

"No, she can't make it," Debbie said through gritted teeth.

"You can go, Debbie. I know you're worried about your dogs."

"That's okay, Mom."

"I'll be fine. I'm going to watch some television and try and take a nap."

Reluctantly, Deb agreed. She made sure her mother had everything she might need: her phone, the remote control for the television, a fresh glass of Pepsi, her word search book, and a pencil. She stepped back and looked at the table. "I think everything is there. Did you want to go to the bathroom one more time before I leave?"

"Would you stop with all the fussing?" her mother said. "Go let your dogs out before they destroy your house."

"All right," Deb said, still hovering.

Finally, Darlene looked up at her and said firmly, "Goodbye, Debbie!"

She nodded and said as she walked out, "I'll call you later, Mom."

There was no reply.

"Mom, do you still have the electric roaster?" Debbie asked a week later when she stopped over at her parents' house. She'd arrived late morning after she washed the floors at her house and took her dogs for a walk.

Darlene frowned. "Electric roaster?" She sat in her recliner, her broken leg elevated on two pillows, leafing through the circulars of the Sunday paper. The incentive spirometer lay in her lap. Debbie, though hopeful that her mother was using it, was also doubtful. Her lap might be as far as the plastic device had traveled.

Debbie nodded. "That old one. You remember. The one that used to belong to your mother? The one that sits on a small cabinet."

"Oh that," Darlene said. "It's up in the attic."

"I remember those roasts as being the best. Or am I imagining it?"

"No, you're not imagining it. It did a beautiful job on any cut of meat."

"I was thinking of making a roast for dinner tomorrow," Debbie said. Being here every day since her mother came home from the hospital, Debbie had learned that her parents hadn't met a bag of frozen or canned vegetables that they didn't like. It was disheartening to see them eating separately, her father at the kitchen table when he was home and her mother in her recliner.

There wasn't much she could do about that but maybe she could make them a proper meal.

"It's a lot of work. And I don't know if that old thing even works."

"Can I try?"

"Look, Debbie, there's pot pies in the freezer, just make those."

Debbie persisted. "Can I see what condition it's in?"

"Go for it," her mother said. "But the bulb is out in the attic, you'll need the flashlight."

"I've got my phone, I'll use that."

She was surprised her mother had been so agreeable. She'd braced herself for an onslaught of protestations that never came. On her way to the attic, she stopped in the kitchen and rooted around for a lightbulb, finally locating a dusty one way in the back of a cabinet, shoved behind an old cigar box. She wiped it off with a cloth and made her way to the second floor. At the end of the short hall was a heavy wooden door that led to the attic. She passed her old bedroom, not bothering to look in. It had remained the same since she'd left home, but every available space was now covered with her parents'—mainly her mother's—accumulation of things over the years.

She was hit by damp air when she opened the attic door. She flipped the switch at the bottom of the stairs and just as her mother had told her, there was no light.

She turned on the flashlight on her phone and carefully made her way up the steep, narrow staircase. Years ago, before Debbie was born, the steps had been painted brown. That paint was now chipped and worn from the passage of time. She wondered when her parents had last been up here.

Carefully, she managed to reach the bare bulb hanging over the top of the landing without tumbling down the staircase. After she swapped out the bulb, she made her way back to the bottom and flipped on the switch, illuminating the attic in light.

Smiling, she said to no one but herself, "Voilà."

She climbed up the steps and stood with her hands on her hips, looking around. Her immediate thought was she should have left it in darkness. The space was packed with cardboard boxes and junk. And everything was covered in dust. She stepped forward and walked right through a thick cobweb. It slashed across her face, and bits of it ended up in her mouth.

"Ew, *pfft*." She tried to dislodge the nasty bits from her mouth, swiping at her tongue several times, not even remotely wanting to venture a guess as to what it was.

The smell of mildew was faint, but it was there. She discovered a dead mouse and had to clamp her hand over her mouth to stifle a scream. At the far end of the space was the only window, but it was blocked with boxes stacked high. The first thing she did was shift those boxes and after a struggle, she managed to get the window open to air the room out. Immediately, cool air blew in. She stepped away breathless, scanning the dimly lit area for any sign of the old electric roaster.

In the far corner, next to the aluminum Christmas tree that had been her grandmother's, were boxes marked *Christmas* in her mother's boxy handwriting. As much as she would like to go through each one and look at everything, she reminded herself that she was here on a mission: to find the roaster.

By the time she spotted it, her hands were grimy with dust. There was a stack of large cardboard boxes that had to be moved for her to get to it. She went to lift the first one, and it was practically immovable. She tried again. She wiped off the top of the box as best she could. In the less-than-ideal light, she was able to make out the word *Judy* in her mother's handwriting at the top corner of the box.

Confused, she dragged the box down from its perch on top of the others and managed to get it to the floor. She slid her fingernail along the taped seal, which had gone brittle with age, and opened it up. Inside there was a stack of vinyl albums. No wonder it weighed a ton. On top was an album by Aretha Franklin, *Runnin' Out of Fools*. The album beneath it was *Meet the Supremes*. She couldn't imagine these were her mother's. From her recollection, her mother had been a fan of the Rolling

Stones and Led Zeppelin back in the day. She closed the box up, not wanting to get sidetracked. The next box was also labeled *Judy*, as were the rest of the boxes in the pile. She shoved them aside and made a mental note to look through them at another time.

There, against the wall, stood the electric roaster. She carried the top, a small oven, and then the bottom, a cream-colored cabinet, over to the top of the stairs where the light was better. It brought back memories of the Sunday roasts her mother used to make on rare occasions when she was a kid. This piece had occupied a place in the kitchen downstairs. The bottom cabinet had been filled with all sorts of kitchen items. She didn't know when it had been relegated to the attic. But who knew when things were retired. One day, they simply weren't used anymore and then banished to storage in an attic, a basement, or a spare bedroom. Or put out to the curb.

Carefully, she carried each piece down the stairs to the second floor and then transported it downstairs to the kitchen.

"I found it!" she announced triumphantly as she stepped off the last step of the staircase.

"What kind of condition is it in?" her mother asked from her recliner.

Debbie inspected it. Other than dust, it appeared all right. The front needed a good scrub, and a toothbrush would clean up the grooves of the dial nicely. There was a detachable electric cord inside that was covered in black cloth with gold specks on it. It seemed to be intact. "I think it's all right. It only needs a good cleaning," she said.

"Be careful. That's from the 1940s. Let's not burn the house down in all the excitement," her mother warned. "This is the only asset your father and I have."

"I'll be careful."

"I need to go to the bathroom, and I need something for pain," Darlene said. "My leg is throbbing."

"You should take the pain pill first and then wait fifteen minutes before you go to the bathroom."

"I'll go the bathroom first," her mother replied.

"But the nurse said you should take the pain relief before any activity."

Darlene closed her eyes and the muscles along her jaw worked overtime. "I can't wait."

Recognizing the telltale signs of an imminent outburst, Debbie hurried over to the recliner. "All right, bathroom it is."

After she assisted her mother to and from the bathroom, she helped her get comfortable in the recliner, gently lifting her casted leg and laying it on the pillows. Her mother only winced once. Deb went to the kitchen for the prescription painkillers and a glass of water. She handed both to her mother. Darlene poured out one tablet into her hand, popped it into her mouth, and washed it down with a good sip of water. Debbie spied the pill organizer she'd bought and filled, and lifted her eyebrows when she noticed some compartments were empty, meaning her mother was taking her prescribed meds. Best not to say anything, she thought.

Her father walked in, bundled up in the heavy cardigan Debbie had gifted him the previous Christmas. The smell of alcohol was faint on him, which meant he might be reasonable.

Beneath her breath, her mother muttered, "Just terrific."

Jerry scratched the back of his neck and looked around.

"Dad, did you have lunch?" Deb asked.

He shook his head.

"Would you like me to make you a sandwich?"

He tilted his head back and forth, considering her question, and said, "Sure."

Debbie paused. "Mom, I have a quick question for you."

"You ask an awful lot of questions," her mother said sourly. "And there's no such thing as a quick question."

"When I was up in the attic, I found a lot of boxes marked *Judy*." Beside her, her father stiffened. "Who's Judy?" she asked.

"Oh boy," Jerry said in a tone that sounded like he'd just received bad news. "I'm outta here." And without another word, he turned and walked out the door.

Debbie, confused by her father's abrupt departure, turned her gaze back to her mother and asked again, "Mom? Who's Judy?"

Darlene let out a long sigh. "My sister."

Debbie was speechless for a moment. She hadn't even known her mother had a sister. Was there a long-lost aunt in another part of the country somewhere? "Sister? Where is she?"

"Judy's dead," her mother said flatly. "We left her back in 1975."

That answer only left Debbie with more questions.

CHAPTER THIRTEEN

Over the next few days, Debbie's mother refused to shed any more light on the subject of her late sister. The only thing she got out of her was that Judy was a younger sister. But when Debbie pressed, her mother blew up and said, "I don't want to talk about it!"

When she got her father alone—which meant walking over to the Dog Days Bar—she questioned him, figuring the alcohol would loosen his tongue.

"Oh no you don't, Debbie," Jerry said, tipping back a bottle of Genny and taking a large gulp. "I made a promise to your mother fifty years ago that I would never mention Judy's name again. And that is *one* promise I always kept."

"Why all the secrecy?"

Her father was no less mysterious with his reply, shrugging and saying, "You know how your mother is."

"Can you tell me how she died?"

"She got hit by a car," Jerry said.

Debbie went to ask another question, but her father put up his hand. "I've told you enough. Your mother will kill me if she finds out. Now go on. Surely you must have a dog to walk or a cat to feed."

As she left the bar, she pulled out her phone and called her sister.

"Did you know that Mom had a sister?"

"No, I did not," Dawn said.

"It's very mysterious," Debbie said. If she expected a sympathetic ear from her sister, she was sadly mistaken.

"I hope you're not stupid enough to ask Mom a lot of questions about this sister," Dawn said.

Debbie bristled. "Not too many."

"It's your funeral. You know how she is," her sister said, and hung up.

She didn't bother calling her brother, assuming he'd tell her the same thing Dawn had told her.

But it only left her more intrigued. She figured there were ways around her mother's awkwardness.

"Mom, that attic is a mess, you should really get it cleaned out," she said as she carried in the tray with her mother's Sunday dinner on it. The electric roaster had cooked the meat to perfection. But it was still eighty years old, and Debbie kept an eye on it while it was cooking. She had prepared the roast as Darlene instructed, adding a little vinegar to tenderize it. She sat in the empty recliner next to her mother and tackled her own plate. "Oh, this is yummy."

"It certainly brings me back," Darlene said quietly. "My mother and grandmother used that roaster all the time. A bad meal never came out of it."

This softening of her mood was as rare as an interstellar alignment. Debbie was tempted to ask her about Judy but left it alone, thinking it was nice to enjoy a moment together.

"How come you stopped using it?" she asked instead, spearing a piece of carrot with her fork.

Her mother shrugged. "I don't know. You kids moved out and it was just me and your dad, and it was a lot of work."

"I get it. I live alone. I rarely feel like cooking a nice meal for myself."

"What do you do for your dinners?" her mother asked.

"Grab something on the way home. A taco or a burger."

"You should get those chicken pot pies," Darlene said. "They're tasty and filling."

"I'll keep that in mind."

They ate in silence for a few moments, until Debbie asked, "Mom, why don't you let me clean that attic out for you?"

"No, don't bother. There's too much junk up there. Plus, I can't have you running up and down the stairs asking me every five minutes whether I want to throw something out."

"Well, if you leave it, it'll be Dawn who decides. And she'll probably get a dumpster and throw everything out," Debbie told her.

Her mother didn't seem too bothered by that thought. "A dumpster might be all it's good for."

"I feel like I could be more useful around here," Debbie said, looking around, only too aware of the dining room table staggering beneath the weight of junk, which set her teeth on edge.

Her mother sighed, forking a piece of roasted potato into her mouth. "Knock yourself out, then."

Debbie looked at her mother, trying to gauge her mood. It was always varying degrees of grumpy. She nodded toward the plate in her lap and dared to ask, "How is it?"

Before her mother could respond, her father yelled from the kitchen, "It's delicious!"

"She didn't ask you, Jerry!" Darlene yelled back.

It had been enlightening for Debbie to see that every interaction between her parents was tense and at times, explosive. Had they always been like this? She couldn't remember. Growing up, there always seemed to be some kind of turmoil going on, with their mother at the center of it.

Finally, Darlene said, "It's not bad." She set her half-finished plate on the table next to her.

It was as good a compliment as Debbie was going to get from her mother.

After she washed all the dishes, she put the roaster back together and tucked it into the corner of the kitchen, out of everyone's way, especially her mother's. The last thing Darlene needed was another broken bone.

Debbie made her way to Coffee Girl and found Angie out on the floor, going around to the tables and talking to the customers. Debbie approached the counter and ordered a flat white and a lemon tart. Once she swiped her card through the reader, she was given a stainless steel table stand with the number eight on it.

Erica was in her forties and had worked at Coffee Girl for years. "We're super busy. I'll bring your order out as soon as I can," she said with a smile.

"No problem, Erica."

It was nice to get out of her parents' house. She gave the arm of her coatigan a quick sniff and hoped the smell of cigarette smoke wasn't too overbearing.

From behind her, Angie laughed. "Girl, why are you smelling your arm?"

Debbie stepped closer to her. "Do I reek of cigarette smoke?"

Angie shook her head. "Not at all. I take it you're coming from your mom's house."

"Yes."

"How's she doing?"

"The usual. Giving the physical therapist who comes to the house a hard time, making my father's life miserable, and refusing to do her exercises. Other than that, she's fine."

Angie laughed. "You've got your hands full."

Debbie sighed. "You could say that."

"Come on, let's get you a table."

Angie secured a small single table at the long banquette against the far wall. Debbie slid onto the comfortable booth-like seat. Her friend sat in the vacant chair across from her.

Debbie looked around and felt guilty. "I don't want to keep you from your work."

"I've got five minutes. I feel like we haven't spoken in forever," Angie said.

"I know, I'm sorry. How are you? How's Tom?"

A smile spread across Angie's face. "I'm fine. He's wonderful. We're great."

"I am so happy for you," Debbie said truthfully.

"Thanks, Debs, I know you are. How's caregiving one oh one going?"

"It's going. She's challenging. I try to stop in every day to see if she needs anything, and then I get sucked into the vortex and end up spending a few hours there."

They were interrupted by the appearance of Erica with Debbie's order. She set the flat white and the lemon tart in front of her.

"Thanks."

"Enjoy," Erica said, and went back to the counter to help the next customer.

"But wait until I tell you this," Debbie said to Angie. She took a sip of her flat white. "Mm, that tastes good." She set her cup down and said, "My mother had a sister."

Angie's eyes widened, and she leaned forward on her elbows. "What?"

"Can you believe it? Apparently she died a long time ago. Her name was Judy," Debbie said. She explained how she'd been in the attic looking for the roaster when she stumbled upon the mysterious boxes.

"What happened to her?"

Debbie shrugged. "All I know is that she was hit by a car fifty years ago. My father told me that part, but he wouldn't say anything more. Said he promised my mother he'd never mention it. I tried asking my mother, but she shuts right down, says she doesn't want to talk about it. I can't get any information out of either of them. They clam up."

"That is strange."

Debbie shook her head, picked up her fork, and tasted a piece of the tart, loving the tart lemony flavor. "Oh, that is nice."

Angie laughed. "You say that every time you get it."

"It's always true! Anyway, I can't get my aunt out of my mind. I don't even know where she died. Was it here in Lavender Bay?"

"Go to the library and go through the newspaper archive."

Debbie grimaced. "That would be twelve months of newspapers."

"You have a name, start there." Angie looked around. "Look who just walked in, Edna Knickerbocker and Edith Bermingham. Ask them. I bet Edna knows, she knows everything that has ever gone on in this town."

Debbie turned her head in the direction of Angie's gaze. It was hard to get used to seeing the two elderly sisters meeting for coffee. Wonders never ceased. For years—*decades*—they'd not spoken to one another, but had a recent détente.

"I'll ask them on my way out," she said, taking another mouthful of her lemon tart.

Angie stood. "I've got to get back to work."

"All right, I'll talk to you later."

Angie paused and said, "What's going on with you and Jim?"

"Sadly, nothing."

"I thought you had a good time with him?"

"I did, and he's a great cook, which is a plus, but I've been so busy with my mother that I haven't had a chance to see him again."

"Why don't you tell him that?"

"What? Why?"

"Because he thinks you're not interested."

"Oh," Debbie said. "Maybe it's just as well." She decided for vague.

But her friend was on to her and tilted her head to one side. "Don't be like that, Deb. There's no reason you can't have a happy relationship."

"I have a happy relationship with my dogs and cats," she countered.

"I mean with a man. I can't recommend it enough," Angie said.

"It sounds like a testimonial."

"Maybe it is," Angie said with a grin, and made her exit.

When Debbie had finished her coffee and tart, she slid out of the seat, pulled on her coatigan, and made her way through the maze of tables to Mrs. Knicker-bocker and Mrs. B.

"Hello, Debbie," Edna and Edith said in unison.

"Good morning, ladies. How's everything?"

"We're fine," Edna said, and her sister nodded in agreement.

"Do you mind if I join you for a moment?" Debbie asked.

"Of course not," Mrs. B said.

Debbie cast a quick glance around and borrowed a vacant chair from a neighboring table.

As she sat down, she was aware of the scrutinous gaze of both women.

"I was wondering if you remember when my mother's sister was killed," she started.

Mrs. B threw a hand to her chest and said, "Goodness, I wasn't expecting that."

"Nor I," Mrs. Knickerbocker said to her sister.

"It was a long time ago," Mrs. B said.

"It happened in 1975," Debbie said, hoping to jog their memories.

"I remember that," Edna said. "It was in August. We had a terrible summer that year: unrelenting heat. And that poor girl was run over by a car out on the highway."

"How old was she?" Debbie asked.

"She wasn't that old. Maybe eighteen or nineteen. Those kinds of tragedies, although they do happen, don't happen that often in a town like Lavender Bay, so you'd remember it," Mrs. B said.

"What she was doing out on the highway at that time of night was something we couldn't figure out. In those days, hitchhiking was a no-no," Edna said. "Too many young women ending up in a ditch across the highways and byways of America."

"That's colorful," Edith said.

"Sad too," Edna said. "At that time, I was working over at the Dog Days Bar at night and the jelly factory during the day. It was all anyone talked about for a few weeks."

Debbie thought that was how it was: A tragedy happened, everyone talked about it and nothing else, and then it receded into the background until it faded out altogether, and all that was left was a few cardboard boxes of belongings sitting in a dusty attic.

"Did you know her?" Debbie asked.

"Not really," Mrs. B said.

"We knew of the family, but that was about it," Edna added. "There was a nice write-up in the paper about her with a photo next to it. I remember thinking she was a lovely girl."

Debbie had a hard time wrapping her head around the fact that these two women were talking about a blood relative of hers whom, up until recently, she'd had no idea existed.

She stood and thanked them, encouraged by the reconciliation of these two sisters, thinking that maybe there was hope for her own family.

Chapter Fourteen

The day was slipping by, but Debbie had one more stop to make before going to the library to search for information about her aunt. What Angie had said about Jim thinking she wasn't interested bothered her. And that surprised her. She asked herself, *Am I interested?* and after thoughtful debate, decided she was. After all, the terrible marriage had been almost two decades ago. She was certain she wasn't the same person she was back then. And she could do a lot worse than Jim Sloane.

It was an overcast autumn day with a definite chill in the air. Wet, decaying leaves were gunky underfoot, and the only plus was that at least it wasn't raining. All the shops along Main Street had put away their Halloween decorations, and a few had Thanksgiving displays in their windows. There were even a couple that had skipped straight to a Christmas theme.

Debbie wasn't a big fan of Christmas. She knew a lot of people took it seriously. She thought of the Cooks and the Campbells. If the holidays were an Olympic sport, then Louise and her sister, Gail, could medal in it. She supposed your childhood memories of Christmas decided whether you loved it as an adult or not. She was envious of those people who looked forward to it as much as they did as a child. Growing up in her household, her father was always bombed at Christmastime, and her mother was always in a bad mood. Like so many life events in the Melvin household, it was just another thing to be gotten through and gotten over with.

As she approached the Ink Stain, a young woman was exiting it, leaving Debbie to wonder what kind of tattoo she'd gotten. Or maybe she'd simply had her ears pierced. When she pushed through the door, Jim was showing a client, a man in his forties, through to one of the rooms off the main area. It was lit up, and it reminded Debbie of an examination room in a doctor's office.

Jim's face was full of surprise at the sight of her. "Debbie."

"Hi, Jim."

He turned to his client. "Go on in, Carl, and make yourself comfortable. I'll be in in a minute."

Now that she was here, she didn't know what to say. She should have prepared for this, but she knew why she didn't: If she had thought about it too much, she would never have stopped.

"I know I haven't seen you lately," she started, "But I'm busy with my mother. She broke her leg."

"Angie told me. I didn't want to bother you," Jim said.

She lowered her voice, aware of Carl in the other room with the door open, probably listening. It's what she would have done. "You're not bothering me."

He smiled. "Glad to hear it. Would you like to come over for dinner again sometime soon?"

"I would like that. I'd have you over for dinner at my house, but I'm not much of a cook."

"Don't worry about that. Can you make a sandwich?"

"Sure, but my specialty is bagels and cream cheese."

"I like bagels." His laugh was easy and downright attractive, now that she thought about it.

"That's good. Someday I'll have you over for bagels and cream cheese."

"It's a date."

"It is," she agreed, and with a huge smile on her face, she waved goodbye and exited.

The Lavender Bay Library was over on Lincoln Avenue, not far from Ben Franklin Elementary School and McKinley High School. At one time that made it convenient for students, but now that everyone had research at their fingertips with their phones, she wondered if students even used the library anymore. She probably hadn't been inside since she was in high school herself, which was almost twenty-five years ago.

The hush of the interior immediately slammed her back to her high school days. And the first thing that came to mind was a memory of her and Angie huddled in the stacks, reading old copies of Sidney Sheldon. The librarian had first shushed them, and then eventually asked them in a whisper to leave. They had.

Tentatively, she approached the desk, looking around as she did. The place had been renovated since she'd last been inside. It was done up in white and gray, and skylights let in natural light. A few people sat at computer terminals, and there were kiosks where you could check out books and request them as well. The library had definitely moved into the twenty-first century. She approached the information desk. A man sat behind it with his eyes fixed on a computer screen, but he turned his attention to her and smiled. "Can I help you?"

Debbie returned the smile. "I hope so. Do you have archives of *The Lavender Bay Chronicles*? I'm looking specifically for August 1975."

He nodded and stood. "That narrows it down. Do you have a library card?"

She shook her head. "I don't."

"You'll need a card to access the computer."

"Oh."

"You can sign up for one right now."

"How long will it take to arrive?" she asked.

He appeared confused, as if he didn't understand the question.

She clarified, "I mean, it comes by mail?"

He gave her an indulgent smile. "No, you'll have it right now."

"Oh." And then, "It's been a long time since I've been in the library."

"Don't worry about it. We're always here if you need us."

She filled out and signed the form quickly, and the librarian handed her a shiny new card in hues of lavender.

He pointed out the back of the card. "There's your library account number right there. Use that to log in to any computer, and the last four digits of the card is your PIN."

Debbie nodded. "Got it."

"Would you like me to walk you through how to use the archives?"

"If it isn't too much trouble."

"Not at all. Usually, to use a computer, you have to call ahead or go online to book one by the hour. But there are a few available now, so I'll put you in for the hour."

"Thanks, I appreciate that."

He led her to an unoccupied terminal, and she took a seat.

He walked her through accessing *The Lavender Bay Chronicles* archives, how to search by date and event, and even how to zoom in and out to read the tiny print.

Debbie thanked him and got to work, trawling through the newspaper in search of information on her mother's sister. She was sidetracked by the movies that were showing back then: namely *Jaws* and *One Flew Over the Cuckoo's Nest*, both of which she'd seen several times. She read with great interest the lost-and-found columns, wondering if the lady ever found the diamond watch she lost at the beach. It was either long gone or someone else was enjoying it. She scanned every headline and the accompanying opening lines of each article. It was a slow, tedious process. And having to go through the whole month of August—assuming Mrs. Knickerbocker had the month right—meant she was going to need more than an hour. As she read bridal announcements, she studied the black-and-white photos of the brides from 1975, looking young and hopeful. There were all the sports scores of the summer baseball teams, from Little League to adult men's league. Most of the teams were sponsored by the Dog Days Bar. She wondered if her father ever played but somehow doubted it.

It turned out there was no need for her to search through the entire month. The article she'd been looking for was on the front page of the August 9th edition. The headline read *Local Girl Hit by Car and Left for Dead.*

Debbie quickly scanned the article and then went back to the beginning and read it again slowly:

Judith MacNamara, 18, of Adams Street, was found on the highway in the early hours of the morning. A passerby found her on the side of the highway, the apparent victim of a hit-and-run. She was pronounced dead at the scene.

Miss MacNamara was a recent graduate of Lavender Bay High School, where she excelled in English and Math and belonged to the drama club and the debate club. She is survived by her parents, Mr. and Mrs. Leonard Mac-Namara, and an older sister, Darlene MacNamara.

Police are asking any witnesses to please come forward.

Funeral arrangements to be made at a later date.

Debbie leaned back in her chair and blinked several times, trying to digest all this information. What a horrible way to die.

She leaned forward to study the black-and-white yearbook photo of her aunt that accompanied the article. Even though it wasn't in color, Debbie recognized the red hair the MacNamaras were famous for. She wore it in the style of the time: bangs, parted down the middle, and feathered back on both sides. She wore a prim plaid blouse buttoned to the neck with a ribbon around the neckline. Although she bore a strong resemblance to Debbie's mother, her fashion choices were as far from Darlene's as possible. Debbie had seen a few photos of her mother from back in the seventies. Lots of red hair, halter tops, flare jeans or cropped shorts, and always holding a cigarette and sometimes a beer bottle. Maybe that was why her mother was adamant about not talking about her dead sister: maybe they were so different that they didn't get along. She thought of her own siblings and had to admit, hand on heart, that she wasn't close with either of them. She always considered Angie more of a sister than Dawn.

She scrolled through subsequent editions, searching for any follow-up articles. There was a report a few days later that the Lavender Bay police were still searching for witnesses to the hit-and-run of Judith MacNamara, but so far no one had come forward. They even suggested that someone might have hit her and, with it being in the middle of the night, thought they'd hit a deer. Regardless, they'd like to talk to them.

Weeks later, another follow-up article, now relegated to page three, revealed that the police were no further ahead. The high school was hosting a memorial assembly in Judith's honor. Debbie wondered if her mother and her grandparents had attended. She couldn't see her mother attending such an event, but maybe she had been different back then. She couldn't even be sure her mother would attend her father's funeral when the time came. It was anyone's guess.

As she walked out of the library with printed copies of the articles, she wondered how she could get her mother to open up about her aunt without setting her off.

Because she wanted to know what happened that night back in 1975.

CHAPTER FIFTEEN

Debbie decided a change of scenery was necessary, and she showed up at coffee morning at Louise Cook's house with a box of donuts in hand. She needed a break from dealing with her mother, where every question was taken the wrong way and every response was dissected. She understood why her father spent most of his days at the bar. After weeks of caring for Darlene and spending time with her every day, she was ready to join him.

As usual, the driveway of the house on Heather Lane was packed with cars, with the overflow out on the street in front of the house.

"Deb's here," Louise called out as she entered through the back door. Deb stepped into her waiting embrace and closed her eyes. It felt good to be hugged by Louise. It always made her feel better.

Louise's rescue cat, the one-eyed, three-legged Peter, stood carefully from his bed. He'd found a loving home with Louise, and he was thriving. Deb had fostered him and was delighted that he remembered her. She stooped to get closer to him, stroking his back and telling him how big and brave he was. He purred under her attention.

"Don't even think of it, Debbie," Louise teased. "You can't have him back."

Debbie laughed.

"I can't imagine my life without him," Louise went on.

Five minutes in and Debbie could already feel the lift in her mood. The air here in this house on Heather Lane was definitely different from her parents' home over on Clover Drive; it wasn't so rife with tension.

She was disappointed to see that Jim wasn't there. She'd been looking forward to seeing him, even fussing with her appearance a little bit.

She took a seat between Gail's younger daughter, Suzanne, and Nadine.

"How's Herman?" Debbie asked Nadine. Nadine's rangy dog was a hoot, taking on the unofficial role of mascot when Nadine opened her inn after she moved back to Lavender Bay.

"He's fine. Loves having all those guests to make a fuss over him."

Debbie laughed.

From the other end of the table, Gail asked, "How's your mother?"

"She's all right. Coming along." No sense in telling them how she was abrasive toward the physical therapist, or how she was hit-and-miss with the exercises and then couldn't understand why her progress was so slow. They already knew she was difficult. No need to spell it out for them.

Gail and Louise had agreed to use this Sunday morning to discuss the upcoming holidays. The sisters alternated hosting Thanksgiving and Christmas each year. They sat next to each other on one side of the table. Gail wrote *Thanksgiving* on a notepad.

"All right, let's talk turkey," Louise said.

There was laughing and joking around the table, and it made Debbie's heart ache that this wasn't her own family and that they could never be like this. In her wildest dreams, she couldn't picture herself sitting around a table with Dawn and Darren, laughing. Not after that disastrous brunch.

"Debbie, can we count on you for your sweet potato casserole?" Louise asked.

She nodded. "Yes, of course." Her family did Thanksgiving but not in the traditional sense. It was usually a serving of chicken pot pie for everyone and a frozen Sara Lee cheesecake or a Pepperidge Farm cake for dessert.

And her father took off soon after dinner for the bar, which was open three hundred and sixty-five days a year.

Everyone around Louise's table spoke at once, with many sidebars going on and everyone seeming to understand it all, as if they all spoke fluent Cook and Campbell. The ache in Debbie's heart continued to blossom and began to put pressure on everything surrounding it. It was an ache and a longing for something she'd never have: a sense of belonging with her own family. Every holiday was crummy and she couldn't help but wonder if her aunt had lived, if things might have been different. Maybe an uncle or a cousin or two? How awesome would that have been?

"Debs, where'd you go?" Angie asked. "You look far away."

She gave her friend a quick smile.

"Any luck finding out anything about your aunt?" Angie asked softly.

Debbie shook her head.

"What's this?" Esther asked, leaning across the table toward them.

Silence descended around the table as they all looked at Debbie. Embarrassed, she pushed a stray lock of her hair off her forehead and cleared her throat, getting her emotions under control.

"I only recently learned that my mother had a sister who was hit and killed by a car back in the summer of 1975."

"That's awful," Maureen said.

Louise appeared thoughtful. "Oh, my goodness, that's right. Judy MacNamara. Hit-and-run."

"I don't think they ever found the driver who did it," Gail added, looking at Louise for confirmation. Louise shook her head. "No, they didn't."

The two sisters exchanged a look and then lowered their heads. Debbie narrowed her eyes at them, wondering what that was all about.

"Did you know her?" she asked.

"She was in my year at McKinley. We graduated together," Louise told her.

This surprised Debbie. "What was she like?" The need to find out more about this aunt was becoming a driving force in her life.

"She was quiet and shy," Louise replied. "We didn't have any classes together. But she was a sweet girl."

She must have been adopted, Debbie thought, thinking of her own mother. "Mom doesn't want to talk about it," she said.

"I can imagine it must be very painful for her, even after all this time," Louise said softly.

Gail looked at Louise and said, "I don't know what I'd do if anything ever happened to you. I don't think I'd ever recover."

Louise smiled softly at her older sister. "Same here."

"Speaking of your love and devotion for each other," Maureen started. "You two still owe us an explanation."

"For what?" Gail asked.

"You told us once that you weren't always close and that it was the summer of 1975 that changed everything," Esther said.

"It was a strange summer indeed," Gail said.

"A lot happened that summer," Louise added softly.

"It sure did."

Louise cast a sympathetic glance at Debbie. "And not all of it was good."

"Come on, tell us," DeeDee prompted.

Louise and Gail looked at each other.

"I suppose we should tell them what happened," Gail said.

Louise nodded. "It's time."

Part Two

Gail and Louise

CHAPTER SIXTEEN

1975

Louise Sturges stood at the foot of the staircase and yelled up, "Come on, Gail, I'm hungry!" She should have gone with her parents, but she said she'd wait and drive over with her sister. At eighteen, it didn't look too cool to be driving around with your parents on a Sunday afternoon. Her stomach rumbled and she decided she'd rather be fed than look cool.

"Wait a minute!" came the reply.

They were heading over to Sam and Joy Ruggiero's house for Sunday dinner. The Ruggieros were longtime friends of their parents', and when they were younger, they went every Sunday. But as they all got older and Sam and Joy's brood of three expanded to include grandchildren, Gail and Louise's mother, Diana, had told Joy they'd come only once a month. Sam and Joy had protested vigorously, but Diana wouldn't budge, claiming she and Mark had decided to dedicate Sunday afternoons to a drive and dinner out somewhere along the way.

Despite her determination to let their family friends spend most of their Sundays with their own growing brood, Louise knew that decision had been hard on her mother. She loved the Ruggieros with all her heart. Their house was the first place she'd stepped out into public after the industrial accident at the Cheever Aviation plant during the war that had caused her to lose a part of her scalp and left her disfigured for life.

Louise glanced at her watch, a thick leather band with a red strawberry embossed on it. Joy served dinner promptly at one o'clock. It was now five minutes to, and the Ruggieros lived in the next town over; they weren't even in Lavender Bay.

Louise spotted Gail's car keys on the table by the front door, and an idea popped into her head.

She called up again. "Gail, so help me, if you don't come down right this minute, I'm taking your car and going over myself!"

"You wouldn't dare!"

"Watch me."

Fed up, Louise grabbed the satchel she used as a purse and picked up the keys on her way out, letting the wooden screen door slam behind her. She didn't possess a driver's license. She hadn't gotten around to it. Her parents or Gail drove her everywhere she needed to go.

Although she'd never driven, she'd seen everyone else do it a million times; it couldn't be that difficult, could it?

The early afternoon sun beat down on her face as she stepped off the porch. Overhead, the sky was a cloudless blue. She couldn't remember the last time it had rained. Gail's pale blue 1966 Ford Falcon was parked in front of the house, out on the street. Louise slung her satchel between the two front seats and situated herself behind the steering wheel. She froze for a moment, not sure what to do. She leaned over slightly to the right and tried the first key in the ignition, but that didn't work. Most likely it was the key for the doors and trunk. The second key fit, she turned it in the ignition, and the car came to life. A smile of satisfaction creased her face. She stepped on the gas pedal maybe a little too hard, because there was a long *Vroom* sound. She eased up.

She took hold of the gearshift on the side of the steering column and attempted to put the car into drive, but she couldn't get it to move. She frowned as she fooled with it, but the thing wouldn't budge. The sound of the porch door slamming alerted her that her sister was on her way. She tried the gearshift again; she'd love to take off and leave Gail behind. That would serve her right.

But Gail opened the driver's-side door, leaned over her sister roughly, and pulled the key out of the ignition. "Get out!"

Louise didn't trust her sister. She'd leave her standing on the curb and take off, so she picked up her satchel and climbed over to the passenger seat. In that short time, the back of her dress felt sweaty and sticky from the vinyl seat.

Gail jumped in wearing heavy blue eyeshadow and lip gloss and reeking of Charlie perfume. She wore a lavender cotton skirt and a sleeveless blouse.

"You're coming in strong with the perfume, Gail," Louise said. "Unless you're trying to pick up Sam or Sam Jr."

Gail looked over at her and narrowed her eyes. "Shut up. I should leave you right here and let you find your own ride."

"Stop talking and let's go!" Louise said, motioning with her hands. "I'm hungry!"

"When are you not hungry?" Gail demanded. She started the car, threw it in drive, looked over her shoulder, and pulled out onto the street. "You're a bottomless pit!"

That was true. Louise ate indiscriminately and all the time, whereas Gail always seemed to be on some kind of diet.

Neither sister spoke as they made their way to the highway and headed south. Gail booked, and they weren't that late. When they arrived at the Ruggieros', Joy was just serving up the first course.

Their mother glared at the two of them and tapped her wristwatch, arching one eyebrow in a silent rebuke. Diana Sturges, now almost mid-fifties, was still considered an attractive woman. Sharp cheekbones, clear, bright eyes, and long legs were her best features. Tanned from the summer sun, she wore a headscarf, as always, to cover the extensive scarring on her scalp from an accident during the war. Outside of her bedroom, she was never without a head covering.

Louise shrugged and glanced in Gail's direction so their mother knew exactly who to blame.

Sam Ruggiero, patriarch of the Ruggiero family, stood up and broke into a wide smile. "Look who's here, Miss America one and Miss America two."

Louise giggled and Gail mumbled, "Sorry we're late, Sam. My fault."

Sam waved them away. "Don't worry about it." And then with a grin, he added, "I know how it is, Gail. You have to spend a lot of time on your hair to get it to look just right." Still grinning, he said, "I spent hours on mine this morning!" And he brushed his hand over the top of his bald dome.

Everyone burst out laughing except his wife, Joy, who shook her head, pursed her lips and said, "Quit horsing around and let's eat." She positioned herself at the head of the table in front of two large pans and a huge pot of sauce and meatballs.

His response was another laugh. You couldn't offend Sam. He was all about laughter and having a joke. There was nothing mean about him. Louise agreed with her mother's assessment that he was probably the kindest man they'd ever known, aside from their father.

"Grab a seat, sit down before your dinner gets cold," Sam said.

There were two vacant seats on opposite sides of the table, and Louise was glad she didn't have to sit next to Gail. She took the seat next to one of the Ruggiero grandchildren, a ten-year-old boy named Lucas. She smiled and asked him how he was doing. Shy, he only nodded.

Gail had taken the chair next to Lucas's mother, Rose, who was Sam and Joy's only daughter.

Louise looked around the table. All the regulars were there: the Sturgeses, Sam and Joy, the three Ruggiero children and their spouses, who were in their late thirties and early forties, and all their kids. It was loud, busy and boisterous, and Louise loved it. She hoped someday to have a house full of kids herself. It sure looked like a lot of fun.

"You girls got boyfriends yet?" Sam asked, accepting a plate from his wife. It was laden with manicotti, meatballs the size of baseballs, and a liberal amount of sauce. Sam wasn't tall, maybe five five, and Joy wasn't even five foot. Their mother had told them that when they drove to the plant in Cheever during the war, Joy always had to sit on a telephone book to reach the pedals and to be able to look out over the steering wheel. The Ruggieros had hearty appetites, and Joy always seemed to be cooking.

"Are the boys beating a path to your front door?" Sam asked.

Gail shook her head. "No, I don't want to be tied down."

He burst out laughing. "Why not?"

"I want to live a little first," Gail said.

"What about you, Lou?" Sam asked.

"No, no one yet," she replied, though she was hopeful.

"You'll never land a man dressed like that," Gail said. "You look like you just walked out of *Little House on the Prairie*." Unlike Gail, who liked flashy and fashionable, Louise opted for a plain and simple style, like Laura Ashley. Her current dress was from the Prairie collection.

"I love that show!" Sam said. He poured some of his homemade wine into his glass and passed the bottle around the table.

"I do too," Louise said. "It's so nice and wholesome."

"It makes me want to puke," Gail said, pouring wine into her glass.

"Gail, can you choose some better words, please," Diana scolded. Next to her, her husband, Mark, laughed to himself as if he'd given up on the idea of his oldest daughter being less bold and forthright.

Gail shrugged and sipped her wine.

"What do you like to watch, Gail?" Sam asked.

"I like *Police Woman*."

"I do too!" Joy said, finally taking her seat and starting her own dinner. "She's so smart and pretty."

"And independent," Gail added.

"Women shouldn't be cops," Sam opined. "Too dangerous."

"Sam, do you watch *The Waltons*?" Louise asked.

Sam forked a section of manicotti into his mouth. He nodded and after his mouth was clear, he said, "I love that show too. It's all about the simpler times of this great country. 'Goodnight, John Boy. Goodnight, Mary Ann.'"

"Mary Ellen!" Joy and Rose reminded him in unison. Joy shook her head. "He can't get that right. We tell him constantly, Mary Ellen, not Mary Ann."

Sam laughed so hard he shook. "Close enough." He looked at Louise. "Am I right?"

Laughing, she nodded. She couldn't argue with him.

"After dinner, we'll take you down to the basement. The kitchen is finished," Sam said proudly. Over the winter, he had informed them that they were building a second kitchen in the basement because during the summer, the kitchen upstairs was too hot to cook in.

"You finally got it done?" Mark said from across the table.

"Finally. We were waiting on my cousin Dominic to tile the floor. But it's finished. In fact, this meal was cooked down in the new kitchen," Sam said.

"You must find it much cooler down in the basement."

Joy nodded. "It's wonderful. It's so cool on these hot days. The only problem is running up and down the stairs, but it is better."

"She was sweating her weight off upstairs in the kitchen. She was barely casting a shadow. I couldn't send her outside on a windy day," Sam said in mock seriousness.

There was laughter right around the table.

"But seriously," Joy said, "it does make a difference, it's a joy to cook down there. It's not only cool but it's quiet too."

"I even got her a little radio so she could listen to the oldies," Sam said. "It's important to keep the cook happy."

Joy laughed, but she shook her head. She was used to her husband; they'd been married almost forty years.

More laughter. Louise decided if she ever did get married, she'd marry someone like Sam: kind and *funny*.

Chapter Seventeen

G ail could barely move for all the food she'd eaten. After dinner, she'd refused espresso and biscotti, not that she didn't like them, but she had no more room. She'd have to seriously diet for the rest of the week. The manicotti was delicious, and despite fretting over what all the food would do to her waistline, she cornered Joy in the kitchen when she was helping to clear the table and asked her what she put in the ricotta cheese—it was so tasty it was practically addictive.

Joy smiled at Gail, taking the stack of dirty plates from her. "Mint and basil." Then she winked. "But keep it to yourself. I can't let all my secrets out there."

"Understood."

After the table was cleared, Gail took the linen tablecloth outside and shook it over the porch railing, then neatly placed it back on the dining room table. She looked over at her sister, who had Rose's youngest, a baby not even one year old, in her lap, cooing to it and talking in funny voices. The baby giggled in delight, trying to shove her fist into her mouth, drooling all over everything.

Diana and Rose had joined Joy in the kitchen to do the washup, and Gail found a dish towel and helped out with the drying. As there were five of them to wash and dry, including the oldest granddaughter, Jeannie, it didn't take long.

Mark, Diana, Sam, and Joy retreated to the chairs in the shade beneath the old oak tree out back, and Gail made her way to the front porch. Her head was pounding. The previous night, she'd been out late at the new disco up in Cheever. They had nothing like that place in Lavender Bay. She wished they did, as the drive to Cheever was long and driving home at two in the morning was tricky. She'd gone with a few of her girlfriends, and they'd danced all night. The balls of her feet were killing her, and she had a headache the size of Lake Erie, but it had been worth it. She'd had a great time. She'd even suggested to her friends that they drive up later that night but was met with resistance: "Who goes out on a Sunday night?" She didn't see what the problem was. The marquee outside the building touted that it was open seven nights a week. Somebody must be going up there on Sunday nights or they wouldn't be open. Their county's drinking laws mandated that bars close at two in the morning. She wished she lived up in

Buffalo; she'd heard closing time up in that county was four a.m. Staying out until four in the morning, dancing and drinking, sounded wild to her.

She took a seat on the front porch, relishing the shade. There was a large sycamore tree that added extra shade in addition to the porch roof. It had to be ten degrees cooler. She looked at the cars on the street, musing about how their chrome shone with a sharpness because of the sun.

Rose stepped outside, still wearing an apron over her clothes. Gail had always liked Rose. She remembered when they were children, Rose had always been so kind to them, treating them to ice cream cones with her hard-earned babysitting money. Rose was not much taller than Sam, but she was very attractive, with dark eyes and eyebrows and an abundance of thick black hair. She'd kept her figure after having five kids. Her husband, a television repairman, was currently inside, watching some baseball game on the television.

"It feels good to get off my feet," Rose said, sitting down in the other chair.

"Amen," Gail added. "I was out dancing all night. My feet are killing me."

"Ahh, I remember those days well. Out all night, dancing. All the music."

"Do you miss it?"

"No, not really." Rose crossed one leg over the other, swinging it gently. "When I was your age, I remember it was all I wanted to do. I actually used to feel sorry for my mother and father, stuck in the house all the time."

"I know. I think my parents lead boring lives," Gail said. "They like to play chess and watch the news, go to the movies, go for drives."

Rose affected a shudder. "Checkers is more my speed."

"Mine too. My poor father. He tried to teach Louise and me how to play chess, but it was hopeless. It wasn't that we weren't smart enough, it's just that we weren't interested."

"But anyway," Rose said, "I don't miss the nightlife. I think as you get older, you're more content to remain at home. Plus, you're doing different things, like raising children and working."

"I don't plan on getting married until I'm at least thirty," Gail said with conviction.

"I said that once too," Rose said with a laugh. "A long time ago. But by the time I was thirty, I had three kids already."

"Is there happiness in being a housewife?" Gail wondered out loud. There had to be more to life than cooking, cleaning, and raising children. And she wasn't going to feel guilty because she wanted a life outside of family.

With a shrug, Rose said, "Mom always loved cooking and cleaning. The only job she ever worked was at the aviation plant with your mother during the war. After that, she was happy being with us kids and staying home."

"She does it so well!" Gail said.

"That she does." Rose's expression turned wistful. "If I had the chance, I'd stay home with my kids instead of working at the bank. These days, no woman goes to work to get out of the house. She goes to work because she has to."

Gail didn't know if she agreed with that, but she respected the other woman's opinion. Everyone had to decide for themselves what was best for them. She could easily see Louise being a stay-at-home mom. But it wasn't for her. She wanted a career.

"I heard the Rolling Stones are coming to Buffalo in August, will you go?" Rose asked.

"I like the Stones but not enough to stand with eighty thousand people in the August heat." Gail paused and added, "Besides, I like disco music best."

"I do too! It's so upbeat and you can dance to it. Where's the young crowd going out these days, anyway?"

"There's a place up in Cheever, a new disco called Flashes. Have you heard of it?"

A shadow passed across Rose's face. "I have. Be careful. I've heard rumors that there are a lot of drugs passing through there."

"Really?" Gail feigned surprise. She'd seen it firsthand. Only last night, she went into the ladies' room and walked in on a couple of girls snorting a line of coke off the bathroom counter. They'd paid no attention to Gail or the other girl that had come in behind her. There were some people at the disco who were as high as kites. She steered clear of them. She was there to dance and enjoy the music. She considered herself mature enough not to get involved in any of that.

"You know not to turn your back on your drink, right, Gail?" Rose said. She had an air of *older sister* about her.

"I do. I'd never leave my drink unattended," Gail told her. She'd heard too many horror stories of mickeys being slipped into drinks.

"Good girl."

Gail was just about to ask her not to mention the drugs thing to her mother when Rose said, "I was telling your mother about the drugs issue at Flashes. She was horrified."

She groaned inwardly. That would be the end of that. Her mother was pretty strict. Her father, who was a softy, was so in love with her mother that he went along with everything she decided, always adding, "Your mother knows what is best." It could be quite maddening at times.

"Mom comes from a different generation," she said.

"I bet times were a lot simpler in their day," Rose said. "I have no idea what it's going to be like when Natalie and Maggie are older and going out. I shudder to think about it."

Gail had nothing to add.

As if on cue, Rose's daughter Natalie emerged from the house. "Dad says we're going home."

"Are we?" Rose asked.

"Do I have to go?" Natalie asked. "It's summer. Nonnie and Poppy said I can stay overnight if I want."

"If they said it's all right, that's fine," Rose said. She looked at Gail. "Now, if I could convince a few of the others to stay, that would be great."

Gail laughed, thinking she should be heading off herself.

"I want to stay by myself," Natalie said.

"I bet you do," Rose said. "I wouldn't mind staying here by myself either." She stood, brushed her daughter's thick black hair away from her face, and went inside. Gail followed them.

Louise handed the baby back to Rose.

"You're a natural with children, Louise," Rose told her.

Here we go, singing Louise's praises. "I'm leaving, Louise, are you coming with me or do you want to go home with Mom and Dad?" Gail asked. One look out the kitchen window and it was obvious that her parents had planted themselves beneath the shade of the old oak tree and wouldn't be leaving anytime soon.

"I'll go with you," Louise replied.

"Run back and tell Mom and Dad we're going," Gail said.

Louise scowled. "Why don't you tell them?"

"I'm driving and if you want a ride home, you'll do as I say."

"Forget it then. I'll wait and go with Mom and Dad."

"Fine," Gail said, storming out the back door. By the time she reached the group out back, she realized that Louise was at her side. Now what was she up to?

She said her goodbyes and hugged Joy and Sam, thanking them for dinner and promising she'd see them soon.

Louise hugged them too—why, Gail wasn't sure, as she wasn't leaving yet—and then took off like a shot and ran toward the house. Gail shook her head and made her way around to the front of the house. When she neared her car, she saw that Louise was sitting in the passenger seat, her satchel in her lap.

"Why, you little . . ." she huffed as she sat in the car.

"Oh, don't swear, Gail," Louise said. "It makes you less attractive than you already are."

Gail leaned back in her seat and studied her sister. The farm dress, the satchel. "You know, Lou, if they're ever recasting for Miss Beadle on *Little House*, I think you should try out for it."

Louise stuck out her tongue at her.

"That's nice. Really grown-up," Gail said.

Louise went to say something, but Gail cut her off. "Look, no talking. I'll give you a ride home but if you annoy me in any way, shape, or form, I'll pull over and drop you off by the side of the highway."

"You'd make me walk home in this heat?" Louise asked, appalled.

"You've got a thumb, don't you? Besides, eventually Mom and Dad would pass by. You could catch a ride with them." She pulled out and drove down the residential street.

"Sometimes, Gail, you're nasty."

Gail pulled over immediately. "Out you go, Lou."

"All right! I'm sorry!" Louise wailed.

Gail examined her nails as if she might pull out a nail file any moment. Finally, she looked over at Louise and said, "Want to try it again?"

The ride was quiet all the way back to Lavender Bay. When Gail parked the car in front of the house on Peony

Lane, Louise jumped out and slammed the door so hard the car shook.

"Hey!" Gail called out as her sister stormed into the house. "Such a moody little thing," she muttered under her breath.

CHAPTER EIGHTEEN

Flashes, the popular disco in Cheever, was located in an old warehouse. Some genius had gotten the place for a song. After refurbishment, you never would have known that it had recently been a rusted-out old building with broken windows and water leaking everywhere, exterior walls covered in graffiti, weeds sprouting through cracks in the asphalt parking lot.

Now it sported the largest dance floor this side of New York State. Black UV lighting throughout cast a purplish hue over the interior. On the floor was a black carpet with a confetti design. The sunken dance floor was right in the middle of the interior space with a large strobe light suspended over the center of it. On the north and south ends of the building, bars with mirrored glass shelving holding every imaginable form of alcohol and liquor ran the length of the walls.

Gail had arrived twenty minutes ago, alone, having lied and told her mother she was going to hang out at a friend's house. She had told no one where she was going, not even Louise. She was still mad at her sister, who annoyed her to no end. She didn't want to sit at home at night, even if it was a Sunday. She wanted to dance. And there were always enough girls on the dance floor that she could hang on the periphery of some group. There was some unwritten rule that it didn't look *right* for a young woman to go to a bar by herself. But as she was there to dance, she didn't care.

Still, she approached the bar with some trepidation. She elbowed her way through the crowd until her arm was resting on the bar. She kept raising her hand to get the bartender's attention. Finally, he stopped in front of her and took her order. After he set a Harvey Wallbanger down in front of her, she paid him and told him to keep the change. The guy next to her vacated his space, and that allowed her to turn and put her back to the bar, sipping her drink while she observed everything going on around her. The dance floor was crowded, which was good; she'd be able to dance to her heart's content. But first, she needed a little liquid courage before venturing out there by herself.

"Has anyone ever told you how pretty you are?" said a voice next to her.

Without missing a beat and before getting a good look at the speaker, Gail clapped back, "Does that line ever work?"

He burst out laughing and said, "Usually."

She shrugged and turned to face him.

The first thing she noticed was how handsome he was. He appeared to be in his late twenties and had a headful of thick hair as black as midnight and dark, mysterious eyes. He also had a mustache, which Gail found intriguing. She'd never kissed anyone with a mustache before. Not that she'd done a lot of kissing. He was tall, but not too tall, perfect for her own height of five two. He was dressed in the current style: a tan leisure suit with a print shirt. He wore a thick gold herringbone chain around his neck and a signet ring on his ring finger. She'd never met a man who wore jewelry aside from a wedding ring, and she thought it was a bold statement.

"Can I get you a drink?" he asked with a nod to her glass, which was still full.

Boldly, she said, "Not yet."

His cologne was heady, something she didn't recognize but liked all the same. It definitely wasn't Brut, which seemed to be what all the men were wearing these days. Some smelled as if they'd rolled around in a barrel of it. He leaned in, and the front of his shirt was open to his navel, allowing her to practically count every dark hair on his chest. She tried not to stare.

He held out his hand. "I'm Rick."

She shook it. His grip was firm and warm, and his hand dwarfed hers. A tingling sensation traveled up her arm. "Gail."

"I've never seen you here before," he said.

She shrugged. She believed a woman should never reveal too much about herself. That she should keep things private and retain an air of mystery.

He looked around. "Are you here alone?"

"I was supposed to meet up with my friends, but they're not here yet," Gail lied. She hoped her expression was one of disappointment.

"Then I guess this is my lucky night. I hope your friends never show up."

"Do you come here often?" she asked.

"When I can," he said. He leaned up against the bar. "I like the energy this place gives off."

Gail looked around and had to agree. The energy was frenetic; the place buzzed with dancing, loud music, and even louder conversation. Who knew a Sunday night could be so much fun?

"Are you ready for that drink yet?"

She looked at her almost-finished drink, now watered down from the melted ice. "I think I am."

With a subtle lift of his finger, Rick got the bartender's attention. When he approached, he leaned in and spoke loudly over the volume of the music. "One Harvey Wallbanger and a gin and tonic. Tanqueray, please."

The bartender nodded and went about preparing their drinks. Rick pulled out his wallet and Gail tried not to stare, but it was hard to miss all those bills tucked neatly inside. They weren't ones. He snapped his wallet shut and she looked away, not wanting to be caught staring. The bartender placed their drinks in front of them and Rick paid for them, tipping him generously.

Rick lifted his glass and clinked it against Gail's. "To new friends."

She smiled, returned the clink, and took a sip.

"Jive Talking" started playing overhead, and she began to tap her feet to the rhythm of the music.

"Want to dance?" Rick asked with a grin.

"I'd love to!"

"What the lady wants, the lady gets," he said. "Follow me!" She took a quick sip of her drink and followed Rick as he led them to the dance floor.

The crowded floor was a perfect square. Three sides of it were surrounded by a black wrought-iron railing topped with a narrow ledge where people could sit and set their drinks down as they watched the maneuvers on the dance floor. Gail stood there holding her drink, her purse slung over her shoulder, and felt encumbered.

"Come on, you can set those down here," Rick said, and with a wave of his hand he headed toward the corner of the dance floor. He showed her a space beneath the ledge where she could set her drink and lean her purse against the railing. Relieved of the two items but keeping them within reach, she started dancing with him, moving to the rhythm of the music, aware of his gaze firmly fixed on her. The song ended, and the music segued into "Get Down Tonight" by KC and the Sunshine Band. They kept dancing, Rick moving closer to her and putting his hand on her waist. He moved like a dream, loaded with rhythm, and it felt like they'd been dancing together for years. She paused momentarily to catch her breath and take a sip of her drink.

"Kung Fu Fighting" was next. By the end of the third set, Gail was almost breathless. Almost. And she could feel a fine sheen of perspiration dotting her brow.

"Let's slow it down," the DJ's voice boomed overhead.

Frankie Valli's "My Eyes Adored You," floated out overhead, and Gail decided this was her cue to exit.

"Don't you want to dance?" Rick asked, smiling.

She shook her head. She liked him. He checked a lot of boxes, but she was aware that she'd begun to sweat and despite a heavy application of Secret deodorant, she didn't want him up close and personal. At least not yet.

This time she led the way, stepping off the dance floor and making her way back to the bar, ready for another drink. As much as she loved the Harvey Wallbangers, her mouth was parched and she needed something more refreshing.

As she approached the bar with Rick trailing in her wake, she spotted an opening and picked up her pace as fast as her high heels would allow, landing in the vacant spot before anyone could beat her to it. She leaned forward and lifted her arm to signal the bartender.

"I love this women's lib stuff," Rick teased.

The bartender approached and Gail said, "A large glass of Pepsi, loaded with ice." She looked at Rick, who shook his head and said, "I'm fine, thanks."

When the Pepsi appeared, she pulled out her wallet, but Rick laid his hand on her arm. "I'll get this."

She looked at him with steely determination. "Thank you, but I can pay for my own drink."

He threw up his hands, but his grin indicated he wasn't offended.

Although it was the custom for the man to pay the way—drinks, dinner, whatever—Gail felt that if women were to be truly independent, they needed to start bearing some of the financial burden. And although a glass of Pepsi certainly wouldn't bankrupt him, it was the principle of the matter.

If he hadn't been standing right next to her, smelling all wonderful of male scent and heady cologne, she would have gulped the entire glass in one go. Exercising restraint, she took a few sips. It was when he disappeared into the men's room that she drank the entire glass, cooling off and asking for another.

Rick reappeared as she sipped her drink, waiting to see what the next song would be. Neil Sedaka's "Bad Blood" came on. "Want to dance?" she asked.

"Sure."

They found themselves back in the same corner on the dance floor. Gail set her purse and drink down and turned her attention to Rick. After three dances, he made moves to exit, but she pulled on his sleeve, dug her heels in, and laughed. "One more?"

"I can't keep up with you. You've got quite a bit of stamina."

There they stood, at a standstill, with people dancing around them and the strobe light flashing above them, until she acquiesced and let him lead her off the dance floor. Once they stepped up into the main bar, he leaned into her, his voice warm against her ear. "Let's find somewhere more private. Quiet." He lifted his gaze and met her eyes, and she found she couldn't refuse him.

He led her away from the flashing lights and loud music to the booths at the far end of Flashes. They seated from two to four people and were intended for those who didn't care about dancing but wanted to hang out. But right now, Gail could plainly see that they were mainly occupied by couples who were making out openly, in front of everyone. Her eyes widened.

With a casual shrug, he said, "What do you say we get comfortable and take a break from dancing?"

It was enticing. He was handsome. He was a great dancer. And he smelled terrific. But Diana Sturges didn't raise any fools.

"Another time, maybe," she said coyly. She glanced at her wristwatch. "Besides, I have to go."

"Don't go, not just yet," he said.

She shook her head. "I really have to; I'm going to turn into a pumpkin pretty soon."

He grinned.

It was near midnight, and she still had a long drive back home. She'd told her mother she was going to a friend's house, and with that came the assumption that she wouldn't be out late.

Boldly, he reached forward and pushed her hair back off her shoulder with a finger, staring at her, almost mesmerized. "Come on, I'll walk you to your car."

"Thank you."

He pushed through the crowd to the exit and opened the door, allowing her to step outside first. The night air was warm and offered scant relief from the heat inside.

"I'm right over here," she said, digging through her purse for her keys as she walked.

"Hey, be careful, watch where you're going, you'll trip and fall," he said, motioning to her footwear. "I don't know how you women walk in those things."

"It is definitely an art and a skill," Gail said with a laugh. Keys in hand, she closed her purse. As she reached her car and unlocked the door, she said, "It was nice meeting you, Rick."

"How about a little kiss to end our night?"

Resolute, Gail shook her head. "I don't kiss on the first date." She smirked and said, "And this wasn't even a date."

"I suppose not." He paused and scratched the side of his neck with his forefinger. "Maybe I'll see you around again."

"Maybe," she said, non-committal. She slid into the driver's seat and closed the door gently. Quickly, she rolled down the window. "Goodnight, Rick."

He tapped on the roof of her car. "Drive safe."

As she pulled away, she watched him in the rearview mirror, standing there, hands on hips, waiting until her car disappeared from sight. She smiled to herself. She'd played it cool. Didn't fawn all over him because of his attention. She'd played hard to get, and she was so proud of herself.

Oh, she'd definitely be coming back to Flashes. And she planned on seeing him again.

Chapter Nineteen

One of the reasons Louise liked her part-time job at the Quirk and the Quill was that she was allowed to listen to music while she worked. The owner, Loretta Jablonski, kept a little transistor radio behind the counter, and had told Louise she could keep it on as long as it wasn't too loud. Mindful of her boss's instructions, Louise had found the sweet spot where it was loud enough for her to hear in the back of the shop but not so loud that customers complained.

Earlier that morning, the monthly delivery of stock had arrived, and cardboard boxes were stacked up in the back room. Loretta hated unloading boxes and putting everything out on the shelves, so that job always fell to Louise. She didn't mind. In the back room, she sliced open a box with a box cutter, peeked in, and carried it out front to the relevant shelf.

The layout of the shop was shotgun style. If you walked through the front door and looked straight back, past the shop interior and the dim, shadowy back room, you could see right out the back door to the parking lot. Currently, both doors, front and back, were propped wide open for the cross breeze. But it was so still outside, without the slightest movement of air, that she was doubtful of any breezes today, cross or otherwise. She'd worn a thin cotton dress and still felt sticky.

The bell over the door tinkled, signaling the arrival of a possible customer. She pushed the box out of the way with her foot so no one would trip over it.

She made her way to the front of the shop. She was always conscious of the cash register behind the counter and tended to guard it with her life. It had been robbed once, back in 1971, and Loretta constantly reminded her to keep an eye on it.

She stopped in her tracks at the sight of the most handsome man she'd ever seen in her life, a dead ringer for Burt Reynolds. To Louise, Burt Reynolds was the standard by which all men should be compared, looks-wise, that was. For other important qualities like intelligence and kindness, her father was her barometer. But the other thing was that any thought or mention of Burt Reynolds immediately reminded her of his centerfold in *Cosmopolitan* a few years ago. Gail had a copy hidden between the mattress and box spring of her bed, and Louise had snuck a peek when she wasn't home, to see what all the fuss was about. Just thinking about him stretched out seductively on that bearskin rug with nothing on, a cigarillo between his teeth, made her blush furiously.

She approached the customer. "Can I help you?"

He smiled, revealing lovely teeth. "I'm looking for a pen."

"Any particular kind?" she asked.

"Preferably a Cross." He stepped closer to her, and she could have sworn the heat was rolling right off of him. And it had nothing to do with the weather.

Cross was the most expensive brand of pen Loretta carried in her store. She said there was no need to carry anything fancier; it would only serve to tempt people who were up to no good. Besides, if Cross pens were good enough for the White House, they were good enough for the residents of Lavender Bay. Louise preferred the fountain pens with their fancy nibs that you had to refill with an ink cartridge. She loved that lovely indigo color.

"We have a selection right over here in the case," she said, indicating to him that he should follow her.

Past the front counter was a locked glass display case featuring Timex watches and Cross pens. Louise couldn't figure out why watches were being sold in a stationery store, and she didn't ask Loretta as she didn't want to be viewed as impertinent.

"As you can see, we have a large collection," she said. They stood next to each other and peered into the glass. Everything looked lovely beneath the overhead lighting of the case. It tempted her to buy a pen too, but she could never afford such a thing on her part-time salary.

"Let me know if you see anything you like," she told him. She didn't want to be one of those busybody shop people who hovered. She found nothing more annoying when she was shopping and a saleslady stood right next to her as she browsed through racks of clothing. It was intimidating.

She turned slightly and he said, "I'll take that one right there."

"The silver one?"

"That's the one, with the gold pocket clip."

Louise pulled the ring of keys from the pocket of her dress and unlocked the glass case, opened it, and pulled out the case that held the pen. "Would you like to browse?"

He shook his head. His cologne was heavenly. Not too overpowering. Something subtle but nice. The only cologne she was familiar with was Old Spice. It was what her father wore. She gave him a gift set every Christmas.

He followed her to the counter, where she set down the pen and began to write up a sales slip, placing a carbon between the white and yellow copy.

On the radio, "It's Good to Be Back Home Again" started playing. Louise smiled; John Denver could release an album singing the telephone book and she would buy it.

"Do you like John Denver?" he asked.

"I do," she gushed. *Tone it down, Lou.*

"I like him too," he said. "He's so wholesome. Just what this country needs right now."

"I couldn't agree more," she said. She'd spent her childhood with cartoons on the television punctuated with images of the Vietnam War on the news. And then the previous year, the President of the United States resigned. As young as she was, she'd known it was a pivotal moment in American history. Her parents had been glued to the television during those days. But now, maybe they'd turned a corner. The last chopper had left Vietnam in April, and there was a new man in the Oval Office.

"My favorite song of his is 'Sunshine on My Shoulder,' " he said. Up close, his dark brown eyes were warm and kind.

"I love that one too!"

She totaled up the cost of the pen with tax and told him the cost. "Would you like me to gift wrap that?" she asked.

He grinned, his smile magnetic. "No, thank you." He paused. "I'm Richard, by the way."

She extended her hand across the counter. "Louise. Pleased to meet you."

When her hand made contact with his, it was like a magnetic force. Reluctantly, and without removing her gaze from his, she pulled her hand away.

He opened his wallet and handed her a couple of bills. She returned the correct change, counting it out backward as she laid it in the palm of his hand. She put the sales receipt in the little brown paper bag with his pen.

"Thanks, Louise, it was lovely meeting you."

"You too."

As he headed out the door, she called out to him, "Enjoy your new pen!"

He turned slightly, grinning, and her heart melted. "I will, thank you."

She watched him go, thinking they had never had anyone like that in the shop before. And they probably never would again. Sighing, she went back to work. Those boxes weren't going to unload themselves.

Chapter Twenty

Gail ventured out to Flashes in Cheever whenever she could, sometimes with a group of friends and sometimes by herself. Sometimes she saw Rick, and sometimes she didn't. It seemed to be hit-and-miss. Her parents continued to be none the wiser. She gave them a variety of excuses as to where she was going, usually *to a friend's house*. And she definitely did not tell Louise. Lately, the two of them hadn't been getting along.

Today was her day off from the small grocery store where she worked part-time. It was a job she hated, but it provided her with pin money. She was on her way to the beach to meet some friends and work on her tan. She carried a large macramé bag over her shoulder, which held her beach towel, a bottle of Hawaiian Tropic, a comb, a small transistor radio, and an ice-cold can of Tab wrapped in tin foil.

She was on a new diet. Unlike her sister, Gail put on weight easily and always had to be mindful of it.

Currently, she was on the grapefruit diet for eighteen days. She'd never been crazy about grapefruit, but she was managing to stick to it so far. She was hoping to lose ten pounds before the weekend. She had a cute little halter-top dress she'd picked up on sale, and it would look better if her shoulders were tanned and her collarbones more pronounced.

When she arrived at the beach, she was happy to see that it was crowded. School was out for the summer, and it looked like every kid in Lavender Bay was either on the beach or in the water. As she trod through the heavy sand, she looked down at her feet, the sand dulling her navy blue Dr. Scholl's. She hoped the sand wouldn't chip her nail polish. She walked the length of the beach and was unable to spot her friends anywhere. She stood at the surf, her sandals in her hand, letting the warm water of the lake wash over her hot feet. She scanned the beach and then the water for any sign of her friends, but with no luck.

They said they'd be there. It was possible that they'd tried to call the house, but her sister had been on the phone all morning with one of her friends. She didn't want to look like a total loser, alone on the beach, but she had no choice but to make the best of it. She spotted a slightly older woman, maybe in her late twenties, stretched out in her bikini on a low teal-and-white-striped plastic chaise. She approached the woman, who was also there by herself, and staked out a spot next to her, thinking this could be the singles' club.

She laid out her beach towel, which she'd got at half price with coupons saved from the purchase of Hawaiian Tropic. With the amount of it she went through, she should have bought stock in the company.

She spread suntan oil all over, never tiring of the sweet coconut smell. It was a scent that would remind her of the beach for the rest of her life. Next to her, the single lady turned onto her stomach. She undid the string of her bikini top, and Gail thought that was a little daring but noticed she had no tan lines on her back. The other woman had a nice, even tan, and that made Gail a little envious. Not one to be outdone, she did the same, lying on her stomach and undoing her bikini ties. She felt the girls give way and hoped she could get it tied when she needed to turn around. She got comfortable, decided after a while that she liked the freedom of her top loose, and pulled the newest edition of *Cosmopolitan* out of her bag. It was a magazine that was considered contraband in their house. Her mother did not approve. But Gail loved it and when she was in a good mood, she let Louise borrow it to read. Sometimes. But not lately.

She was eager to read the article about how to lose twenty-one pounds in fourteen days. She was flipping through the pages when she heard a voice behind her.

"Gail? Gail Sturges?"

She anchored her untied bikini top with her hand and looked over her shoulder, but the sun was in her eyes, and she couldn't make out who it was. There were two guys there, standing over her. As quickly as she could, she tried to tie the string of her bathing suit behind her, thinking she should have practiced this at home first.

"Uh, do you need some help with that?" asked the male voice.

Her eyes widened. "Um no, I got it."

As she struggled, she thought maybe if she held the top in place with her hand, she could possibly turn around without revealing one of her best features to the general public.

Suddenly, she felt the string being pulled tight and a female voice asking, "Is it in place?"

"Yes, thank you." It was the woman from the lounger next to her. She'd tied it tight, and it was going nowhere.

Gail turned around and sat up. She said to the woman, "Hey, thanks."

The woman, who had a pretty face to go with her perfect body, smiled and said, "No problem. Anything for the sisterhood."

Gail turned her attention to the two guys. "Oh, hi. Hugh Campbell, right?" Or she thought it was him. She remembered him vaguely from high school. He was two years ahead of her. But his family had moved away or something like that. The only thing she remembered about him was that he'd played basketball for the school team. "What are you doing here?"

"My family has moved back to Lavender Bay." A distant memory of his father being transferred for work floated in front of her.

Feeling at a disadvantage on her back on the blanket with Hugh and his friend standing there towering over her, Gail stood as gracefully as she could. Hugh had gotten taller since she'd last seen him. His friend wasn't as tall and where Hugh was dark, his friend had reddish-blond hair.

"I'm Gail Sturges," she said to the friend, who grinned.

"I know who you are," he said. "Hugh's told me all about you." Hugh elbowed him so hard he let out an *oomph*.

She wondered what there was to tell. He'd only been a passing acquaintance in high school. A nod as he passed by in the hallway.

"This is my soon-to-be ex-friend, Martin Cook," Hugh said firmly.

Gail laughed. *Boys will be boys*, she thought. An image of Rick came to mind unbidden. He'd never engage in such silly games.

"Are you going to college?" she asked Hugh.

"I am," he explained. "I graduate next May."

"What in?"

"I'm prelaw."

A lawyer. Hmmm. She turned to the other guy. "And what about you? What do you do?"

"I'm graduating with Hugh."

"Prelaw?"

"God no." He visibly shuddered. He looked up at his friend, who was scowling. "Um. Sorry. I'm a math major."

"What will you do with that? Teach?"

Martin Cook looked appalled. "Let's hope not."

It was all well and good to stand there talking, but she couldn't see the point. They seemed friendly enough, but she wasn't interested. What surprised her was how she measured them against Rick, whom she'd only met a few times. These boys seemed, well, like boys.

"It was nice seeing you," she said, trying to move them on their way so she could get back to working on her tan. She thought she heard a chuckle from the woman on the chaise.

"We're going into the water," Hugh said. "Do you want to go with us?"

Now she definitely heard the woman next to her laugh. It seemed to go over their heads.

"I'll sit this one out," she said nicely.

"All right. We won't be long," Hugh said.

She watched them walk off toward the water, and it appeared that Hugh was giving Martin a thorough talking-to. Hugh Campbell was certainly handsome, but she wasn't attracted to him in that way.

Next to her, the blonde in the bikini said, "I think you've got an admirer."

"Do you think so?"

"Oh definitely. I couldn't help but hear the whole conversation. He's quite smitten."

"I don't know," Gail said, her voice trailing off.

"You could do a lot worse."

"Maybe I'm not in the market."

"Then don't be here when he comes back."

"You think he'll be back?" Gail asked.

The blonde nodded and said knowingly, "He's going to plant himself here after he gets out of the water."

Gail fretted. "He's a nice guy, and I don't want to hurt his feelings . . ."

The blonde let out a tired sigh. "I've been there."

"Thanks for the tip," Gail said, and she quickly packed up her things and threw them into her bag, stopping briefly to shake the sand off her towel.

She bid goodbye to the woman and as she walked away, she glanced toward the water and saw Hugh and Martin way out in the lake, almost up to their shoulders. Even from that distance, she could tell that Hugh was watching her leave. And she felt bad.

The following weekend, she went out to Flashes on a Friday night with some friends. She was disappointed not to run into Rick, but spent the night dancing and drinking with her friends and had a blast. As they were heading toward the exit at the end of the night, she felt someone touch her arm and turned, smiling when she saw it was Rick.

She stopped mid-stride. Ahead, her friends stopped and looked back at her. "Go on, I'll catch up," she said. They looked at Rick and grinned.

"We've got to stop meeting like this," Rick teased.

Coyly, she looked up at him from beneath her eyelashes.

"Did you not want to meet me anymore?" she asked.

His mouth fell open. "Of course not! Running into you is the highlight of my night. I always look out for you when I come here."

She smiled and threw her head back. "Do you, now?" She turned slightly, the exit in sight. "I've got to go. My friends are waiting."

"You are really playing hard to get, Gail," Rick said.

"Am I?" she asked, already knowing the answer. The last two times she'd run into him, they'd danced, had a few drinks, flirted, and still she said no when he tried to convince her to sit down with him in one of those booths in the back.

He laughed and reached for her, pulling her close to him. He leaned in and whispered into her ear, his breath warm against her skin. "You know you are."

She took a step back. "Hold on a minute." She dug through her purse and pulled out an old receipt and a pen and scribbled down her phone number. "Look, Rick, if you're serious, call me. Take me out to dinner or something. A proper date."

There was a new restaurant she wanted to try out, and then maybe they could take a romantic stroll on the beach.

"You're right. I think that would be a wonderful idea." He took the slip of paper, studied it, folded it carefully, and tucked it into his pocket. He leaned in to kiss her, but she stepped back. She wagged her finger at him, laughing. "Naughty, naughty."

"Gail, you're driving me crazy!"

That's the plan.

"I've got to go, I've got to work in the morning," she said. The manager at the grocery store had put her on the opening shift and that meant a seven a.m. start, which meant she'd have to get up at five thirty to do her hair and makeup.

"I'll call you," he promised.

"Good." Satisfied, she leaned forward and kissed him softly on the lips, then pulled back and dashed for the door before he could respond. She had to get home. Grinning, she stood at the door, at what she considered to be a safe distance, and waved and blew him a kiss goodbye. From where she stood, she saw his grin. Quickly, she slipped out the door before she could change her mind about leaving.

Chapter Twenty-One

Louise walked to work that morning. With her hair parted down the middle and her long blond locks flowing, she felt the heat of the sun on her scalp and was sorry she hadn't worn a hat, but she hadn't wanted to mess her hair, as it was as near to perfect as she was going to get it.

She'd spent the previous evening at her friend's house. A group of them had sat on the porch drinking beer the girl had taken from her father's refrigerator in the garage, and it wasn't long before the conversation had turned to boys and sex, or *around the bases* was the code they'd used.

Louise felt like the odd man out. Admittedly, she was old-fashioned. And as they spoke and laughed about having reached first, second, and even third bases, she felt weirdly uncomfortable. What made things even more awkward was the fact that she had nothing to add to the conversation. No personal experience. First, she didn't like baseball. Second, all this talk about boys and bases made her dizzy. She'd gone to her senior prom with a neighbor, but the evening had ended in a chaste kiss. She'd been on dates, but nothing serious. They never called back. It wasn't that she was unattractive, but one date had asked her if she was a prude. That had hurt. Just because she wasn't throwing it around out there didn't make her a prude. But like those girls branded because they slept around, maybe she'd been branded because she didn't want to do things she felt uncomfortable with. Or wasn't ready for.

Despite the bright sunny day, she felt a bit down. Were all men only after one thing? She was only eighteen. Her mother had advised both of her daughters to be cautious.

She said hello to Loretta as she entered the shop.

"Louise, you're a dream employee. You always arrive ten minutes early," Loretta said with a smile. She was heavily pregnant and when she had the baby, Louise would be working more hours to help cover her maternity leave.

Her parents had raised her to take pride in her work no matter what the work was.

She made small talk with Loretta for a few minutes before her boss left her a short list of tasks to do while she left to go to the bank and then to her doctor's appointment.

She looked at the list and decided she'd take it one item at a time. There was always a sense of satisfaction in taking a pencil and crossing a line through a task, job done.

Systematically, she went through the store and took inventory of the stock in hand, ticking off boxes on the order sheet to indicate what items were needed and in what quantity. She ordered double of everything, per her boss's instructions. Loretta was already getting ready for August, when sales of back-to-school supplies would go through the roof.

Louise was distracted by the arrival of a customer. She looked up and couldn't hide her surprise when she recognized Richard. After last week, she figured she'd never see him again. After all, he didn't seem the type to need an excess of stationery supplies, and the Cross pen he'd purchased would last awhile.

She walked to the front of the shop and set her pen and order form on the counter.

He grinned when he saw her. "I was hoping you'd be here today."

She smiled, not sure what to say, but it wasn't necessary as Richard continued talking, for which she was grateful.

"You know, I have to admit that I came in here yesterday and was disappointed that you weren't here."

"I only work part-time," Louise explained. Inside, a glow filled her at the thought that a man as handsome as this had come in looking specifically for her.

"Then that's my bad luck."

"Were you looking for something in particular?" she asked, twisting her hands together. Despite the incessant heat, goosebumps broke out on her arms.

"No, nothing specific. I've got my pen and I'm happy," he said with a laugh. "I was walking by and thought I'd stop in and say hello."

"Hello," she said softly. She wished she were witty or a great conversationalist. She wished at that moment she were more like Gail: outgoing and always clever. Her older sister would know what to do. And what to say.

"What time do you get off work?"

"This is my long day," Louise explained. "I'm here until six."

"Ouch!"

She smiled. "I don't mind. I like working here."

"You do?"

She wondered if she'd given the wrong answer, but she found her voice and said, "Yes."

He smiled easily. "It's important to like a job you're working at."

"Do you like your job?"

He tilted his head back and forth. "Most days. Except on beautiful days like this when I would rather be outside in the sunshine."

"I think everyone feels like that," Louise added.

"Maybe you have to work until six, but do you get a lunch break?" he asked.

"I do. But I bring my own and eat it in the back room." An image came to mind of her baloney sandwich wrapped in wax paper in a brown paper bag. Pathetic.

"Can I take you to the diner for a quick lunch?"

She laughed. "It would have to be really quick, I only get twenty minutes," she said. There was only one diner in Lavender Bay, and it was at the other end of Main Street. It would take her twenty minutes to walk back and forth. "And anyway, I can't leave today. The boss isn't here. I'm the only one holding down the fort."

"Okay, maybe that won't work after all," he said. "When do you have your next short shift?"

"Next Tuesday. I finish at two," she said.

"Would you go to lunch with me then?" he asked.

"I will."

The bell over the door rang and two young men walked in. Louise sighed at the interruption. The gods were cruel to interrupt her singular romantic interlude.

Richard took it as his cue to leave. "All right. Until then. I look forward to it."

"Me too."

And he winked at her and turned and exited, brushing past the two guys who'd just come in. She didn't give them a second glance, her focus firmly on Richard as he walked by the shop window.

Not knowing the intent of the new customers, she parked herself on the stool behind the counter. The transistor radio belted out Captain and Tenille's "Love Will Keep Us Together."

The two men tentatively approached the counter. A stationary shop didn't get a lot of young men as customers. Three in one day and in the space of half an hour had to be some kind of record for the Quirk and the Quill.

"Are you looking for something?" she asked.

Both stepped up to the counter. One was tall, muscular, dark-haired and dark-eyed. The other was shorter, with reddish-blond hair, a fair complexion, and blue eyes. To Louise, both were attractive.

"Not in here, but I was hoping you could help me with something," said the tall dark-haired fella.

She smiled. "I'll try."

"Are you Louise Sturges?" he asked.

This caught her off guard, and she was surprised and wary by equal measures.

"I am," she said hesitantly.

"Good," he said.

She wondered if she should be worried about being alone in a shop with two men, but she wasn't getting a bad vibe off of them. And she was someone who trusted her instinct.

"I'm Hugh Campbell and this here is my friend, Martin Cook," he said.

Louise lifted up her hand in a small wave to the friend, thinking she liked the way his eyes looked. They were the prettiest blue.

"We're on a reconnaissance mission," Martin said. There was a spark of mischief in his eyes, and she decided she liked that too.

In a mock serious tone, she said, "Oh, I see."

Hugh frowned, rolling his eyes at his friend. Martin appeared to take his friend's reaction in his stride. "You're Gail's sister, right?" Hugh asked.

"I am."

"Can you tell me one thing?"

"I'll try," she said, not wanting to fully commit.

"Well, maybe two things," Hugh said.

"Come on, Hugh, spit it out," Martin said. "We can't take up all of Louise's time." And he winked at her.

She laughed.

"Does your sister have a boyfriend?" Hugh asked.

This was a surprise development! "No, she does not," Louise replied.

Hugh's face broke into a wide, happy smile.

Oh my, she thought, *he's got it bad.* "Um, how do you know my sister?" she asked, suddenly feeling slightly protective.

"I was ahead of her a couple of years in high school."

Martin interrupted, rocking back and forth on his heels, hands in his pockets. "The condensed version, Louise, if you will: Hugh moved away and then he moved back. And here he is, still carrying a torch all these years later for Gail Sturges."

Through gritted teeth, Hugh said, "Stop clowning around, Martin, this is serious."

"Apologies," Martin said, affecting a serious face. "There's nothing funny about love."

Louise burst out laughing, and Martin laughed along with her.

Hugh asked, "Does she work somewhere? I mean, here in town?"

Louise could have been sisterly and not told him, but she said, "At the little grocery store." Her sister hated her job. Hated the dusty place, the old, yellowed sales banners and most of all, the smock she was forced to wear that covered up her fashionable clothes beneath. Louise would love to see the expression on her face when Hugh and Martin showed up and there she was, trapped behind the register with no escape.

Hugh frowned. "Is that place still open? It was teetering on the brink of despair when I lived here years ago."

"It's still teetering, and Gail works there, now full of despair."

Martin snorted, covered his mouth, and said, "Sorry."

Louise smiled at him, thinking she really liked this guy. He was so easy to get along with.

"Do you know if she's there today?" Hugh asked, hopeful.

"To be honest, I'm not sure." Although they lived in the same house, they were not up to date on each other's work schedule.

"Come on, Martin, let's go," Hugh said, heading to the exit.

Martin grinned at Louise as if they shared a secret. "Oh, okay."

Louise laughed again.

"Come on, quit clowning around," Hugh said in a harried voice.

As Martin followed Hugh out, Louise heard him say, "Do you think this is a good idea, Hugh? She didn't seem that interested the other day when you saw her at the beach."

"I don't assume anything. If she's not interested, then she can tell me."

"I hope you know what you're doing," Martin said as they stepped out onto the sidewalk and into the bright sunshine.

Louise smiled to herself. That last hour at work had been most interesting. If it could only be like that always. With a gentle sigh, she returned to her task of taking inventory and filling out the order form. An hour of her shift had passed, and she'd yet to cross anything off her list.

Chapter Twenty-Two

Gail was stretched out on her bed, wearing only a pair of shorts and a tube top, reading the current issue of *Glamour*, when there was a knock on her bedroom door.

"Come in," she said, not looking up from her reading.

Louise floated in wearing a pale yellow sleeveless cotton dress that fell to her ankles. Her blond hair fell straight down on either side of her shoulders. On her feet were a pair of flat sandals. The word *wispy* came to mind. She took after their mother's side of the family, whereas Gail felt she was channeling some stout peasant ancestor from her father's Pennsylvania Dutch relatives.

"What are you doing?" Louise asked.

Gail held up her magazine. "Take a guess."

Without an invitation, Louise sat on the floor and crossed her legs. "I need some advice."

Curious, Gail set the magazine down. This she had to hear. It must be serious if Louise was coming to her. She couldn't remember the last time her sister had searched her out for advice. She usually went to their mother. If she was approaching Gail, it had to be about men. Or a man.

"Shoot," Gail directed.

"There's this guy coming into the Quirk and the Quill," Louise started. "I think he likes me."

"How so?"

"He's been in twice—er, three times, once when I wasn't there—to see me," Louise told her.

This led Gail to wonder what kind of man hung out in a stationery shop. She'd never seen that article in any of the glossy magazines she read. Her immediate conclusion: super nerd. He had to be. And without a doubt, perfect for her waiflike sister.

"Do you like him?" she asked.

Louise's features softened. "Yes. He's dreamy."

"That's good." She'd have to see him to believe it, but she set that aside for the moment.

"Anyway, when he comes in, I'm all tongue-tied and I end up looking like an idiot," Louise confessed. "I don't know what to say to him. I'm not used to this kind of attention."

For the life of her, Gail couldn't understand why men weren't beating a path to their front door. Her sister, despite her pioneer getups, was beautiful. Gail had advised her more than once that she should put on a bikini and show off her wares. At the time, Louise had scrunched up her nose and shaken her head, opting for the one-piece. Gail didn't know where all this modesty had come from. If she had her sister's body, she'd be parading around in a bikini all the time!

"That's easy," she said with authority. "Ask him about himself. Any question, likes, dislikes, his opinion on current affairs and politics. That sort of thing. Men love talking about themselves." She'd gleaned all this information from the many women's magazines she'd read.

"Oh," Louise said with a frown. "Is that all? It's that easy?"

"Yes. Like I said, men love to talk about themselves," Gail prattled on. "Ask him if he has any hobbies. Does he follow sports?"

Louise made a face and said, "Yuck."

"Accept the fact that most men, if not all of them, follow sports," Gail told her.

"What else?"

She appeared thoughtful for a moment. "A couple of things. Don't hang all over him, don't hang on his every word. Remember you're an independent woman in your own right."

"I am?" Louise asked.

Gail looked at her younger sister. "Well, maybe not yet. But you're on your way. Look, Louise, it's 1975, we don't have to be the little woman anymore. We want to be equal with our partners."

"We do?"

"Yes!" If she impressed anything on her sister, it was going to be this. That they were to be treated as equals in any relationship and that they had just as much value as a man.

"All right," Louise said.

"Look, honey, we're not living on the prairie or the mountain," Gail said gently.

"I know, but sometimes I wish we were. Things seemed kinder and simpler."

"They only show you the good parts on these television shows. But trust me, in the middle of the night in the month of January, you are not going to want to be running to an outhouse in the backyard."

Louise's brow furrowed. "I hadn't thought of that."

"Don't forget that. And taking the clothes down to the stream to wash them on a washboard."

"Ew."

"Right."

There was a long pause as Lou appeared to digest all of this. It was not uncomfortable by any means. It was companionable. The way it used to be.

"He's asked me to lunch," Louise said.

"Lunch?" To Gail lunch dates were for older couples, and her sister was barely eighteen. "How old is this guy?"

Louise shrugged. She hadn't a clue. "He's more mature."

"He's not over thirty, is he? Mom and Dad will never go for that," Gail warned her.

"It's nothing like that. But I'd say he's in his late twenties."

Gail wondered what kind of freak of nature this guy was that he didn't offer to take her sister dancing or out for a drink instead of a lunch date. "Where's he taking you?"

"The diner in town."

Cheapskate, Gail thought but said, "When?"

"Tuesday after work," Louise said.

That was too bad as Gail was scheduled to work in the place called hell on Tuesday. Otherwise, she'd be a fly on the wall in the diner. She wanted to see who this guy was and make sure he was good enough for her sister.

"Now, I've given you plenty of advice to work from," she said.

"Thanks." Louise stood up and made to leave. Gail picked up her magazine and resumed reading.

Louise halted at the door, hand on the doorknob. "I forgot to tell you, but someone came into the Quirk and the Quill asking about you."

Gail lowered her magazine and frowned. "Who?"

"A guy named Hugh Campbell."

Gail rolled her eyes. "Oh no."

"Do you know him?"

"He was two years ahead of me in high school. To be honest, I don't really remember much about him other than he was a basketball star for the team."

"Basketball? Yuck."

"I ran into him at the beach the other day. He was with some friend."

Louise brightened. "Martin Cook. He was nice."

Gail eyed her sister but continued. "I had to leave. I think he likes me."

"Oh, he likes you all right. He was asking questions."

Gail bristled. "What kind of questions?"

"If you had a boyfriend. Where you hung out."

"You didn't tell him anything, did you?"

"He seemed nice. I didn't get a threatening vibe off of him."

"I didn't either, but that doesn't mean I want to go out with him."

"Why not?" Louise said. "He's quite handsome."

Gail wasn't ready to admit that she was more interested in Rick over at Flashes. *That* she wanted to keep to herself, if only for a little while longer.

"I don't think Hugh is my type." She paused and asked, "What did you say to him?"

Louise faltered, tracing the wood grain of the door-frame with her index finger. "I might have mentioned that you work at the grocery store."

"You didn't! How could you? Now I'll never get rid of him," Gail groaned.

"You worry too much. He won't hound you at work."

"Thanks a lot!" Gail said, and she snapped the magazine shut.

"He actually seemed kind of nice. Why don't you give him a chance?" Louise pleaded. When her sister leveled a glare at her, she added, "I'm *sorry*, it won't happen again."

"Get out of my room, Lou."

Without looking at her sister, she jumped off the bed and knelt on the floor to pick out an album to play. Lou left, closing the door behind her. She loved her sister, but sometimes she didn't use her head. She didn't want information about her life passed out to everyone who went into the Quirk and the Quill.

CHAPTER TWENTY-THREE

Gail managed to get someone to switch shifts with her on Tuesday afternoon. The curiosity to see her sister's object of affection was too strong to remain in a place of work she detested. One more year of college and she'd blow this town and never look back.

Although she never went out of the house without her hair and nails done and some makeup, it was hot, and therefore her effort was minimal. Her dark hair was feathered and heavily lacquered with Aqua Net. She applied some Maybelline mascara, thinking the only reason she'd bought it was because of the colors of the wand: pink and green. As she got ready, a Fleetwood Mac album played in the background. There was a spritz of perfume before she left the house.

The diner was at the far end of Main Street and because it was so hot, she drove over and parked about two blocks away so Lou wouldn't see her car and know she was spying on her.

She glanced at her wristwatch; it was a quarter to two. Lou didn't finish her shift for another fifteen minutes. After some thought, she realized Lou would be walking right past her car on her way from work, so she moved it two blocks in the other direction.

As she headed toward the diner, she hoped for a booth in the back where she could observe unobtrusively and make sure this guy was good enough for her sister. She didn't know why she cared, especially in light of her sister telling Hugh Campbell where she worked. Since last week, he'd been in the grocery store twice, standing in *her* line even though at one point he'd been called over by the cashier next to her. The first time, he came through with a loaf of bread. Luckily, that had been quick as there were people behind him in line and he couldn't exactly linger and chat her up. By the second visit, he'd smartened up and placed half a dozen items on the belt. It was an odd assortment: a light bulb, a quart of milk, matches, a bar of Irish Spring soap, a box of Salerno cookies, and another loaf of Millbrook bread.

"How've you been?" he asked.

"Since I saw you yesterday? Fine," she replied.

"You look great, Gail," he said.

"Thank you," she said automatically as she rang up the milk. The bread was missing its price tag, and she knew how much it cost as it was a common purchase, but she held it up to him and said, "I'll be right back, I need to get a price on this." Usually, she'd make her bag boy run and get it but today, she felt like taking a walk. Before Hugh could respond, she slipped out from behind her register and headed toward the bread aisle. As soon as she reached it, she turned around and took the long way back, heading down the shampoo and soap aisle because she liked the way it smelled.

Hugh remained in the same spot. Behind him the line was growing. His discomfort at holding people up was evident by his shifting back and forth on his feet and giving a sheepish smile to the people waiting behind him. As if things couldn't play any more in Gail's favor, Edna Knickerbocker had joined the line and couldn't help but offer commentary.

"Where'd the cashier go?" she wondered aloud. Followed by, "I'm on vacation from the jelly factory, but I've only got a week." And as Gail resumed her position at the cash register, Edna said, "Where'd you go, Gail? We thought you got lost."

"Sorry, Edna, had to do a price check."

A scarlet tinge began to color Hugh's cheeks. She almost felt sorry for him. Almost.

She quickly rang up the rest of his order, took his money, and counted out his change into his palm. The pennies looked quite small in his large hand. It was almost comical.

"I'll see you later, Gail," he said, picking up his brown paper bag of groceries.

Not wanting to encourage him, she'd said nothing.

Relieved that their run-in for the day was behind them, she went back to clock-watching until her shift was over.

Now as she walked into the diner, it occurred to her that she wouldn't be able to sit there and not order something, but there was her current diet to think about. She'd order a Tab and maybe some grapefruit, if they had any. She would have preferred one of their legendary chocolate milkshakes, but she was trying to be good. It was a constant, tiresome battle.

As her eyes adjusted to the change in light, she scanned the interior of the restaurant. Because of the time of day, it was half empty. The very last booth along the front row was vacant, and she headed in that direction. Halfway there, she did a double take when she spotted Rick sitting in one of the booths by himself. She couldn't believe her luck. And it was nice to see that he was as handsome in broad daylight as he was at nighttime.

"Rick!" She could barely contain her glee. She put aside her disappointment that he'd never called her to take her out to dinner.

His head snapped up and his expression was one of shock. Immediately, he slid out of the booth and kissed her on her cheek.

"Fancy meeting you here, of all places," Gail said. Her face hurt from smiling.

"What are you doing here?" he asked. His eyes darted toward the entrance and then back to her.

"I thought I'd stop in and have some lunch," she said casually. "What about you?"

He was dressed differently than what she was used to seeing him in, in jeans and a short-sleeved shirt. *Boy, he's so handsome he could be on television*, she thought.

"I'm meeting someone for lunch," he said. Again, his gaze moved past Gail.

It was at that moment that Louise entered, looking waiflike in a short-sleeved peasant blouse, matching skirt, and a pair of sandals. Her blond hair had a lovely shine to it, indicating a recent wash. She locked eyes with Gail and frowned, confused. But she broke into a smile when she spotted Rick.

Rick shifted nervously on his feet. "It was great seeing you, Gail. I'll see you over the weekend at Flashes."

Gail was smart enough to recognize a brush-off when she saw one. She could feel the muscles along her jaw working overtime.

Louise approached them and tilted her head to one side. "Gail, do you know Richard?"

Richard? Gail thought, and then it dawned on her: Louise was meeting Rick, or Richard, as she knew him.

"I do," she said. "I see him all the time at Flashes. Last time we were there, we won the dance contest, didn't we, *Rick*?"

She turned her attention to her younger sister. "Are *you* here to meet Rick?" she asked, indicating by her tone that she couldn't believe it.

There was a slight tinge of pink to Louise's cheeks. "Yes, as a matter of fact, I am," she said. She turned to him and said sweetly, "Isn't that right, *Richard*?"

Both girls fixed their stares on Rick/Richard, who by this time was beginning to feel like a tennis ball at Wimbledon.

"How do you two know each other?" he asked. His expression was a mixture of confusion, disbelief, and some amusement.

"We're sisters!" they said in unison.

"I knew I had good taste!" he said.

Both looked at him. Louise looped her arm through his and said, "Shall we have lunch?" Gail just about went into orbit.

He didn't answer immediately, but Louise wasn't letting go.

Gail didn't give up so easily, in fact, she stood her ground and dug her heels in. "I'll see you at Flashes, Rick. Looking forward to it."

As Louise slid into the booth and Rick joined her on the opposite side, Gail leaned in and whispered to her sister, "I saw him first."

This time, Louise went the color of scarlet.

Smiling, Gail straightened up, winked at Rick, and marched out of the diner with her head held high. She'd had the last word. And if Lou thought she'd hand Rick over to her and just give up, she had another thing coming.

Chapter Twenty-Four

"Turn it down, Gail, I can't hear my own record player!" Louise wailed before slamming her bedroom door so hard that the house on Peony Lane shook.

From the foot of the stairs, their mother called up, "Turn down both record players or I'll turn them off!"

The volume of the music from Gail's room lowered immediately, but you could still hear the words to Patti LaBelle's "Lady Marmalade," which was her all-time favorite song. Across the hall, you could just as easily hear Gordon Lightfoot's "If You Could Read My Mind" from Louise's room.

Gail's bedroom door opened, and she shouted, "Louise, you little tattletale!" and launched her hairbrush against her sister's bedroom door.

Their mother marched up the stairs and opened both doors. "Turn off both those record players right now and step out here."

Diana waited, arms folded across her chest. Louise appeared first and leaned against the wall of the hallway, piqued.

Gail soon appeared as well, her abundant dark hair freshly feathered and falling just past her shoulders.

Her mother took one look at her halter top and cutoff jeans and said, "Your father will never let you out of the house wearing that top. Not with your midriff showing like that. Best to change your outfit now."

"This is the style, *Mother*," Gail said pointedly.

"Forget that for a moment. Are the two of you still fighting over that boy?"

"He's not a boy!" Gail protested.

"He's a man!" added Louise.

Diana raised her voice. "I don't care if he's Gazoo from *The Flintstones*, no man is worth fighting over." She appeared thoughtful for a moment and added, "Except for your father, of course."

"I saw him first," Gail said tightly.

"Even so, he asked me out," Louise said in mock sweetness.

"Stop it!" Diana said. "I'm disappointed that the two of you would let a man come between you. I thought you had more sense than that."

Gail looked down at the floor as if there was something interesting on the carpet, remembering that her mother had asked her to vacuum it earlier that morning. And she hadn't.

"Now, this fighting is going to stop right now. Take a good look at each other," Diana commanded. When neither moved, she said again, "Look at each other." Both lifted their heads, locked gazes with the other, and narrowed their eyes. "This is the person you're going to know the longest in your life. After your father and I are gone, you will only have each other. You must learn to be friends and get along. Please don't fall out over a man. Don't do that. Your relationship is too important. You don't want to end up like Edna and Edith."

When neither said anything, she said, "Where are you going tonight?"

Louise spoke first. "I'm going wherever Gail is going."

Gail erupted. "No, you're not! You do your own thing."

"I can't, I don't drive!" Louise shouted.

"Whose fault is that?" Gail demanded. "You've failed your driving test three times!"

Before Louise could explode, Diana threw up her hand and spoke sternly. "All right! There's no need for that. Wherever you're going, Gail, you're taking your sister with you."

"Mom!" She was going to Flashes that evening to look for Rick, and she certainly didn't want Louise tagging along. Three would definitely be a crowd. If she and

Louise showed up together, would that force a show-down? A little spark of doubt niggled her: would Rick choose Louise? The slight, lovely, willowy Louise?

"That's it. You'll have to take Louise with you. I insist." There was no use arguing with their mother when she used that tone.

Gail tilted her head back and groaned. "My life is so awful."

"Now it really isn't, so don't exaggerate," Diana said.

Gail looked at her younger sister and said, "Wipe that smug smile off your face, Lou, or I'll knock it off myself."

"Gail!" her mother warned. "I'm of half a mind to ground you both and make you stay in tonight."

"On a Saturday night?" Gail protested.

"In summer?" Louise added.

"Go get ready and get out of here before I change my mind," Diana said, and she left them, marching down the stairs to the peaceful company of her husband and their interrupted chess game.

"When are we leaving?" Louise asked.

"Ten minutes," Gail replied. "Is that what you're wearing?"

"No, I'm going to change right now," Louise said.

Gail slipped into her room and closed the door behind her. She headed toward her closet to pick another outfit. She decided on the navy blue halter dress. Her shoulders were tanned, and all that grapefruit had enhanced her cheekbones. She waved a can of hairspray around her head, took one final look in the mirror, and decided she was ready.

She met Louise out in the hall. Lou was wearing a brand-new Gunne Sax dress, a busy affair of peach and lace. It made Gail dizzy.

"How did you afford a Gunne Sax dress?" she asked.

Her sister smiled slyly. "Unlike you, I save up my money for something nice."

"Well, good for you," Gail sniped and without another word, bounded down the stairs, followed by Lou.

Both sisters paused in the living room and took in the familiar tableau of their parents: hunched over the small table that held the chessboard, play in progress, their mother resting her face on both hands as she studied the board, and their father with his pipe clamped between his teeth.

"Going out, girls?" he asked.

"For a little while, Dad," Gail told him.

"Where are you going?" Diana asked, looking up.

She shrugged. "Not sure yet."

"Please don't go to that bar in Cheever, Flashers or whatever it is," Diana instructed.

"Flashes, Mom."

Diana looked at Mark. "I've heard there are a lot of drugs there. People doing drugs right in front of everyone."

Mark looked over at his daughters and took two quick puffs of his pipe. "No Flashes tonight, girls. You heard what your mother said."

"Okay, Dad," Louise said.

"Come on, let's go," Gail said.

"Not too late tonight," their mother called out after them. "We're going to Sam and Joy's tomorrow for Sunday dinner." She followed up with the same question she asked every time they went somewhere: "Do you have your dime in case you have to make a phone call?"

"Yes," they answered back, as always.

Gail thought she might give Sunday dinner a miss but said nothing. They walked down the front steps and over toward Gail's car.

"What are you wearing on your feet?" Gail asked with a scowl.

Louise stopped on the sidewalk, lifted her foot, and turned it sideways so the bottom was visible. "Ballet slippers. They're super cute. And very comfortable."

"You're going out in those? They look like bedroom slippers."

"Look at *your* shoes," Louise said. "How can you even walk in them?"

Gail extended her leg, showing off her new pair of Candies. The heel was impossibly high, they had no strap, and her toes peeked out the end. She'd seen them in a magazine and had coveted them. "It's not difficult at all when you're used to walking in high heels. Besides, they make my ankles look skinny and my legs longer."

Louise huffed, "For Pete's sake."

"Pete's got nothing to do with it. Get in the car."

Before Gail started the car, she looked over at her sister. "I'll drop you anywhere you want to go. But you're not coming with me." There was no way she was dragging Louise all the way to Cheever with her, especially in that getup.

Louise leaned back against the seat and folded her arms across her chest. "Oh, yes, I am. I know you're going to Flashes because you want to see if Richard—"

"Rick," Gail interrupted.

"—if he's there, and if you don't take me with you, I'm going to tell Mom you went. And then you won't be going anywhere for the rest of the summer." Louise wore a self-satisfied smile.

"You little snitch."

"Come on, start the car, let's go," Louise said.

"When we get there, you go your own way. We don't know each other. And we're not leaving until I say it's time to leave."

"I wonder if Richard will be there," Louise wondered, her expression soft and dreamy.

"We'll find out." And then, adding a dig, she said, "He's a great dancer. You're not much of a dancer, are you?"

Louise fumed.

Even though it was dark, it was still hot and humid out. There'd been no rain in Lavender Bay for more than a month. You weren't even allowed to water your gardens or lawns for the foreseeable future. Their mother had got the notion of taking the old Radio Flyer wagon down to the beach, filling up two containers with lake water, and dragging the wagon through the sand and back home to water her roses and the few vegetables she had in the backyard.

The current dilemma was whether to roll down the windows or not. If they didn't, they'd be a sweaty mess by the time they arrived. But if they did, their hair would be ruined. Gail opened the vent window and suggested that her sister do the same.

The highway was a straight run to Cheever, which lay north of Lavender Bay. The traffic was light, and the buildings, stores, and plazas thinned out until there were only copses of dense trees on either side of the road. There were plenty of deer grazing next to the highway and Gail was mindful, thinking how a colleague of their father's had hit a buck the previous week and the car had been destroyed. The two sisters had felt sorry for the deer; how awful it must have been for him. But now, Gail realized this was the only set of wheels she had.

"Why couldn't you get a car with air conditioning," Louise complained, fanning herself with a map she pulled from the glove compartment.

"Why don't *you* buy a car with air conditioning," Gail shot back.

"I don't have that kind of money."

"Come on, Lou, you have more money than God. You never spend it."

"I'm trying to save it."

"For what?"

Louise shrugged. "Maybe a place of my own someday."

Gail scoffed. "I can't see that happening. It's not like there are a lot of apartments in Lavender Bay. Unless you're looking to rent one of those little cottages." She cast a quick glance over at her sister, who shrugged again.

"Don't you want to live on your own?"

"Sure I do, but I'm sensible. I'm not going to be able to afford it working at the grocery store," Gail explained. "I don't want to be tied to that job because I have to pay rent and utilities."

They drove on for the next few miles in silence. It was Gail who spoke first.

"How was your lunch with Rick?"

Louise nodded. "Good. *Richard* is a lovely man." She paused. "We talked about a lot of things. Did you know that he doesn't like the Buffalo Sabres?"

Gail's mouth hung open. The hockey team had lost the Stanley Cup against the Philadelphia Flyers back in the spring. Talk like that in these parts of New York State was treasonous. But at the same time, it irked her that Louise knew this about him, and she didn't. She went for nonchalance and shrugged. "I know. He told me."

Louise burst out laughing. "You liar! He never said anything to you about it. Actually, he went on about how much he loved the Sabres, how next year they'd win it, and how he'd gone to all the home games during the playoffs."

Furious, Gail immediately pulled her car off to the side of the highway, not even bothering to put her indicator on. Once she turned the car off, she turned to her sister and said, "Let's call a truce about Rick."

"Richard," Louise added with emphasis.

Gail sighed, "Whatever. Look, I thought about things. I think if *Richard* is there tonight, we should ask him to make a choice. Which one of us he wants." She'd given it careful deliberation.

"It's not right for him to be dating us both," Louise conceded. "It's only going to end in tears . . . for one of us."

With that tacit agreement in place, Gail started the car and pulled back out onto the highway. And for the rest of the drive, they spoke no further.

The parking lot at Flashes was packed. Gail drove around several times and finally took one of the few vacant spots left in the back row.

"Maybe you could drop me off at the door," Louise said.

Gail snorted. "I'm not your chauffeur. You can walk like me."

"But the gravel will ruin my ballet slippers."

"You should have worn more appropriate footwear."

Louise mimicked what Gail had said in a high voice, tilting her head from side to side.

Gail looked over the roof of the car and said tightly, "Keep it up and you and your ballet slippers can pirouette all the way back to Lavender Bay."

Louise muttered something under her breath and then said, "Wait a minute." She pulled out a tube of Kissing Potion and applied the clear, thick gloss to her lips.

"Why don't you wear proper lipstick or gloss?" Gail asked. "What put it into your head that a guy wants to kiss a girl who smells like bubble gum?"

Louise shrugged. "I like it, that's all."

Without another word, they headed off toward the building, Gail trailing behind as she navigated the loose gravel in her Candies.

As they got close, Louise headed for the wrong door. Laughing, Gail called over to her sister, "You can go through the delivery door if you want, but I'm going in the front door."

Even from that distance, she could see Lou's annoyed expression, and that made her laugh.

As they walked into the club, the noise increased exponentially. Overhead, Donna Summer's "Love to Love You Baby" blasted out from the loudspeakers, and Gail began to move her hips in rhythm with it.

"Gail! That's scandalous!" Louise said behind her.

Gail turned on her. "Lighten up, Laura Ingalls."

Both scanned the crowd for the object of their affection but there was no sign of him, and both girls deflated.

"Come on, let's get a drink and do some dancing," Gail said. She couldn't shake the feeling of disappointment and briefly wondered if they'd somehow scared him away. Maybe he didn't want the drama. Despite all this, she was determined to have a good time.

Chapter Twenty-Five

Louise had never been to Flashes before, and she wasn't sure if she liked it or not. The noise level was so high she couldn't hear herself think. Plus, there was this resounding bass that made the floor vibrate beneath her. Her footwear could not absorb it, and it made her feel off-kilter and slightly nauseous. She kept all this to herself, knowing Gail would berate her for it. She was loath to admit it, but she preferred the Dog Days Bar back home. It was small, and she knew everyone who frequented the place. What she loved best about it was the jukebox in the corner. Edna Knickerbocker, who tended bar in the evenings, made sure the guy who serviced the jukebox kept it loaded up with all the most recent hits. Edna's favorite song was Johnny Mathis's "Chances Are," but the jukebox also held some of Louise's favorite artists like John Denver, Jim Croce, Harry Nilsson, and Gordon Lightfoot. Although Dog Days was a dump, it was more intimate, unlike this big, cavernous space with its futuristic purple lighting and that relentless vibration beneath her feet.

Over her shoulder, Gail yelled, "Come on, let's get a drink." And she elbowed a path through the crowd. As they edged up to the bar, she said to Louise, "I'll get this round, and you can get the next. What do you want to drink?"

"Grenadine and Squirt."

"That's basically a Shirley Temple," Gail said, shaking her head.

"I know, but I like it."

Gail got the attention of the bartender, leaned in, and ordered a round of drinks, but Louise couldn't hear what was being said. She was too busy looking around the place for somewhere to sit as her feet were killing her already.

Gail pivoted and faced her, holding two cocktails in her hand. She handed one of them to her sister.

Louise frowned. "What is this?"

"It's a gin squirt. Don't worry, it has some grenadine in it and a little bit of gin. A grown-up drink."

Louise ignored the barb and approached the drink with a skeptical expression. Why couldn't she just have what she wanted? She'd never had gin before. She sipped it carefully and nodded several times. "Not bad." She gestured to the highball glass in her sister's hand. "What are you drinking?"

"A Harvey Wallbanger. Try it." Gail pushed it toward her.

Louise took a sip and scrunched up her nose and shook her head. "Ew. Orange juice. No thanks. I'll stick to the gin squirt."

But Gail wasn't listening; she'd started to walk away, working her way through the throng, leaving Louise no choice but to follow her. As they neared the dance floor, Louise spotted a bunch of circular booths on the other side of the bar. "Look over there, there's somewhere to sit."

Gail turned and glared at her. "I did not come here to sit down. I came here to dance, listen to music, and drink. Besides, you can't go back there."

"Why not?" Louise asked. Immediately, her back was up. She hated it when Gail told her what she could and couldn't do. She'd been doing it since they were little. Being the oldest, Gail was naturally bossy.

"Because it's where couples go to sit," Gail explained.

"Why is it okay for them to sit but not me?"

Gail sighed as if her younger sister were a simpleton. "They go back there to make out."

Realization dawned on Louise. "Oh." And then, "Have you ever been back there?"

With a smirk, Gail said, "That's for me to know and you to find out."

Before Louise could think of a snappy comeback, her sister wound her way through the crowd and stepped down onto the dance floor, tucking her drink and purse along the raised platform next to the other purses and drinks. Louise did the same.

Over the din of the music, Gail said, "Always keep an eye on your drink so no one slips a mickey into it."

"I know that," Louise snapped. "I'm not stupid."

"If you say so," Gail said, and she began to dance to the beat, closing her eyes, moving her hips, and snapping her fingers.

For a minute, Louise stood there, not moving and feeling foolish. She wasn't big into dancing, which was another reason she preferred the Dog Days Bar. There was no dance floor there, so there was never any worry about dancing in front of strangers and possibly making a fool of yourself. Self-conscious, she looked around and saw that all the other girls there were dressed more like Gail, and that she in her Gunne Sax dress and ballet slippers was conspicuous. Terrified of looking like an idiot, she watched Gail's dance moves and mimicked them as best she could. By the end of the second song, she wanted off the dance floor. She felt as if she were on display. But Gail kept dancing. When the fourth song ended, Louise picked up her now-empty glass and purse and said, "I'm going to the bar to get another drink."

"Hold on, this is my favorite song," Gail said, and she kept dancing.

"You say that about every song!"

"Wait!"

"No," Louise said firmly. She knew her sister. It wouldn't be one song. It'd be about ten more. "Look, I'll make my way to the bar and when you're finished, join me. It's my turn to buy."

"Okay."

Louise made her way off the dance floor, almost tripping up the two steps but recovering quickly, grateful that she hadn't fallen. She tried to make her way to the bar, but she kept getting pushed back in the crowd, like one of those powerful waves on the lake when the current was strong. Frustrated, she began to barge her way forward and at last had the bar in sight. She couldn't understand how Gail enjoyed this place. It was awful.

She edged her way between two burly guys at the bar but had to stand sideways. Tentatively, she put up her hand to get one of the bartenders' attention, but they kept sailing right past her, oblivious. The two men that she was squeezed between finally realized they had company and looked down at her.

"Hello there, little lady," said the one.

"Hello there yourself," she said.

"I suppose you want a drink," said the other.

"It would be nice."

The one put up his hand to signal the bartender, who appeared in front of them.

"What'll you have, half pint?" asked the other.

Recognizing a fellow fan of *Little House on the Prairie*, Lou burst out laughing. "I love that show!" He indulged her with a smile like the kind an adult would bestow on a child. "A gin squirt please," she said. By now she'd realized they must be brothers. They were big, bulky men, and they kind of reminded her of linebackers who'd gone to seed, although they weren't that old. Maybe in their mid-twenties. They both had naturally curly auburn-colored hair that they wore longish. Both wore square-framed glasses.

The one ordered Louise's drink and made a gesture with his finger indicating they'd like another round as well. While they waited for the drinks, the one on her left said, "I'm Chet, and this is my twin brother, Arnie."

"Hello, Chet, and hello, Arnie. I'm Louise, but my friends call me Lou." She smiled at each of them.

"Hello, Lou."

And then, both brothers put a thumb up to their temples, wagged their fingers, and squealed, "Hee-Haw!"

Louise burst out laughing and clapped her hands. "I love it!"

The bartender slid two bottles of beer and a tumbler of gin squirt across the bar to the trio. Louise reached for her purse, and Chet shook his head. "We've got this one, Lou."

"I can't let you pay for my drink," she protested.

"You can and you will," Arnie said, lifting his bottle to his mouth.

Louise settled in their company. They were good fun, and it was much nicer than being out on the dance floor. She enjoyed their company so much she almost forgot about her aching feet, one of which had the start of a blister. She didn't give Gail another thought, figuring she was still out on the dance floor. She took another sip of her drink, reminding herself to slow down, and turned her attention to the twins, trying to discern subtle differences that would allow her to tell them apart if she were ever to meet them again.

CHAPTER TWENTY-SIX

Gail made her way through the entire club in search of Louise. She couldn't find her anywhere. There was a moment of panic when she wondered if she'd left with someone else. But Louise wouldn't be that stupid. Or at least she hoped not.

And then, about thirty feet ahead of her, she spotted the lacy peach dress. Louise was exiting the ladies' room and heading toward the bar. Her carefree attitude indicated she hadn't been missing Gail. Or looking for her. For a brief, dark moment, Gail wondered if Lou had run into Rick and had been spending time with him. She'd kept her eye out for him but hadn't seen him all night. She moved faster through the throng, elbowing her way through.

As much as she loved her new shoes and all the dancing, her feet were killing her. If Rick was a no-show, then they might as well think about heading home. She could barely disguise her disappointment. And the fact that her sister was definitely not looking for her only further soured her mood.

She closed the gap between herself and Lou and called out her sister's name, but it was lost in the music. Her sister didn't even turn her head. Gail's impatience increased tenfold. She finally caught up with her, intercepting her.

"Where've you been?"

"I've made some friends. I've been hanging out with them," Lou told her, cheery.

"This isn't kindergarten, Lou! I've been looking all over for you," Gail fumed. "I thought something happened."

"Nothing happened. I'm still right here." Louise frowned. "What could possibly happen? Come on, I'll buy you a drink. I want you to meet Arnie and Chet."

But as they approached the bar, Gail spotted Rick. And a second later, so did Louise.

He wasn't alone. He sat on a barstool next to a tall, lithe blonde in a red dress and strappy gold sandals. They sat sideways, Rick's legs flanking the blonde's so they were thigh to thigh.

"Isn't that . . ." Louise started.

"Yeah, it is," Gail said, feeling like a fool.

"I guess we're not the only ones on his string," Lou said.

"I guess not."

"What should we do?"

"Give me a minute. I'll think of something."

Boy, how quickly they'd been forgotten. Gail ran the gamut of emotions, from disappointment that she'd been had to that ever-lingering sense that she just wasn't good enough. A good look at the beautiful blonde left her with that feeling of lacking, that she could never measure up. It didn't come around often, but when it did, it was like blunt force trauma.

"Why, that dirty dog," Louise said. They both stood in the middle of the club, staring at him. He leaned toward the blonde, pushing her hair back, and Gail reddened. He'd used the same move on her.

"Should we confront him?" Louise asked.

"Not yet."

"Come on, let's get that drink I promised you," Lou suggested.

Her ego wounded, Gail followed Lou to the bar but at this point was ready to wrap things up. It was after midnight. The club would be closing within two hours. Louise introduced her to Arnie and Chet.

"You two don't look anything alike," Chet said.

Gail had seen these guys here before. Big, heavyset, they seemed all right. She never saw them anywhere other than belly up to the bar. Only Lou would make friends with them.

Gail and Lou stood close and kept their gazes locked on Rick and his lady friend. "It makes me so angry," Lou said.

"Me too," Gail replied.

With a nod toward Rick at the other side of the bar, the guy on the right, who Gail thought was Chet—or no, maybe it was Arnie—said, "How do you know Rick?"

It took her a moment to process that these two knew Rick. Finally, she said, "Just from coming in here." She wasn't about to admit she'd been played.

Louise went to say something, but Gail elbowed her sharply in the ribs to shut her up.

"Do you know him?" Gail asked, now on a quest for information.

The other brother said, "Yeah, he's our next-door neighbor." His tone indicated he wasn't a big fan.

"Really?" Louise asked, incredulous.

"Yeah, he's a class A jerk. He's here all the time. A different woman every week."

Gail's cheeks reddened, and she was glad for the dim lighting.

"He's got a wife and two kids at home," Arnie said.

"Oh." Louise's voice sounded like the bottom had just fallen out.

Gail suddenly felt sick.

"What's his wife like?" Louise asked.

"Karen's real nice. She deserves better," Chet replied.

"He spends all their money on clothes and going out," Arnie told them. "She's had to borrow money more than once from our mother to buy formula and diapers."

Louise was outraged. "That's awful!"

He has a wife. And babies? Gail wanted to throw up. What kind of man didn't provide his wife and children with the necessities? She had really misjudged him, and she hated herself for it. Furious, she looked at her sister and said, "Come on, Lou, it's time for a showdown."

"We'll be right back, fellas," Lou said to the twins, and she followed her sister. Gail walked with determination over to Rick and the blonde.

"Hello, Rick," Gail said.

He looked surprised to see them. Although why, she didn't know. He knew she came here regularly.

"Hello, Richard," Lou said, crossing her arms over her chest and trying—and failing—to look imperious.

He laughed and stuttered, "H-Hey there. How are you?"

Gail eyed the blonde, who was even more stunning up close. She could be a Breck girl. "Who's your friend?" she asked Rick.

"This is Cindy," he said.

"Cindy, hi. I'm Gail, and this is my sister, Louise. How long have you known Rick?"

"Richard?" she asked. She had the bluest eyes Gail had ever seen. "I only met him last weekend. He asked me out on a date. Why, is there a problem?"

Rick interrupted, laughing nervously. "There's no problem here. Gail and Louise are old friends of mine."

Gail snorted and next to her, Louise scoffed.

"It was great seeing you gals again," Rick said. His smile was tight, and Gail sensed he'd prefer they took it somewhere else.

Cindy looked baffled.

Lou nudged Gail. "Come on, Gail, he isn't worth it."

But Gail wasn't finished. She was going to speak her piece. She directed her words to the woman. "Look, you're a pretty girl. This guy's a lowlife. He's got a wife and two kids at home. You can do so much better."

The blonde didn't know what to say, but her gaze swung from the sisters to Rick, and her eyes narrowed. "Is this true, Richard?"

Rick glared at Gail, which was answer enough for Cindy. She jumped off her barstool, grabbed her drink and purse, and said to Gail, "Thanks for the tip."

"Wait a minute, Cindy, I can explain," Rick said hurriedly, but his pleas fell on deaf ears.

Gail had had enough, and turned and walked away with Lou. They returned to the bar, and the brothers confessed to watching the whole confrontation, saying it was about time Rick got what was coming to him.

Gail should have felt victorious, but all she felt was hollow and tired. The brothers bought another round of drinks. Gail yawned and set hers on the table.

The brothers seemed friendly enough, but by the fifth *Hee-Haw!* Gail had had enough. It was time to go home. She was about to suggest to Louise that they leave when her sister leaned into her and whispered, "Look who just walked in."

Gail followed her sister's gaze and saw Hugh Campbell and Martin Cook near the entrance. Hugh stood a head above everyone else. His gaze swung in every direction, searching for something. Or someone. Could he have come all this way in search of her? Her ego had taken such a beating with Rick's duplicity that there was no way she could believe that.

"I'm ready to go," she said.

Louise peered at her watch on the thick leather band with the embossed strawberry and tried to read it in the dim light. Her eyes went big. "It's almost one!"

Gail was relieved her sister didn't put up a fight. She was anxious to depart before Hugh spotted her. Maybe if it were another night, she'd be in a better mood, but now she only wanted to get home. And they still had a considerable drive back to Lavender Bay.

They said quick goodbyes to Chet and Arnie and promised to return, though the luster of Flashes had now faded for Gail. At that moment, she was doubtful she would ever come back. But she might change her mind by next Saturday night. On the way out, she steered clear of Hugh and Martin and was relieved that she was able to exit without being spotted.

She ignored her hurting feet and raced through the parking lot, eager to get home and get into her bed. Behind her, Louise pleaded for her to slow down, but Gail didn't stop until she reached her car. She was waiting in the driver's seat by the time Lou caught up and slid in next to her.

Without a word, Gail started up the car and pulled out of the parking lot.

CHAPTER TWENTY-SEVEN

Louise didn't say anything for a while. She could tell by her sister's mood that she didn't want to talk. She supposed Gail was disappointed to find out that Richard had a wife. Louise was too, but her contact and involvement had been minimal. From what she gathered, Gail had spent more time with him—even if it was at a disco—and obviously, the sting had been greater.

Despite it being the middle of the night, the air was heavy and warm. They both rolled down their windows, no longer caring what happened to their hair. Her pillow wouldn't mind what her hair looked like when her head hit it, Louise thought.

"Can I turn on the radio?" she asked.

Gail shrugged. "I don't care."

Louise reached forward and turned the knob but kept the volume low. She hung her hand out the window, letting the warm air float over it, and watched the landscape pass by. The trees along the side of the highway were now hidden in darkness. There were no deer to be seen. She yawned, longing for her bed. It would take about half an hour to get home, and they'd only been driving for five minutes. Possibly, she could doze off on the way, but that felt disloyal to Gail. Plus, she didn't want her sister falling asleep at the wheel. She glanced in her direction. Gail was gripping the steering wheel, staring straight ahead, lost in thought.

Suddenly, the car jerked and sputtered. Louise sat up straight and asked, "What's wrong?"

Gail looked at the dashboard. "I don't know." As the car continued its violent shaking, she slowed down and headed for the shoulder. As she pulled off the highway, the car gave one final shudder and died. The radio went silent, and the dashboard lights and head-lights went dark.

Louise stared at her sister. "What's happened?"

"I don't know, Lou! I'm not a mechanic."

"Start it again," Lou suggested.

"It's still in drive. The key is turned on," Gail said. She threw the car in park and turned the car off and then turned the key again, attempting to turn it over. She tried this several times, but nothing happened.

Louise looked around the empty highway, the black sky, and tried not to panic. "What do we do?"

Gail sighed. "I don't know."

Louise pulled out her change purse. "I've got my dime."

"Look around. Do you see a payphone?"

Lou bit her lip.

Gail tried one more time to get the car going. With no success, she leaned back and said, "We've got two options. We can sit here and wait for someone to pass by, or we can start walking."

"I vote for staying here until someone passes by," Louise said.

Gail decided they should walk. Or at least start walking. They headed south along the two-lane highway in the direction of Lavender Bay. Certainly, someone would pass them. Hopefully a patrol car from the county sheriff's office. She couldn't imagine walking all the way back to Lavender Bay. That would take all night. And neither of them sported the proper footwear for such an endeavor.

The noise from the crickets in the tree-lined fields on both sides of the highway was loud and obnoxious. In the distance, a train chugged along the tracks, its lonely whistle blowing through the night. They walked along the shoulder of the road, where the pavement ended. It was a wide enough strip for a car to pull over, but it was dusty and full of stones.

"What time is it?" Gail asked.

Louise peered at her watch as they stepped into the pool of light from the next streetlight. "It's twenty after one."

Gail stopped. "That's it? We only left twenty minutes ago?"

"I'm afraid so."

"Why does it feel like it should be so much later? It feels like four in the morning."

Louise shrugged and they resumed walking.

"Have you ever seen the highway empty before?" Gail asked. She stopped, turned, and looked in the direction they'd come from. Behind them and ahead of them lay only darkness. She stared for a moment, hoping to see headlights, wishing them into existence.

Louise rubbed her shoulders as if she were cold. "I don't like it. It's too dark. Almost creepy."

"Come on, let's keep going."

"I don't even see the sign for Lavender Bay."

Gail hadn't the heart to tell her that wasn't in their immediate future. They'd probably be walking for the rest of the night. They'd roll into the house at dawn, and she'd have to explain that they'd gone to Cheever anyway, not heeding their mother's warning. She'd be caught out for lying. She stepped awkwardly on a large stone and winced as her ankle bore the brunt of it. As for her car, she'd have to get it towed to Edwin Knickerbocker's garage. She hoped it wouldn't cost too much to fix. She'd be forced to pick up more hours at the grocery store. The thought of that alone depressed her.

"Are you disappointed in Rick?" Lou asked.

Gail stiffened. With the car breaking down and the long walk home, she'd temporarily forgotten about him.

"I'm more disappointed in myself that I was seduced by a married man," she admitted.

"You're not the only one," Louise said. "What a jerk."

Gail sighed. "What a jerk is right."

"How can a man with a wife and kids be out on the prowl?" Louise asked.

Gail looked at her sister for a moment, raising an eyebrow at her turn of phrase. *She must be reading my* Cosmopolitan *magazines again.*

"It happens." But it would never happen again to Gail Sturges, that much she'd decided. She'd never let another man make a fool of her. And she certainly had no intention ever again of being the other woman, not even with harmless flirting.

"Men can be so terrible," Louise said. There was a mixture of disappointment and anger in her voice.

Gail yawned, wishing her bed weren't so far away. "Says the one who's only met one."

"I meet men all the time at the Quirk and the Quill," Louise protested. Her vehemence was full-on considering the time of day.

Gail snorted. "Sure, older men who clip pens to the insides of their pockets."

Louise didn't say anything.

She looked forward along the highway as it disappeared into the darkness. "As soon as I finish college next spring, I'm out of here."

"Gail, don't say that. Don't leave Lavender Bay."

"Why do you care if I leave or not?"

"Two reasons. First, if you leave, I'm afraid you'll never come back. And second, you're the only sister I have."

Gail put her sister's argument aside for the moment and circled back to the topic of Rick. "I feel like I made a fool of myself with Rick. All those times at Flashes, it was me and him, dancing and drinking all night." She was so glad now that she'd never let him talk her into sitting down in the back for a make-out session. Her stomach flipped at the thought of that. So much for playing hard to get. He'd played her!

"Oh, me too! He walked into the shop just like they do in the movies, and I was all swoony over him. It was like Burt Reynolds walked into my life," Louise said.

Swoony?

"And there's the two of us, fighting over some man who didn't even deserve us," Gail said with a sigh.

"That's for sure."

She stopped walking, relieved to give her feet a break. "Let's make a pact to never let a man come between us again."

Louise gave a short, sharp nod of her head and thrust out her hand. Gail shook it, thinking her sister was a strange little bird. She was so naïve and needed to be protected from all the Richards in the world.

"My feet are killing me," Gail said.

"So are mine. I can feel every stone on the bottom of my foot."

Gail looked back again, disappointed not to see any headlights. "Come on, we might as well walk on the road, it's smoother."

"But what if a car comes?"

It was painful that she sometimes had to spell out the obvious. "Then we'll get back on the shoulder."

She walked down the double yellow line of the two-lane highway. She removed her shoes, emitting a loud sigh of relief, and carried them in one hand.

"You're going to ruin the bottom of your feet," Louise said as she limped over to the yellow line to join her.

"They're already ruined." With a nod toward her sister's feet, Gail asked, "How are your slippers holding up?"

Lou stopped on the double yellow line, lifted her foot, and twisted it to look at the bottom of it. The sole of the ballet slipper was black, and there was a tear forming in the middle of the sole.

"Oh darn, I just bought these. I'll have to throw them out," she wailed.

They walked on in silence, going from one pool of illumination to the next, but there was a break between each in which they walked in total darkness, with only the stars in the sky above them providing any kind of light. At first, Gail counted the pools of light as she walked, for something to do and as a marker. But when it appeared to be interminable, she gave up.

"What time is it?" she asked.

Louise peered at her watch in the darkness. "It's too dark, I can't see what it says."

As soon as they reached the next pool of illumination, Louise lifted up her arm and looked at her wristwatch. "It's ten minutes since the last time you asked."

Gail tried not to be disheartened by this. Her feet hurt and her legs ached. Plus, they were nowhere near Lavender Bay.

"Look, headlights!" Louise said, pointing north, sounding as if she'd uttered the magic words.

Gail turned. In the far distance were two small orbs of light that were growing bigger. She almost sighed with relief. Hopefully, if the driver would drop them off at the turnoff to Lavender Bay, everything would be fine.

She was going to have to do something their mother had warned them against for years.

"Come on, let's get in the light." Gail ran forward to the next swathe of light on the highway, ignoring her protesting feet. Louise ran after her.

The two of them limped and hobbled toward the shoulder.

A white panel van approached. Boldly, Gail stepped off the shoulder and stood on the edge of the highway, arm extended, thumb out.

"Gail! Mom doesn't want us hitchhiking!"

Looking over her shoulder, Gail said, "Do you want to walk the rest of the way, or do you want a ride home?"

The van drove past them, and Gail dropped her arm in frustration.

Twenty feet ahead of them, the vehicle stopped. It idled in the darkness, its exhaust loud, its red taillights like two glowing bars in the night.

"Come on," Louise said, and she broke into a run. Gail followed her, relief filling her. Finally, a ride home!

CHAPTER TWENTY-EIGHT

As they neared the van, Gail saw that it was dirty, and mud covered the tires. The only sounds were the idling engine, the rumbling exhaust, and the relentless din of crickets. With all the exuberance of a child with a new toy, Louise reached the open window of the passenger side first.

"Thank goodness! We need a ride to Lavender Bay. Our car broke down and we've started walking home. But we'll never make it in these shoes."

Gail arrived at the open window and peered in. There was only one passenger seat, and behind it was an open space. It was relatively clean, but it looked beat-up. Her gaze traveled to the driver, whose countenance was highlighted by the dashboard lights.

"Was that your car back on the highway?" he asked.

"Yes," Gail said.

"Lavender Bay?"

"Please."

He was middle-aged, on the other side of forty, with dark hair that hung over his ears and thick glasses. His hand rested on the steering wheel, and Gail glimpsed a thin wrist.

"Hop in, I'll give you a ride home." He leaned over and opened the door.

"You're a lifesaver!" Louise said. Gail wished her sister would temper her enthusiasm. After all, they didn't know this guy. Louise jumped in to stake her claim on the passenger seat and announced, "I guess you'll have to ride in the back, Gail."

Before she even got into the van, Gail became aware of the smell: a combination of body odor and unwashed human. She had one foot on the sidestep when she looked over at the driver and froze. He sat there staring at them, and it wasn't so much a grin on his face as a leer. An involuntary shiver went down her spine. Her mouth went dry, and she whispered to her sister, "Get out."

Louise's smile disappeared. "What?"

"Come on, get in," the guy said. His pleasant tone had turned surly.

"Get out, Lou," Gail whispered, tugging on her arm.

Louise saw the troubled expression on her sister's face and began to slide out of her seat, but the driver was quicker, grabbing hold of her left wrist.

"Not so fast. I offered you a ride. Now get in." He had a firm grip on Louise's wrist. Even in the shadowy interior of the van, the fear on her face was evident as she tried to pull free.

Gail jumped up into the vehicle, leaning over Lou, who was half on and half off the seat, and began to pound on the driver's hand, trying to release his death grip. She punched and scratched at the arm while he swung at her with his free hand, grazing her chin with his fist. Finally, terrified, she sunk her teeth into his wrist. He howled and released his grip on Louise, who half slid, half fell out of the van. As Gail jumped from the van, he grabbed a hank of her hair and pulled it. She landed hard on her knee on the gravel shoulder.

Louise crouched over her as she lay on the pavement in agony. "Are you all right? Are you hurt?" Her voice was full of panic.

"I've hurt my knee," Gail said. The pain made her shaky and nauseous. Perspiration broke out on her brow.

The driver pulled the passenger door shut and took off but braked hard about ten yards away. Ahead of them, the van idled, the rumble of its engine reverberating through the night.

"Can you stand?" Louise asked, keeping her eye on the back of the vehicle.

"Why is he just sitting there? Why doesn't he move?" Gail asked out loud.

Finally, the white van peeled away and sped off, its red taillights disappearing into the night. Both sisters stared after it. Once it was gone, the tension in Gail's body began to slowly uncoil and loosen.

"Help me up, Lou." However, she realized she was missing a shoe. "Where's my other shoe?"

Lou leaned over and peered around. "I don't see it. It's too dark."

"Try to find it. I can't walk with one shoe," Gail told her.

Louise walked a few paces back and forth, bending and looking into the grass, but shook her head. "Forget about it. It's gone."

It took a few efforts to pull Gail to her feet, but Louise had a strength in her that belied her slight stature. The effort to stand cost Gail, though. The pain shot from her knee up and down her leg. She bit her lip to keep from screaming.

"Lean on me," Louise said.

Gail put her arm around her sister's shoulder. Every step she took, she winced in pain.

"What do we do now?" Louise asked.

"We hope and pray someone else comes along, because there's no way I'll be able to walk," Gail said, drawing in some deep breaths. The pain was incredible. They might have to wait all night until daylight, when the traffic would increase and surely, someone would help. "And let's hope the next car that stops, it's not a perv."

"What if no cars come?" Louise said, panic in her voice.

"Someone will eventually come along. Flashes closes at two; there'll be people there from Lavender Bay." Gail thought for a moment. "If not, you'll have to walk on ahead of me and get help."

Lou's body stiffened. "I am not leaving you alone. There is no way we are splitting up tonight. Not after what just happened."

"Let's go back to my car then," Gail suggested. "At least we can sit down."

"Can you make it?" Lou asked, concern lacing her voice.

"I'm going to try."

"Why are you carrying one shoe?" Louise asked.

"Because I'll have to come back and look for the other one."

"Whatever," Louise grumbled.

They hobbled along, Gail leaning on her sister for support and trying mightily to keep the weight off her affected leg. She had to grit her teeth to soldier through the pain. She'd need to see a doctor tomorrow, of that there was no doubt. She only hoped she hadn't broken something.

Breathless, she said, "Listen to me. We can't tell Mom and Dad about this."

Lou frowned. "Why not?"

"Because Mom is going to kill me." She was already in trouble for going to Flashes, and if her mother found out she'd been hitchhiking and put her and her sister in danger, the punishment would be just about forever. Forget about leaving Lavender Bay, she'd never be able to leave her room.

"We'll tell them I fell because of the shoes and landed hard on the gravel," Gail told her.

"Are you sure?" Louise said. "We really should report this to the police. What if it happens to someone else? To another girl who's alone?" She visibly shuddered.

Gail hadn't thought about that. "All right. But don't say anything yet. Let me figure something out."

Gail grunted in pain, winced, and said, "That's it for me. I can't go any further."

"Oh no."

They were standing in the blind spot between two streetlights, in total darkness. Louise eyed the next pool of light, just out of their reach.

"Can you try to go a little further so we can at least get out into the light?"

Gail shook her head. "Help me down to the ground. I can't stand." She ignored all the stones that had embedded themselves in the bottom of her feet.

Very carefully, Louise helped lower Gail to the ground. Gail hung on to her sister's arm, her hands sliding down the length of it as Louise lowered her slowly to the shoulder of the road.

She landed on her bum and grimaced. "You're stronger than you look, Lou."

But Louise was looking off in the distance, toward Lavender Bay. She lifted her arm and pointed. "Look! A car."

Gail looked over her shoulder and sighed at the approach of twin headlights from the south.

"Hopefully we'll have better luck this time," she said.

"Drat," Louise whispered, shrinking back along the shoulder of the road.

"What?" Gail asked, and a little pit of dread formed in her stomach.

"It's him. The guy in the van."

"Get down, Lou," Gail said, yanking on her sister's dress. "Maybe he won't see us."

That was a possibility. They were in between the highway lights. Louise crouched next to Gail. The van sped past them, but soon slammed on his brakes and swung his vehicle around so that it was southbound again.

Gail whimpered. She wouldn't be able to defend Lou; she couldn't even defend herself. She issued a silent prayer. First for help and then a promise that she would be good for the rest of her life and look after Louise if they made it out of this alive.

For whatever reason, Louise thought this was the time to rifle through her purse.

"What are you doing?" Gail demanded.

Louise triumphantly held up a fountain pen. She uncapped it. "I'm going to stab him in the eye if he comes near us."

Gail held her hand out. "Give me the pen. I'll stab him in the eye, and you run as fast as you can."

"I'm not leaving you!"

"Don't be stupid. I can't go anywhere. And if you don't do as I say, I'll kill you myself."

Before they could get into further debate, the van picked up speed and headed toward them.

"He's trying to hit us!" Louise shrieked. With the strength of two men, she dragged Gail off the shoulder of the road and into the high grass.

The van just missed them, its tires kicking up gravel and spraying them with stones. The driver slammed on his brakes as the back end of the van swung wildly close to them, filling the air with loud screeching and the smell of burnt rubber and exhaust. Once the van was righted, it now faced north. It idled for less than a few seconds before coming at them again. With a grunt and a groan, Louise pulled Gail further away. But before he reached them, he slammed on his brakes again.

Suddenly, a sweep of headlights behind the girls caught their attention.

Another car.

CHAPTER TWENTY-NINE

As the pair of headlights grew larger, the van sped off, passing the approaching car and disappearing into the night.

Gail heard a whimper and realized it had come from her. Louise scrambled to the shoulder of the road.

"What are you doing?" Gail said.

"Getting us a ride home."

"Get down, what if it's another perv?"

"That is statistically impossible," Louise said.

The car, a Chevy Yenko, slowed until it was abreast of them, and Louise started clapping and laughing. "It's Martin and Hugh!"

Gail was so relieved she wanted to cry.

Hugh Campbell sat in the driver's seat with his friend Martin beside him in the passenger seat. Hugh threw the car into park, and both he and his friend jumped out and trotted toward them.

"Say nothing," Gail whispered. "Follow my lead."

Next to her, Louise's nod was imperceptible.

"Gail? Louise? What happened?" Hugh asked. "We saw your car at the side of the road a mile or so back." His voice was full of authority. "We've been looking for you."

"It broke down," Gail said. "We started walking and I fell."

"You look like you've been beaten up," Hugh said with concern. He and Martin exchanged a glance.

"Like I said, I fell," Gail repeated, her voice firm.

"Louise, why do you have stones in your hair?" Martin asked.

"I fell too," Louise lied. She changed the subject. "You two are like our knights in shining armor."

Gail pulled at the hem of her sister's dress and whispered, "Don't overdo it, Lou."

"Are you hurt?" Hugh asked Gail.

She nodded. "My knee. I landed on it."

"She's in agony!" Louise added. "I bet it's broke."

"Thank you, Louise, for your input," Gail said sharply. She looked up at Hugh. "Can you help me up?"

"I can do better than that."

And before she realized what was happening, he scooped her up off the ground.

"Be careful, I'm heavy," she advised him.

He laughed. "Heavy? You're tiny."

In her entire life, she'd never been called tiny. It was the only highlight of a terrible evening.

As Hugh carried her to the car, Martin said, "Come on, Louise, we'll get into the back." He pushed the front passenger seat forward and allowed Lou to climb into the back before following her. Carefully, Hugh helped Gail into the front seat. She noticed two things: He was very strong, and his cologne was wonderful. She became giddy and if she weren't in so much pain, she would have laughed until the end of time.

Hugh leaned against the frame of the car and looked in at her with a smile. "What's so funny?"

She looked up at him, aware for the first time of the kindness and the goodness in his face and realizing how at that moment, she was in need of it. "Lou and I have had a really long night, and I was thinking how I really like your cologne. It smells heavenly. And it struck me as funny."

He broke into a grin. "All right, let's get you home. You might be delirious."

Giddy with relief that the worst events of the night were now firmly behind her, she put up a finger and said, "That's a strong possibility."

Hugh got into the driver's side, looked over his shoulder, and pulled back out onto the highway. Gail went quiet, trying to ride through the waves of pain and also thinking of the story she was going to have to come up with to tell her parents. They'd be in bed by now and she'd have all night to think about it.

With a grin, Hugh looked down at her one shoe in her hand.

"Where's your other shoe?"

"I lost it when I fell," she replied.

"You were walking on the highway in those things? No wonder you fell! Have you lost your mind?"

She gazed out the open window, her head resting in her hand, propped up by her elbow. "Yes, I do believe so."

In the back seat, Martin and Louise spoke in whispers amongst themselves.

"We were at Flashes too," Hugh said.

Gail experienced a surge of guilt. She'd left because she didn't want him following her around. And now here he was, a gallant knight. This Hugh, this take-charge Hugh, was a different beast altogether.

Fifty lashes with a wet noodle when you get home, she told herself.

The sign to Lavender Bay came into view, and she wanted to cry. What a night!

Louise leaned forward and tapped her on the shoulder. "We're almost home."

Gail nodded, too tired and in too much pain to talk.

When they reached Peony Lane, all was in darkness, except for the streetlights. There were no lights on in the front windows of their house, and Gail's shoulders sagged in relief. She just wanted to go to sleep, but her knee nagged at her relentlessly and she wondered if sleep would elude her.

Over her shoulder, she said to Louise, "We're home."

Louise leaned forward, looked at the house, and said, "Oh sugar." She turned to Martin. "It was lovely talking to you. It was the highlight of my night. It's a shame that I'm home now."

Gail huffed, impatient and in a lot of pain.

"I'm sure we'll meet again, Louise," was Martin's response.

Hugh parked the car by the curb. Louise and Martin got out from the driver's side and waited on the sidewalk for Hugh and Gail. Hugh managed to get Gail as far as the porch steps, when Louise stretched out her arm to him.

"I can take it from here," she said. "I'll get her up the steps."

Hugh appeared uncertain. "Are you sure? I don't mind carrying her up."

"Don't let Lou's size fool you. She's got the strength of ten men," Gail told him.

Beside her, Lou giggled.

Gail gave him her best smile despite all the pain. "I really appreciate everything you've done for us, but Lou can take over from here."

He nodded, disappointed. "Do you want us to go in with you?" he asked.

She shook her head. It would be too much of a risk of possibly waking their parents. Her plan was to get on the sofa, go to sleep, and have her knee feel better in the morning.

"Hey, is it okay if I drop by or call you sometime?" he asked, his voice full of hope.

"Yes. Our number is in the book. Dad's name is Mark Sturges."

Even in the darkness, she could see his broad smile.

Off to the side, Martin held Louise's hand and whispered to her.

What's this? Gail wondered. "Come on, Lou, let's go. It's been a long night."

"That's for sure."

They waved goodbye to Hugh and Martin and waited until they pulled away from the curb. Gail decided she liked Hugh's car and the way he drove it: so self-assured. She was going to have to rethink the whole Hugh Campbell thing.

She leaned against the house, and Lou unlocked the front door. She gently turned the handle and then put her finger up to her lips. "Shh."

As if Gail needed to be reminded. "Remember, no mention of the white van," she whispered.

"I disagree."

"I know, but leave it for now. We'll talk about it in the morning."

The house was silent and dark when they walked in, Gail leaning heavily on Louise for support. Lou turned on the small table light by the front door, bathing part of the parlor in a dim amber light. Gail regarded the staircase, knowing she'd never be able to manage it.

"Help me to the couch, Lou."

"Sure."

Bearing her sister's weight, Louise managed to get her to the couch but as soon as she sat, she winced. "Do you want to put your leg up?"

"Please."

Louise pushed the hassock over closer to her sister. "I've got to lift your leg, Gail. I'm sorry."

"Please be careful."

Gently, Louise lifted her sister's affected leg and laid it straight out on the hassock. Gail clenched her teeth.

"You need to go to the hospital," Louise said in a whisper. "You probably broke something. Let me call an ambulance."

"Don't you dare!"

"All right," Louise said sharply.

Gail relented, realizing that her sister was only trying to help and that she, too, had endured the events of the night.

"Do you want me to run up and get your nightgown?" Louise asked.

Gail nodded. "Please. And my pillow." The room was stuffy. "And could you open the windows, it's close in here."

"Sure. You're right, it is." Lou lifted each of the sashes as quietly as she could. She tiptoed up the staircase, assuring Gail she'd be right back.

Gail leaned back on the sofa and sighed. Her knee throbbed and it was going to be a long night. She prayed it would be better by morning but somehow, she was doubtful. And with that, she burst into tears.

CHAPTER THIRTY

Louise took the steps two at a time. In her own room, she quickly shed her dress and slip, threw her satchel on the bed, and kicked off her ballet slippers. She examined them. They were now gray and scuffed and torn. Only good for the garbage. She'd deal with it in the morning. She slipped on her nightgown and went to the bathroom, washed her face, brushed her teeth, and used the toilet. On the way down, she stopped in her sister's room and grabbed her pillow off the bed and her cotton nightgown off the back of the door.

Downstairs, Lou laid Gail's nightgown next to her and put the pillow near the arm of the sofa. Even in the darkness, she could tell her sister had been crying.

"Are you all right?" she asked softly.

"I need a tissue."

"Sure." She handed her the box of tissues from the shelf. "Do you want me to turn on the fan?"

"No, it's too noisy," Gail said as she wiggled out of her dress and bra and threw her nightgown on over her head.

Louise gasped.

"What's wrong?"

"Your knee," Louise said. "It's all black-and-blue." That was putting it mildly. It appeared purple and marbled. Gail looked down at it and started crying all over again.

"It'll be all right. It'll heal," Louise said, trying to reassure her.

Gail shook her head.

"What is it?"

Through her tears, Gail said, "I have to go to the bathroom."

"Okay, I'll help you." The small half bathroom off the kitchen wasn't far.

"I don't think I can walk anymore. But I really have to go." Gail dabbed at her eyes with a tissue and then blew her nose into it.

"You need to go to the hospital," Louise said, frustrated. She was tired, her feet were killing her, she was worried about Gail's knee, and now she had to figure out a way to get her to the bathroom.

"It's too late now. I'll wait until morning."

"That's stupid."

"I don't want to wake up Mom and Dad," Gail explained.

Exhausted, Louise put that argument aside for the moment.

"Lou, I have to pee," Gail said again.

"All right, hold on." She went into the back hall and grabbed the bucket they used for mopping the floors. If she couldn't take her sister to the bathroom, she'd have to bring it to her.

When she arrived with the metal pail, Gail took one look at it and said, "No way am I peeing in a bucket."

"Fine, then," Louise said. She had an urge to drop it on the floor but knew it would make too much noise. "You have three choices. Get up and go to the bathroom, use the bucket, or wet your pants."

Gail's face contorted in pain. "Give me that damn thing." She sat up gingerly.

"Come on, I'll help you."

"I am not peeing in front of you."

Lou's voice was full of exasperation. "Then let's go to the bathroom or wet your pants. I told you to go to the hospital."

Gail's mutterings were born of frustration and pain. Finally, she said, "Give me the bucket."

It took a few minutes and a lot of "ow, ow, ow," but she managed to get Gail to a standing position, and she placed the bucket between her legs.

"Go ahead." She looked away but held the bucket firmly in place. Her sister peed for a long time. So much so that Louise giggled.

"What is so funny?" Gail asked sharply.

Louise tried to stifle her laughter. "It reminds me of a racehorse, that's all."

"Thanks a lot," Gail said, and started laughing too.

"Jeez Louise, how much did you drink tonight?"

"Apparently a lot." Gail chuckled through her pain.

"Finished?"

"I need toilet paper."

Louise was able to reach the box of Kleenex and handed it to her sister. When she'd finished, she set the bucket down and helped Gail back onto the sofa. She plumped the pillow and put it behind Gail's head. "Do you want some aspirin?"

"Not now."

"Are you comfortable?"

"As much as I can be."

"In the morning, you're going to the hospital," Louise said firmly.

"We'll see."

She carried the bucket to the bathroom, emptied it, washed it out, and put it on the back porch. Yawning, she went up to bed and lay down on top of her bedspread. It was too warm to get under the covers. Sleep escaped her, however, as she wondered if Gail was all right and if she needed anything. Finally, she gave up, took her pillow with her, and went back downstairs. As she suspected, Gail was still awake.

"What's wrong?" Gail asked.

"Nothing, but I thought you might need something," Louise said, throwing her pillow on the floor. She lay parallel to the sofa. When she was a kid, she always stretched out on the floor to watch television. It had been a while, but it would be all right.

"I can't get comfortable," Gail complained.

"You need to go to the hospital," Louise said again.

"It's too late now."

That kind of thinking wasn't logical to Louise, but she kept her mouth shut. She supposed with everything that had happened that night and the fact that they were well past exhaustion, logic had flown out the window.

As she lay there on her back with her hands folded on top of her chest, she stared at the ceiling. The one thing she was trying to forget came into sharp focus. She could still smell the burnt rubber of the tires and the exhaust blowing up in their faces. And then shame settled around her like a heavy fog. She'd jumped into the van ready, willing, and eager to go off with a stranger. There had been no thought involved at all.

"I think we may have dodged a bullet tonight," Louise said into the darkness. She knew her sister was still awake because she kept shifting around on the sofa, groaning and muttering.

Gail sighed heavily. "We did."

"It was scary," Louise said. There, she'd said it out loud.

"It's hard to believe that there are people out there who want to do harm to another human being." Gail practically choked on the words.

Louise swallowed hard. That man had definitely wanted to harm them. What would have happened if they weren't together? If Gail had been alone coming home from Flashes? She shuddered.

"Do not tell anyone, Lou," Gail said.

"Why not?"

"Because."

"That's not a good enough reason," Louise replied.

"For now, it has to be," Gail snapped. "Now go to sleep. I'm beat."

As Louise dozed off, her thoughts ran the gamut: how she hadn't liked Flashes and probably wouldn't return, the car breaking down, the creep in the van, Gail getting hurt. And Martin Cook. The thoughts of him were welcome, and she tried to keep her focus on those, replaying their conversation in her head. She liked him. All the way home, they'd spoken of nothing and everything in the back seat. More than once, he'd asked if she was okay. As she drifted off to sleep, she reminded herself that she had to speak to Gail again the following day about going to the police and reporting the incident with the creep in the van.

She hadn't been asleep long when she heard Gail calling her. At first, she sounded far away but as Louise roused further into consciousness, her voice was closer.

"Lou?"

She opened her eyes but did not move. "Yes?"

Outside the window, the first light of dawn had appeared, and the living room was shadowy.

"I want to go to the hospital," Gail said. "I'm in a lot of pain."

With a sigh of relief, Louise sat up and said, "Okay. I'll call an ambulance." She stood and stretched, still tired. Her eyes burned. She looked at her sister. "Did you sleep at all?"

Gail shook her head. "I couldn't get comfortable."

After making the phone call, Louise climbed the stairs to their parents' room. She knocked softly and opened the door and slipped in quietly, spotting the familiar figures of her parents beneath their thin cotton bedsheet. The windows in the room were wide open, but with no breeze, the curtains hung still. She walked around to the far side of the bed, where her mother lay on her side, her torso rising and falling gently with her breathing.

"Mom?" she whispered.

Diana's eyes blinked open and she sat up, a frown visible on her forehead, even in the dawn light.

"Louise?" Her voice was low and quiet so as not to wake her husband.

The one side of her mother's scalp was a plateau of rugged terrain. Louise had rarely seen her mother without a headscarf. Over the years she'd had glimpses here and there of her mother's disfigurement, usually by accident rather than Diana's choice. Outside her bedroom, Diana would never go without a head covering. It would be akin to not wearing a bra or panties.

"Mom, Gail needs to go to the hospital."

"What? Why?" Her mother flipped back the sheet and swung her legs over the side of the bed, feeling around for her slippers.

"She fell and may have broken her knee or something. She didn't want you to know."

"That's ridiculous. I'll come right down. I'll drive her."

"I've already called an ambulance."

"That bad?" Diana asked as she stood and grabbed a headscarf from her nightstand. She pulled it on and reached for her housecoat, a thin cotton affair.

"Yes, I think so," Louise said.

Diana leaned over and gently shook Mark's shoulder. "Mark?"

Her husband shifted and his voice was thick with sleep. "Hmm? What? Huh?"

Diana quickly explained the situation, then headed downstairs with Lou.

By the time they reached the parlor, sirens could be heard outside as the ambulance approached.

"I'll show them in," Louise said.

Diana assessed Gail and frowned. "My dear girl, what happened?"

"I had a terrible fall," Gail answered, which was the truth but not the whole truth.

"How?" Diana asked.

Mark made his way down the stairs, still yawning, his hair ruffled and his eyes heavy with sleep.

Louise answered her mother's question. "It was her shoes, Mom. They were too high."

Gail looked at her, her expression one of relief that she didn't blab the whole story. Louise smiled and winked at her.

"I've told you time and again, Gail, that you'll break your neck wearing shoes like that," Diana said.

"I know, Mom, I'm sorry," she said, contrite.

Louise showed the ambulance attendants in. After they assessed Gail, they carefully placed her on the stretcher and carried her out.

"Can I ride with her?" Louise asked.

"Sure," said the one.

"I'll go with Gail, honey, why don't you drive with your father?" Diana suggested.

But Louise was adamant that she wasn't leaving Gail.

Finally, Gail put her hand up as they loaded her into the back of the ambulance. "It's fine, Mom, Lou can ride with me."

And that settled it. Louise hopped up into the back of the ambulance, and Diana promised that she and Mark would follow as soon as they changed their clothes. Louise was oblivious to the fact that she was only wearing her nightgown.

The ambulance doors were slammed behind them and they pulled out of the driveway, heading for Lavender Bay Medical Center.

Chapter Thirty-One

Gail's dancing days were over for the rest of the summer. An x-ray determined she had done significant damage to her knee, tearing the anterior cruciate ligament. The rest of her summer would be spent on crutches and doing rehab. Gail stuck to her story that she'd lost her balance on her Candies and landed on her knee the wrong way. Only she and Louise knew the truth about the creep in the van.

Gail was given medication for pain and for the first time in almost twelve hours, she felt some relief. The emergency room doctor, whom Diana said reminded her of the young doctor on *Marcus Welby, M.D.*, told them that there was no need for surgery and Gail could go home with crutches. She was to be non–weight bearing, with no steps for the immediate future and rehab to strengthen the knee.

"Well, that's my summer then," Gail said with a resigned sigh.

"It could be worse," Diana told her. "You could have broken something."

"What about my car?" In all the commotion, no one had given Gail's car another thought.

"I'll give Edwin Knickerbocker a call when I get home. I'll get it towed and let's see if it can be fixed," her father told her.

"Just think, Gail, pretty soon you'll be going home, and you can boss all of us around!" There was almost a sense of glee in Lou's voice.

"Ha-ha," Gail said.

Louise turned to their mother. "Why don't you and Dad go home and rest up? Aren't you going to Sam and Joy's for Sunday dinner?"

Her mother shook her head. "No, I think we'll cancel."

"Aw, Mom, don't cancel," Gail pleaded. "You love going over there and you love not having to cook."

Diana bit her lip, unsure. Louise stood in front of her. "Seriously, Mom, go ahead. I'll stay here with Gail for the afternoon."

"Are you sure?" she asked Gail. "Why do I feel like I'm abandoning you?"

Gail reassured her. "You're not. Go home. Go to Joy's house. Lou can stay with me this afternoon." She appeared thoughtful. "Actually, Lou, you don't have to stay either. You can go home."

Louise shook her head. "No, I'll stay with you."

It was settled then.

Diana pushed back a lock of Louise's hair and asked, "When did you get so grown-up?"

Louise smiled. "It happened overnight."

Her mother chuckled, headed to the door and said, "I'll be back later."

"Can you bring me some clothes?" Louise asked, still wearing her nightgown.

Her mother laughed. "Sure. We'll drop them off on our way to Joy's house."

"If Joy and Sam want to send dinner over, I wouldn't say no." Her stomach had been rumbling for the last hour. She hadn't eaten since yesterday.

After their parents left, Louise pulled up the chair by the side of the bed, sat down in it, and promptly fell asleep.

Later that evening, Gail was stretched out on the hospital bed, dozing. She would have to stay overnight as they couldn't get her a pair of crutches until the morning. There were still traces of Saturday night's makeup, as evidenced by the mascara smudges beneath her eyes. She'd finally fallen asleep after being awake all night and slept away most of the afternoon.

Louise, now fully dressed, sat in the lone chair in the corner of the room, flipping through a magazine. She'd purchased a current edition of *The Ladies' Home Journal* in the gift shop downstairs. "Can This Marriage Be Saved?" was one of her favorite columns. She'd read so many of them, she felt she was mentally prepared for marriage. At least, she thought so.

"Hello? Lou?" Gail croaked from the bed.

Louise jumped up and set the magazine down on the chair. She stood next to the bed. "I'm here."

"What time is it?"

"It's almost five."

"Can I get a glass of water? I'm so thirsty," Gail said, trying to pull herself up in the bed and wincing for the effort.

Lou poured water into a glass and handed it to her. Gail sipped from the straw.

"I bet you're happy you won't have to go to work for eight weeks," Louise said.

"I would be if I didn't need the money so bad." Gail drained the glass of water.

"More?" Lou asked, holding up the water pitcher.

Gail shook her head and lay back down, sighing.

"Dad said you'll get a small disability payment," Louise said.

"I will?"

Lou nodded. To cheer her up she added, "You'll have the rest of the summer off! That's lucky."

Gail glared at her. "I consider myself a lot of things, but lucky isn't one of them."

Louise had felt nothing but lucky the more she thought about their narrow escape the previous night. But now was not the time to get into an argument with her sister. "Can I get you anything?"

"No. Where are Mom and Dad?"

"Still at the Ruggieros'."

"I hope they bring us something to eat, I'm starving."

"Me too."

At that moment, a hospital aide brought in a tray with Gail's dinner on it. "Time for dinner, young lady."

"Your timing's perfect," Gail told her. She sat back up, and Lou lowered the over-the-bed table so her sister could access it better.

The aide laid down the tray on the table and removed the stainless steel cover. As soon as the hospital employee was out of earshot, Gail groaned. "What is this? Can you tell?"

Lou leaned over and inspected the dish. "Those are peas. And those are mashed potatoes, but they look a little soupy. And I think that's beef." She scrunched up her nose. "But I can't tell. It's kind of gray."

Gail pushed the tray away and lay back down. "Forget it."

Louise pulled her chair up closer to Gail's bed and sat and picked up her magazine. "Lou, you don't have to stay here with me," Gail said. "If you want to go home, it's fine."

"I know, but I want to stay."

"Can you bring me a few things from home?" Her mother had dropped off items of clothing before heading to the Ruggieros', but there were other things Gail needed.

"Sure."

"My makeup bag—"

"Hold on, let me get my notepad." Lou rummaged around inside her satchel until her fingers landed on the pocket-sized spiral notebook. She pulled it and her fountain pen from the bag and briefly thought of how the previous night she'd planned to use the pen as a weapon. Thank goodness it hadn't come to that.

"Makeup bag, what else?"

"My toothbrush. My hairbrush."

Lou looked up. "What else?"

"Perfume."

"Do you need perfume in the hospital? Aren't you going home tomorrow?" Louise asked, thinking it wasn't a necessity. "Which one? Charlie or Babe?"

"Bring Babe. Oh, and some Kotex. I'm expecting that this week."

"Oh jeez, on top of everything else?"

"That's the kind of luck I have."

Quietly, Louise put the pen down and said, "We were very lucky, Gail."

"I don't want to talk about that, Lou. Not now. Not ever."

"Okay."

CHAPTER THIRTY-TWO

The following day, Gail was sitting up in bed, waiting for lunch. She should have been discharged by now, but the orthopedic surgeon had had an emergency and was currently in surgery. She couldn't leave until he signed off on the paperwork. Her mother sat on the edge of the bed and her father paced the room, his unlit pipe clamped between his teeth. She'd tried to call Louise to bring her some McDonalds, but the line had been busy. She was just about to dial it again when Hugh Campbell appeared in the doorway, holding a bouquet of pink roses.

Her father stopped pacing and scrutinized Hugh. He took several puffs from his pipe, forgetting that it was unlit. Diana smiled and stood from the bed, winking at Gail, who could feel the furious blush in her cheeks.

The elderly woman in the neighboring bed, who was ninety and had broken her hip in a fall, piped up. "I hope those are for me, young man."

Hugh laughed and looked unsure, but only for a moment. His stride was purposeful as he approached the elderly woman and pulled one long-stemmed rose from the bouquet and handed it to her.

"Careful of the thorns, ma'am," he told her.

"What a gentleman! They're hard to come by these days." She looked over at Gail, her head framed by a cloud of curly white hair. "You better hang on to this one."

Gail sat up straight in bed, glad that Lou had sent her toiletries in with her parents earlier that morning. She'd done her hair and makeup and was feeling presentable. She pushed the bed table away.

"Hey, you," Hugh said quietly. He handed her the bouquet.

"Thank you, they're beautiful," Gail said sincerely. And must have cost a fortune. She hated to admit it, even to herself, but she'd been hoping to see him again. She wanted to see if her change in attitude toward him was permanent or if it had only been the result of the disastrous Saturday night. The roses in her lap were pushing it into the permanent column.

"I'm sorry, I didn't think to bring a vase." He looked around the room as if one might magically appear.

She hurried to reassure him. "Don't worry. I'll call Lou, she can bring one."

"Mom, Dad, this is Hugh Campbell, he gave us a ride home the other night when my car broke down."

Mark extended his hand. "Thank you, young man, for getting our daughters home safely."

Hugh shook his hand. "No problem, sir."

"Your name sounds familiar," Diana said.

He explained how he used to live in Lavender Bay and only recently returned.

"Oh, I remember now. You were a basketball star."

Hugh looked sheepish.

Mark launched into an inquiry of Hugh's plans for the future. Sensing her daughter's embarrassment, Diana glanced at her wristwatch and said, "I think Dad and I will head home."

Gail mouthed, *thank you.*

"Come on, honey," Diana said to her husband.

"Now? I thought we were waiting until Gail was discharged."

"Who knows how long that will be. We'll go home and have lunch." Diana gave a subtle nod toward Hugh and Gail.

Realization dawned on her husband. "Oh right. I see. Okay, kids, we'll see you later."

"Call us when you get word," Diana said on their way out, "and we'll come back and get you."

"Thanks, Mom."

Gail nodded toward the vacant chair next to her bed.

"Sit down, Hugh."

"Thanks." He sat and with a nod toward Gail's knee, asked, "How's it going?" He stretched out his long legs in front of him.

"You know. Not how I planned on spending my summer," she said. "My future is bright with crutches and physical therapy."

"That's good. You'll need to strengthen that leg."

"Yes. So I can go dancing again."

"But no more impossible shoes," he teased.

Even she had to agree that was probably a good idea. "Most likely not."

A silence seeded and then bloomed between them. Before it got awkward, Gail said, "Thank you for the other night. I still have no idea how we would have gotten home if you hadn't come along." She'd racked her brain, thinking of all the other scenarios where it could have gone wrong.

"I'm glad I was there. Funny, but I was hoping to run into you at Flashes. We must have just missed you."

He had said as much last night, and she felt another stab of guilt at her uncharitable thoughts about him, especially after how much he'd done for them since.

She kept it vague. "That must be it."

"Look, there's something I want to ask you about the other night," Hugh started.

A little knot of dread took hold in Gail's stomach.

Hugh plowed ahead. "Just before we found you and your sister on the side of the highway, a white van sped past us. But the funny thing is, Martin and I both thought he was driving erratically and looking back over his shoulder. It's amazing he didn't hit you."

Gail had no intention of reliving that event. "Gee, I don't know what to tell you," she said, thinking there was a half-truth buried somewhere in that statement.

"He didn't see you girls at the side of the road? He didn't stop?" Hugh pressed.

Gail shrugged, growing tired with the questions. She would only concede one little point. "He offered us a ride, but we refused."

But Hugh wouldn't let it go, making her think maybe she wasn't so keen on him.

"See, I would really hate it if someone had tried to hurt you, or if someone *had* hurt you."

"That's nice," she said flatly.

"You don't want to talk about what happened?" he pushed.

She looked at the roses in her lap. They were a perfect shade of pink. "No, not really." She picked up the bouquet, closed her eyes, and inhaled the fragrance.

"All right, Gail." And she was relieved when he dropped it.

"Where's your sidekick?" she asked.

"When I left the house, he was on the phone talking to your sister."

"Is he staying with you?"

"Yeah, he is. I brought him home with me for the summer. He's staying with me at my parents' house. I think he's sweet on your sister."

This was an interesting development. She didn't know Martin Cook at all; in fact, she didn't even know Hugh that well.

Hugh stayed for half an hour, and then he stood and announced that he had to leave. Gail was surprised to find that she was sorry to see him go. But she kept quiet, thinking he probably had better things to do than hang around in a hospital.

After he left, the woman in the next bed said, "Look, honey, I don't know what happened the other night, but I do know bad things can happen to young women. Don't shut that nice man out and for God's sake, whatever you do, don't bury it. There's been too much of that going on with women for too long."

"I know."

There was a long pause, and the woman asked, "Do you mind if I turn on the television? There's a new soap opera on at twelve thirty on ABC. It's called *Ryan's Hope*. Have you heard of it?"

"No, but go ahead and turn it on." Gail leaned back and waited for her parents to return, hoping to get discharged soon.

CHAPTER THIRTY-THREE

Louise sprayed on a light mist of Love's Baby Soft and replaced the pink cap and set it on her dresser. She took one last look in the mirror and despite the fact that her hair looked perfect, she ran a comb through it one more time.

Martin was coming over after lunch. She really liked him. And it would be her last chance to spend time with him alone as Gail was coming home later that day.

She found her mother sitting in the parlor at her sewing machine, working on a large swathe of fabric. There was a quiet rhythm as the thread and needle went in and out, down along the edge of the material. Diana's attention was glued to the task in front of her, sliding the fabric beneath the machine.

"Hi, Mom," Louise said.

Diana looked up, her face creasing in a smile. "You look very pretty today, honey."

"Thanks. Martin is coming over."

"He's sounds like a nice boy." She returned her attention to her sewing.

"I thought you were going to wait at the hospital," Louise said.

"Your sister had a visitor. Hugh Campbell."

"Oh, he's really nice."

"He brought her a dozen roses."

"Gail will like that."

"She did. Anyway, I thought she might like some privacy. It's a good thing we came home. There's been no word from her yet. Your father hates hospitals."

Lou's gaze traveled to the staircase, and a thought occurred to her. "Mom, how is Gail going to get up the stairs when she comes home?"

"Your father and I talked about that. We're going to bring down the twin bed from the spare room and put it in the dining room. It'll be easier for her to be down here rather than being stuck upstairs. She'll be able to go outside and sit on the porch." She held up the floral fabric. "I'm making a privacy curtain for her so we can hang it between the parlor and the dining room."

"That sounds good." Though Louise was unsure how her sister would feel about being downstairs. They'd soon find out.

"Mom, would you like a glass of lemonade or iced tea?" she asked.

Her mother shook her head. "No thank you, I'm fine."

"Is Dad on his walk?"

"He is."

Louise stepped out onto the porch. The sun was bright, and the air was heavy with heat. She sat on the bottom step and waved to the neighbor across the street.

"How's Gail?" the neighbor called.

"Coming home later," Louise called back.

He nodded and began to coil up his hose.

Martin pulled up in front of the house in his older-model Buick. Although he was staying with Hugh's family for the summer, he had his own car. Louise smiled at him as he got out of the car, slammed the door shut, and whistled as he walked up the footpath.

"Hi, Louise," he said.

She looked up at him and shielded her eyes against the sun. "Hi, Martin." She patted the space next to her, and he sat down.

"What's new?" he asked. He smelled of soap and aftershave. She was so happy to see him.

"Gail's coming home later."

"That's good news," he said.

"Dad and Mom are going to set up a bed for her on the main level because she can't use the stairs for the time being.

"Do you need some help?"

"With what?"

His smile was full of mirth. "Getting the bed downstairs."

"Gee, I don't know."

"I think between the two of us, we could do it by ourselves."

"That's a great idea," she said. It would save her parents from having to do it. "Can we do it now?"

"Sure. Why not?"

"Come on, then." Louise stood and led him into the house.

When they entered the front parlor, Diana looked up.

Martin gave a small wave. "Hi, Mrs. Sturges."

"Hello, Martin, how are you?"

"Fine, ma'am."

"Martin said he'd help get the bed down," Louise said. "I think between the two of us, we could get it set up so you and Dad don't have to."

"That would be a huge help. I really didn't want your father carrying a bed frame down the stairs."

"No problem. Let's get to it," Martin said. "I'll probably need a screwdriver."

"Louise, your father's toolbox is out in the back hall. You can look through that, Martin," Diana told him.

He followed Louise out back, rummaged through the toolbox, and found a screwdriver.

Together, they dismantled the twin bed in the spare room and carried everything downstairs: headboard, footboard, slats, and finally the mattress and the boxspring. They moved the dining room table up against the wall to make room, and then Martin reassembled the bed frame and Louise dressed the bed.

Diana laid the privacy curtain she was working on over the back of the sofa. With her hands on her hips, she stood beneath the arch of the parlor and looked into the dining room. "That's a huge help. Thanks."

They set up some more stuff downstairs, things Louise thought Gail would like to have near her, like her albums and record player. She went through her sister's room and piled things in the hall, and Martin carried them downstairs without complaint.

"Mom, can we do anything else?" Louise asked.

"No, you've done enough. It's such a beautiful day, you two should go down to the beach."

Martin and Louise looked at each other.

"I'm game," he said.

Louise nodded. "Let me get my things." She ran upstairs and threw a bottle of Coppertone and a beach towel into a bag. She put on her bathing suit and wore a cover-up over it. She popped her sunglasses onto the top of her head and flew out of the room. From the hall closet, she grabbed an old bedspread to use at the beach.

Martin opened the car door for her and she slid into the front seat.

"Ow," she said. The seat felt like it was on fire from the sun blazing down on the car.

Martin turned on the ignition.

"Do you need to get your bathing suit?" Louise asked.

He shook his head and laughed. "Nope. I carry all that stuff in the trunk."

She laughed. He must have been a Boy Scout.

It only took five minutes to drive over to the beach, and Martin parked the car in one of the few vacant spots left.

"Leave the windows rolled down," he said.

"Okay."

They got out of the car, and he popped the trunk and pulled out a brown paper bag. "Hold on, I have to change." He climbed into the back seat and changed into his bathing suit. Louise kept her back to the car to give him some privacy. But knowing that Martin was getting naked right on the other side of the glass behind her caused her to blush to the tips of her ears.

He jumped out wearing bathing trunks and a pair of sandals. "Come on." He flung a beach towel over his shoulders.

As they walked, he took hold of her hand. Louise smiled to herself. She liked the way her hand felt in his.

It felt so natural, like she'd been holding his hand all her life.

It took a while to find a vacant spot for the old bedspread Louise had brought along to sit on.

Finally, they managed to find a large enough area, but it was near the shore.

"As long as the tide doesn't come in, we should be fine," Martin said, helping her spread the old bedspread out, squaring it up. They put a shoe in each corner to hold it in place.

Overhead, seagulls cried, circling. One dive-bombed the little boy next to them and flew away with a baloney sandwich in his beak. The little boy wailed.

There was the tinny sound of a transistor radio in the distance, and Louise was sorry she hadn't thought about bringing her own. The two of them sat on the blanket, amidst the tropical smell of suntan lotion.

"Can I talk to you about something, Louise?" Martin said. His legs were stretched out in front of him, crossed at the ankles. He looked toward the horizon at the sailboats that dotted the lake, their masts white triangles against the blue of the water.

"Sure, anything," she said.

"What really happened Saturday night? Hugh and I have a working theory that it was more involved than just your car breaking down and the two of you having to walk home. That something else went on."

She didn't know what to say. She didn't know if she should tell him. But she liked Martin a lot, so she didn't want to lie to him.

Gail was adamant that she didn't want to talk about it. Every time Louise so much as brought it up, she quickly shut her down. Maybe she thought if they didn't talk about it, didn't acknowledge it, then it didn't exist. But in Lou's mind, exist it did. The night before, she'd had a nightmare that she was climbing into the white van again and the driver was wearing only a shirt. And nothing else.

"Why do you think something else happened?" she asked, stalling. She wasn't sure whether she wanted to share this with anyone, even him. They hadn't even told their parents.

"First, I find it hard to believe your sister would suffer such a severe injury falling while she was walking along the road."

"You should have seen the shoes she was wearing," Louise countered.

"When Hugh and I pulled up, there was a van speeding away, and there were skid marks on the road and the smell of burnt rubber and . . . It just seemed like maybe something had happened. Hugh thinks the same thing." He paused and added, "Something felt off."

Louise went quiet. What she really wanted to do was scrub the image of that man and his van from her memory. When she spoke, her voice was barely audible. "Something did happen." She sat on the edge of the blanket, drawing circles in the sand with her finger.

Martin waited patiently. Louise looked up and stared at the water, narrowing her eyes at the sting of tears behind them. *Please don't let me start crying in front of him in public. Please spare me that humiliation. Help me to pull it together.*

Beside her, he said softly, "You can trust me, Louise."

She rewarded him with a smile and blinked the unshed tears away. In her head, her thoughts about what had happened were all jumbled. There were a few moments of silence as she chose her words and finally, speaking very quietly for fear of being overheard, she relayed the events of that awful night to Martin. When she finished, she lifted her head and stared out at the lake, liking the way the sunshine made it look shiny and clean. The sounds of splashing and laughter floated over to her, making her smile. The beach was such a happy place. She had a momentary stab of guilt for soiling it with the memory of that night.

"I'm glad you told me, Louise," Martin said. "It must have been a horrible and scary thing to endure."

His kindness and sympathy almost undid her. She nodded her head vigorously to dispel any reappearance of tears.

"Have you reported this to the police?"

She shook her head. "No. Gail doesn't want to talk about it."

"You need to report it," Martin said gravely. "What happened was terrible and you're both lucky to have survived it. But maybe the next girl won't be so lucky."

Louise nodded. She would never wish for anyone else to experience that terror.

"Maybe you could report it without involving Gail," Martin suggested.

She laid her hand on her chest, fingers splayed. "Me? By myself?"

"I'd go with you," he said.

"You would?"

He nodded. "Yeah, I think it's that important."

"Gail will kill me," she said.

"Can you live with yourself if someone gets hurt? Another girl?" he asked.

She didn't need a mirror to know her face had gone pale beneath her summer tan. She felt it by the way queasiness took hold of her stomach. Suddenly, she felt shaky, as if she were going to throw up.

"I'd never forgive myself."

"Look, Gail has a lot going on right now, but I'll go with you."

"I appreciate that."

"This guy has probably done this before."

"Then why hasn't anyone reported it?" she wailed. It could have prevented a lot of grief for her and Gail.

"Because like you, they're probably afraid and grateful to be alive." What was left hanging in the air was the possibility that maybe someone hadn't survived their encounter with the creep. Maybe the only reason she and Gail had got off lightly was because there'd been two of them. It gave her the shivers.

"His behavior is dangerous. He needs to be stopped," Martin said forcefully.

"You're right. I'll report it."

With that determined, there was no sense in hanging around any longer at the beach. It was as if a giant black cloud had settled in above their heads. Deep down, she knew he was right. Something had to be done about it.

They gathered their belongings and walked to the car. Louise's only request was to stop at the house so she could change her clothes. It hardly felt appropriate to be walking into the police station to report something as serious as this wearing only her bathing suit and a cover-up.

No one was home when they arrived, and her parents' car wasn't out front. But her mother had left a note on the kitchen table saying they'd gone to pick up Gail from the hospital. Louise changed quickly, washed her face with cold water, and brushed her hair. Downstairs, Martin changed in the bathroom.

When they stepped out of the house, Martin took her hand and gave it a gentle squeeze. Louise drew in a deep breath. Although she was scared, she knew it was the right thing to do.

Chapter Thirty-Four

By the time they reached the police station, Louise was a bundle of nerves. Martin opened the door for her, and she took his hand, stepping out.

"You're trembling," he said.

"I'm afraid."

"Nothing to be afraid of. You've done nothing wrong."

The sky had darkened and there was the faint sound of thunder in the distance. She looked in the direction of the lake and saw a wall of black clouds.

The police station was located with all the other municipal buildings at the corner of Primrose and Main. As they reached the front door, Louise's mouth went dry. A sharp crack of thunder behind her made her jump.

Martin laid a hand on her shoulder. "It's all right." He held the door for her and she stepped inside, feeling immediate relief at the coolness of the interior.

"Come on," he said. He took hold of her hand, and they walked to the front desk. A burly police officer manned the counter. Louise knew him to see around town but did not know his name. He looked like he wanted to be there as much as Louise did. Unsure of what kind of reception she would receive, she shrank back a bit.

Martin leaned against the counter.

The officer, whose black name tag read *Sergeant Weitz*, looked up, pencil in hand. "Can I help you?"

Martin said nothing but nodded at Lou.

"I . . . I . . . I need to report something," she started.

"I'm sorry, could you speak up?" the sergeant asked. He even cupped his hand around his ear.

She stepped forward and tried again. "I need to report something." The loudness of her voice startled her, and she almost faltered back.

"Okay." From a cubby behind him, Sergeant Weitz pulled out a form and licked the tip of his pencil. "Name, address, and phone number?"

"Louise Sturges. That's S-t-u-r-g-e-s. 682 Peony Lane. My phone number is Lavender Bay 3982."

"Start at the beginning and tell me what happened."

"On Saturday night . . ." She stopped. What was she supposed to say? How did she explain this?

The sergeant tapped his pencil against the paper and stared at her.

"It's okay, Lou," Martin encouraged.

"We were out late Saturday night, although I suppose by this time, it was early Sunday morning. We were coming back from Cheever—" Here the desk sergeant yawned. Martin scowled at him. And if it wasn't so serious, Lou would have laughed. "My sister's car broke down and we started walking back home."

The desk sergeant continued to tap his pencil against the form. He'd filled in nothing but her name, address, and phone number.

"A man in a white van approached us and offered us a ride."

Here the desk sergeant stopped tapping his pencil. "Did you accept the ride?"

"At first. I got in because there was only one seat in the front. It was empty in the back of the van. Anyway, Gail told me to get out."

"Who's Gail?"

"My sister. But this guy wouldn't let me out. He had me by the wrist." She extended her arm to show him the black-and-blue marks along her left wrist. Beside her, Martin stiffened.

"Gail kept trying to fight him off, but he wouldn't let go of me."

"What happened then?"

"Gail bit him really hard on his hand and he let go and I jumped out, and he pulled my sister's hair so hard as she was trying to get out of the van that she landed on her knee and tore a ligament. She's coming home from the hospital today."

The desk sergeant looked up at her again. "Did you get a license plate?"

Louise shook her head. "I tried. But there was no plate on the back of the van."

"Anything else?"

"After we got out of the van, he turned around and tried to run us down with it."

"Huh." The desk sergeant rubbed his hand along the back of his head and let out a big sigh. "Take a seat over there and I'll get one of the detectives to talk to you." He disappeared through a back door, which swung shut loudly behind him.

Louise and Martin sat on the wooden bench along the wall. Lou leaned against the wall for support. They didn't have to wait long. A middle-aged man soon appeared wearing a short-sleeved shirt with a tie. There were stains underneath his armpits.

"Louise Sturges?" he questioned, reading from the form the desk sergeant had just filled out.

Louise and Martin stood.

He eyed Martin up and down. "Who are you?"

"Martin Cook. I'm her friend. I'm here for moral support."

"Come on then, follow me."

They followed him through the door and Louise was distracted from the purpose of her visit. She'd never been inside a police station. There were a lot of wooden desks occupied by men in suits and some in uniforms. There were also two policewomen in uniform, and Louise, thinking of Gail's favorite television show, made a note to report this to her sister. But only when she summoned up the courage to tell her she'd filed a report.

They spent the next hour at Detective John Hardy's desk. Again, Louise recounted the events of early Sunday morning. Speaking it out loud made it seem all the more real. She and Martin sat next to each other in identical antique oak chairs. Across the desk, the detective sat in the swivel version.

Detective Hardy asked for a physical description of the man, and Louise scoured her memory for any little detail that might help.

"How tall did you say he was?"

"It was hard to tell. He was sitting down."

"What color was his hair?"

"Dark and kind of longish. Covered his ears. He wore square-framed glasses," Louise told him.

"What color were his eyes?"

Louise shook her head. "I'm sorry. It was dark out and he had glasses on."

"Any tattoos or scars or anything else you can remember?" Detective Hardy asked.

Louise shook her head. "No, I'm sorry."

"But you said after you escaped, he tried to run you down with the van," the detective stated.

"That's correct. He tried once but Gail and I got off the road, and then he turned around to try again, but that's when Martin and Hugh came along." She looked at Martin and smiled.

When they were finished, the detective stood, said he'd be in touch, and walked with them to the front door.

"Have there been any other reports of this?" Louise asked.

"Not from Lavender Bay, but I'll be checking with the Sheriff's Department and the surrounding localities between here and Cheever."

Martin drove her home. It had rained while they were in the police station, and the road was slick with water. As Martin drove, he assured her that she'd done the right thing. She hoped so. She was tired and wanted to take a nap. She hadn't taken an afternoon nap since she was four, but the time spent at the police station had done her in. Her parents' car was parked in the driveway, which meant that they were home with Gail.

She hesitated before going inside, thinking now that she'd filed an official police report, there was no turning back. And also realizing that she had no choice but to tell her parents. She didn't know what she feared more: telling her parents or telling Gail. But either way, both would have to happen.

CHAPTER THIRTY-FIVE

Gail was home and she was miserable. Her knee throbbed; it felt like someone was stabbing it.

"Let me get you a glass of water and you can take one of those pain pills they gave you," Diana suggested.

Louise walked through the front door, and Gail let herself be hugged by her younger sister. Despite her misery, she was actually glad to see her and squeezed her tight.

She eyed the temporary setup in the dining room. There'd be no privacy. Her parents liked to stay up late and watch Johnny Carson, and she'd be forced to endure that. She knew she should be grateful to be home, but her litany of complaints continued.

She sat on the twin bed if only to get off her knee. Her mother handed her a glass of water and a pain pill. She popped it into her mouth and washed it back with a gulp of water. On top of the dining room table was a collection of her personal care items: deodorant, astringent for the occasional breakout, hairspray, a basket of her makeup, and her makeup mirror.

"I don't want to stay down here," she finally said.

Her parents and her sister stood in the arch between the parlor and the dining room.

Her father had his unlit pipe clamped between his lips. "Honey, you don't want to spend all your time upstairs."

"And look, Louise brought down your albums and your record player," Diana pointed out. "And I've made your favorite meal for dinner: meatloaf."

From the twin bed, Gail said, "What am I supposed to do? Lie in bed for the rest of the summer?"

"Of course not," her mother said. "You can go out to the porch. And the physical therapist said she'll be showing you how to get up and down the staircase."

"How am I going to wash my hair?" she demanded.

"I'll help you," Louise volunteered.

She was about to complain about the fact that the dining room was too hot when there was a knock at the front door. All three turned to it, and Louise looked over her shoulder at Gail and whispered, "It's Hugh."

Diana opened the front door for him. Hugh ducked to clear the doorframe. In his hand he carried a bag and from where she sat, Gail noticed the familiar logo of the town's bakery. She deflated. Her first thing to tackle now that she was home was a diet. Everyone kept bringing candy to her in the hospital, and she knew she must have put on ten pounds. Lying around was not helping anything.

Hugh chatted for a few minutes with her parents. Finally, he handed the bag to Diana and said, "It's a birthday cake."

Diana looked at him quizzically. Hugh looked sheepish. "I didn't know what to get. And I figured everyone loves birthday cake. I know I do."

"You are so right," Diana agreed. "I'll take this to the kitchen and slice it up."

"I'm going for a long walk, honey, I'll have my cake when I come back," Mark said.

Hugh approached Gail. Diana disappeared into the kitchen, and Louise went upstairs.

Hugh pulled up a dining room chair and said, "I bet you're glad to be home."

"I am," she admitted. The hospital hadn't been fun, and she wouldn't care to repeat the experience.

"Would you like to sit outside? On the porch?" he asked.

She nodded. She was getting used to him. In other words, he was growing on her, and no one was more surprised than she. He was thoughtful and kind. And he meant what he said. But there were other things too. When he laughed, really laughed, he always coughed at the end, as if he had a tickle in his throat. He had the build of a basketball player: impossibly tall, long arms and long legs. He was so opposite her in physique that she didn't understand the attraction. And really, this past week, she wasn't looking her best. It had been hard to style her hair in the hospital. But he still kept coming around.

She managed to get her legs over the side of the bed and carefully stood. Using the crutches, she hobbled out to the front porch. By the time she landed outside, she was almost breathless. She sat, leaning the crutches against the porch railing.

Hugh took the chair next to her.

Diana appeared, carrying two plates of cake.

Gail held up her hand. "None for me."

Diana handed Hugh a plate and set the second one down on the wide porch railing. With a smile, she said to Gail, "In case you change your mind."

Hugh thanked Diana and forked big chunks of cake and frosting into his mouth. Halfway through his slice, he looked over at Gail and said, "Are you sure you don't want some? It's really good."

She shook her head. Of course she wanted a slice of cake, who didn't? "I'm on a diet."

Hugh licked frosting off his fork. "Why?"

"Because I'm getting too heavy for my height."

"How tall are you?"

"Five two," she said.

He smiled, a smear of frosting across his teeth. "I'm six two."

"So what does that make us? Twins?"

He laughed so hard his whole upper body shook and he almost dropped his plate, and soon she was laughing too. She waited and wasn't disappointed: when he finished laughing, he coughed a little bit.

When he finally pulled himself together, he said, "Look, I don't think you need to be on a diet, but then what do I know."

"You don't think I'm pudgy?"

He looked at her as if she weren't making any sense. He shook his head. He stared at her for a moment; there was something going on in his eyes that Gail couldn't read. Finally, he announced, "Actually, I think you're perfect just as you are."

Gail didn't know what to say. But damn, there was a glow inside of her. She rolled her lips together to suppress an out-of-control smile. "Hand me that slice of cake, please."

"That's the spirit!" He grinned and handed her the plate and the fork.

CHAPTER THIRTY-SIX

Dinner was a quiet affair. Louise had a lot on her mind. Her father spoke of who he'd met on his walk, and her mother walked back and forth between the table and stove, serving up meatloaf, mashed potatoes, and green beans. She was extra solicitous of Gail, whose mood had improved with Hugh's visit. The phone rang and Louise practically jumped out of her chair. Her mother frowned.

"Louise? What are you so jumpy about?" her mother asked.

The phone continued to ring. "I'll get it," Louise said. She was afraid it would be the police calling with an update or information, and she hadn't had a chance to tell her parents yet.

She stood and picked up the handset from the wall phone. "Mom, it's for you. It's Laura."

Her mother left her plate, food untouched, and they all listened as she agreed to be a fourth for bridge later that evening.

It was then that Louise decided she'd talk to her father after dinner about the events of Saturday night. Of the three of them, he'd be the easiest.

After Louise had finished washing the supper dishes, Laura Knickerbocker arrived to pick up Diana, who kissed her husband goodbye and told them all she wouldn't be late.

Louise waited until they pulled away from the curb, and she joined her father out on the porch. Gail was lying on the twin bed with the phone, talking to Hugh. The corkscrew telephone cord stretched from the kitchen to the dining room.

Her father puffed on his pipe. *The Lavender Bay Chronicles* sat in his lap, waiting to be read.

"Louise, how are you?"

"I'm all right," she said.

Her father nodded in acknowledgement. His gaze swung up and down the street, taking in the neighborhood. "I always like this time of day in the summer. At the end of a hot day, the sun starting to set, everyone home. It's a beautiful thing to behold."

She laughed. "Dad, you're a poet!"

"Maybe I am." He picked up the paper and opened it.

"Dad, I need to talk to you about something, and it's important."

He smiled. "Then I better give you my undivided attention." He folded the paper back up and set it down in his lap.

"I need to tell you what happened to Gail and me on Saturday night when we went out." Louise said. She dreaded having to tell him this. She was going to have to admit to her father that they'd lied and gone to Flashes against their mother's strict instructions. Louise hated disappointing her father.

Mark sighed. "I figured there was more to this story than you told us."

"Why didn't you ask?"

"I hoped one of you would tell me in your own good time."

As Louise recounted the events of the night, they watched the evening unfold in front of them: the sky was a magnificent colorwork of pink and orange. She didn't hold back; she told him everything. From going to the disco in Cheever to the whole seedy affair with Richard and finally to breaking down on the side of the road and the creep in the white panel van who first offered them a ride and then tried to mow them down when they wouldn't play nice.

When she was finished, she looked over at her father. He puffed furiously on his pipe, and his pallor was ashen beneath his tanned face. For a moment, she regretted telling him, thinking she should have kept her mouth shut.

"Have you reported this to the police?" was her father's first question.

"I went today."

"Good girl." He went quiet again. Louise bit her lip. "Dad?"

"Hold on, I'm thinking," Mark Sturges said.

She waited and finally he said, "I'm glad you told me, Louise. It doesn't change the fact that you both disobeyed your mother twice, first by going to that nightclub she expressly forbade you from going to and second, hitchhiking. We've spent years telling you how dangerous it is to hitchhike. But you had to learn the lesson the hard way."

"I'm really sorry, Dad," she said sincerely. She lowered her head and let out a long sigh, waiting for her punishment to be handed down. In their house, actions had consequences.

"I'm sure the ordeal was very frightening."

"It was terrifying."

"And that was probably punishment enough," her father pronounced.

"Do we have to tell Mom?" she asked, hoping his answer was no.

He pulled the tobacco pouch out of his pocket and refilled his pipe, tamping it down. "Unfortunately, yes. She will have to be told. But not today."

There'd be a slight reprieve, if only for the day.

Although she felt as if a huge burden had been lifted from her shoulders by her confession to her father, a new fear planted and rooted.

Gail. When her older sister found out that she had told their father and gone to the police, she wouldn't be happy. And Louise was more afraid of her sister than she was of her mother.

CHAPTER THIRTY-SEVEN

Louise knocked softly on the wooden arch that separated the parlor from the dining room. "Knock, knock."

"Yeah, come on in," Gail said wryly.

Since all that had happened, they were no longer fighting. Not like they used to. No more hairbrushes sailing through the air or doors slamming. There was peace at last.

Gail was stretched out on the twin bed, her back against the headboard, reading the latest issue of *Cosmopolitan*. She looked up at Louise when she appeared.

Louise nodded to the record player in the corner, its turntable still. "No music today?"

Gail shrugged. "Don't feel like it."

Louise turned a dining room chair around from the table so she could face her sister. She lifted one leg up, resting her foot against the cushion and wrapping an arm around her knee.

"I need to talk to you about something," was how she started.

Gail continued to flip through the magazine. Louise waited, and it was okay because she'd been blessed with an abundance of patience. She could outwait anyone. If she had to, she'd sit there until her older sister had finished reading her magazine.

Finally, Gail heaved a big sigh and looked at her younger sister. "What is it, Lou?"

"First, I'm glad you're healing. You've been very dedicated to your regimen," Lou said. She'd read somewhere that when you were going to provide someone with constructive criticism, it was best to start with a compliment. And although her intent was not to criticize, she thought it wouldn't hurt to soften Gail up with a compliment or two.

"What choice did I have? I want to be the way I used to be."

Lou nodded. "Understood. Look, I know you were angry at me about going to the police. And you were even more upset that I told Dad." Gail's expression was unreadable, and she did not comment. She plowed on. "I just don't understand why. I mean, how could we keep something like that a secret?"

Still Gail remained quiet.

"You go on and on about equality and women's rights," Louise said, "but then you're perfectly okay for another woman to go through what we went through?"

Gail blew up. "I am not okay with that happening to anyone else. So don't say I am, thank you very much!"

Lou blew out a breath, frustrated. "Then why are you so mad at me?"

"I'm not mad at you! I never said I was."

"But you *are* mad."

Gail surprised her by bursting into tears. "I'm not angry at you or anyone else, all right?"

"Then what is it?" Lou asked. She stood, grabbed the box of Kleenex off the dining room table, and handed it to her sister.

"I'm angry at myself." Gail pulled a tissue from the box and wiped her eyes.

"Why?"

"Because I got us into that situation. It was my fault."

"That's not true," Louise protested.

"Isn't it? Whose idea was it to go out to Flashes? Whose car broke down on the side of the road? Whose idea was it to hitchhike?"

"Regardless of the points that led us to that creep, it's not your fault. If anything, it's his fault. We have a right not to be scared by a man."

Gail refused to accept this. "No, Lou, it is my fault. As your older sister, it's my job to protect you and keep you safe. And I failed miserably at that."

Louise blinked several times in disbelief. "What are you talking about? If it weren't for you, I never would have gotten out of that van! Who knows what would have happened. You saved my life, and I won't believe anything else but that."

Gail cried harder. After a moment, she said, "You know what I hate most of all about it?"

"No, what?"

"That for those few minutes, I was at the complete mercy of a man, and he made me feel so powerless and helpless."

Lou looked at her sister with a mixture of love and compassion. "But in the end, you beat him. You won."

"It doesn't feel like it," Gail said with a brittle laugh. "I still have nightmares about it."

"Me too," Louise admitted. She pulled her chair closer to the bed until the legs butted up against it, and she took Gail's hand in hers.

"Deep down, I know it was the right thing to go to the police," Gail said. "I know it was the right thing to tell Mom and Dad. But I hate that something like that happened to us."

"I do too," Louise said. And she thought of all the women out there whose stories didn't end as lucky as hers and her sister's.

"When did you get so brave?" Gail asked.

Lou looked at her. "Everything I learned about bravery, I learned from you."

They looked at each other as they cried. When they settled down and blew their noses, Lou said, "I think Hugh is really nice."

Gail laughed. "I think the same about Martin."

"He's going to teach me how to drive," Louise told her excitedly.

"The man is a saint!"

"If it all works out, we should have a double wedding."

Gail smiled at her sister. "I'd like that."

CHAPTER THIRTY-EIGHT

As summer wound down, Gail's knee improved. She was able to give up her crutches and get up the staircase with the help of tips from the physical therapist. At her final follow-up visit with the surgeon, it was declared that the knee was healing nicely. For the most part, Gail was back to normal.

Unfortunately, the police were no further ahead in their investigation. The detective, John Hardy, had come to the house during her recuperation to interview her. Her parents insisted on being there, and Gail was forced to recount in front of them all the details of that night. And although it was difficult to relive it, it was equally upsetting seeing the effect it had on her mother and father. She'd never forget the expressions of pure fear on her parents' faces. She'd never forgive herself for putting them through that. She made a vow that there was to be no more lying and no more sneaking around. It was time to grow up.

Diana had always been stricter than Mark. And although they agreed that the events of the night had been terrifying, still she roped Gail into helping her with small projects in the house. Some of the rooms needed to be painted, so Gail learned to paint. She did what her mother asked, without complaint. She felt she got off lightly.

At dinner one evening, Diana mentioned that a girl from Lou's graduating class had died as a result of a hit-and-run. When their mother said she'd been found on the side of the highway, Gail and Louise exchanged a glance.

Privately, they wondered if it had been the man in the van. They hoped not. And even though they could not voice it, they knew.

Gail leaned against her dresser, getting as close to the mirror as possible as she applied her mascara. She dusted on some powder, then applied lip gloss, but not too much. Finished, she took a step back and appraised her reflection. She turned halfway, wondered if her butt looked too big in the shorts she was wearing, and then decided it was fine. She grabbed her purse and headed downstairs.

She'd seen Hugh almost every day since that night. And Louise spent more time with Martin. Sometimes they went to the beach, and sometimes they hung out with Louise and Martin at the Dog Days Bar, drinking beer and listening to the jukebox. It wasn't long before the guys started coming over for dinner. As time progressed and Gail's body healed, she and Hugh went for long drives. One time, he picked her up early and they spent all day in the car, driving all the way up to Niagara Falls. By the time they got back to Lavender Bay, her knee was throbbing, but she'd never admit that to him; she'd had too much of a good time. He was funny, intelligent, and solicitous. And most of all, he listened to her, really listened to her and was interested in her opinion on things.

Only last week, she'd boldly said to Hugh, "When I'm back in shape, I would like you to take me out on a proper date."

"What's this then?" he asked, looking over at her from his side of the car.

"You know what I mean."

"You mean like dancing? Dinner?"

They were already going out to breakfast, lunch, and dinner.

She shook her head and leaned her cheek against her hand, staring out the window. As much as she loved music and dancing, she didn't want to do that.

"No, I'd like to do something totally different," she said, unsure of what that was.

"Like what?"

She'd given him her best smile and told him, "Surprise me. I'll leave it in your capable hands."

Today was the day for their mystery date. Hugh had said it had to be put off until she was off crutches. And this fact only intrigued her more.

Her parents sat on the front porch, talking. No doubt there'd be chess later, some television and ice cream, and then they'd finish the night off with Johnny Carson. Both looked up at Gail when she appeared.

"You look lovely," her mother said.

"Thanks, Mom."

"Is Hugh picking you up?" her father asked. But they all knew the answer to that question. Gail and Hugh were an item by this time as were Louise and Martin, who that evening were over at the drive-in in Cheever.

As soon as the words were out of her father's mouth, Hugh's car rolled up in front of the house.

"Speak of the devil," Diana said.

Mark glanced at his wrist. "You could set your watch by him."

As Gail stepped off the porch, her mother said, "Not too late, Gail."

"No, Mom," she promised.

The evening was pleasant. The unrelenting heat of the summer was behind them and although the air was warm, coolness tinged it. She was glad she'd brought her cardigan.

From the curb, Hugh waved and called out hello to Gail's parents. He opened the door for Gail, and she slipped into the passenger seat. It was wonderful not to be dragging those crutches around anymore.

He leaned against the doorframe and said, "Are you ready for your mystery date?"

"I am," she said enthusiastically. She had no idea what he'd planned for the evening, but she was eager to find out.

With a wave, they drove off, but when Hugh reached the end of the street, he pulled over and idled the car at the curb. Gail looked at him, curious. Now what was he up to? She rolled her lips inward to suppress a smile.

He leaned over her, his arm brushing against her leg, which sent butterflies flying around in her stomach. He opened the glove compartment and pulled out a bandana.

"I'm going to need to blindfold you."

"Wait, what? Why?" Gail said, amused.

He leaned back. "I want it to be a surprise."

"How about if you take me at my word that I'll keep my eyes closed and promise not to peek?"

He shook his head, laughing. "Nope. You won't be able to resist."

She held up the bandana and made one last attempt. "But it will mess my hair."

"Sorry, Gail."

She narrowed her eyes at him and said, half joking, "I don't think you are sorry."

"Maybe not," he said with a grin and a shrug.

"This better be worth it." She tied the bandana around her head tightly, covering her eyes. She couldn't imagine what he had planned.

Fortunately, the drive was short because she was starting to feel slightly nauseous. When she felt the car stop and Hugh turned off the engine, she went to pull off the blindfold, but he said, "Nope, not yet."

He got out and walked around to the passenger side, opened her door, and helped her out.

"Step up onto the sidewalk," he instructed.

She followed his lead and soon a door opened. She was hit by a cool blast from an air conditioner and the smell of stale popcorn and something else, unidentifiable and slightly concerning. She frowned. He guided her inside.

"Okay, Gail, you can take off the blindfold."

She pulled off the bandana, and her mouth fell open when she saw that she was standing in the bowling alley. *What?*

She saw the eagerness on his face, and her heart melted. He had only wanted to please her.

"Bowling?" she asked.

"Have you ever been bowling before?"

She shook her head.

"I love bowling. And you said you wanted to do something different."

Now she was laughing. Throughout the week leading up to their date, she had imagined all sorts of scenarios. A champagne picnic. Dinner on the beach. But not this. Never once did the bowling alley enter her mind. She bent over, she was laughing so hard. When she finished, she wiped a tear from her eye, not caring whether her mascara was ruined or not.

"I'll say this for you, Hugh, you have completely surprised me," she said, nodding and looking around.

He was so excited that he'd pleased her that it made Gail like him even more. As she followed him toward the counter to get a pair of unfashionable bowling shoes, she thought to herself, *This is going to work out beautifully.*

PART THREE

DEBBIE

Chapter Thirty-Nine

When Gail and Louise finished their story about what happened during the summer of 1975, everyone went quiet around the table. Most stared at them, mouths hanging open. But for Debbie, a troubling question formed in her mind, something she wasn't yet ready to say out loud.

"Wow," Maureen said, and that broke the spell.

In typical Cook and Campbell fashion, everyone spoke at once, directing questions to Gail and Louise.

"Did they ever catch the guy?" from Esther.

Gail shook her head. "No."

"Did it happen to anyone else?" Nadine asked, a frown etched along her forehead.

"Not to our knowledge," Louise replied.

"That must have been horrible," Suzanne said.

"It was. It was scary. Back then, you didn't realize how unsafe you really were until something happened to you," Louise told them.

"Hopefully, things are different now," Gail said and then, lowering her voice, she added, "or at least improved." But they'd all heard stories and seen things on the news."

"Still, everyone should be cautious, man or woman," Esther said.

Debbie agreed with her. There were bad people out there who wanted to do other people harm. It made her shudder.

The conversation about 1975 continued, and it led to Louise pulling out a few photo albums and laying them in the middle of the table. Everyone stood, including Debbie, to hunch over and go through the pages.

"You two were as different as day and night," Maureen observed.

"We certainly were," Gail said.

"Look at your shoes, Mom," Esther said with a laugh.

"And my skinny ankles," Gail lamented. "They haven't been skinny since 1982." She shook her head and laughed.

"And what kind of vibe are you giving off, Mom?" DeeDee asked with a laugh.

"I loved *Little House on the Prairie*," Louise explained.

"I guess so." Angie chuckled. "You look ready to jump on the next wagon train."

Louise shrugged and smiled.

"You looked so young then," Suzanne said.

"As hard as it is to believe, Lou and I *were* young once," Gail said.

They went through every page of the photo albums, and it stung a little for Debbie. If there were photo albums in her mother's house, she wasn't aware. Of course, they could be buried under a mountain of debris or packed away in the attic. But her mother didn't strike her as the type to keep a photographic record of their lives: births, baptisms, first day of school, graduations. If there were no photographs, did it refute the memory? Although it caused some discomfort for Debbie to be looking at other people's family albums when her own family was lacking in that department, she enjoyed it nonetheless, if only to see the younger versions of Gail and Louise.

Debbie was determined to learn more about her Aunt Judy, and the only way to do that was to get at those boxes in the attic. Her mother had reluctantly agreed to let her clean it out, likely to get her out of her hair. She liked—for lack of a better word—having Debbie around but sometimes, Debbie suspected her mother would like her to go to another room.

She climbed the steps, the overhead bulb illuminating most of the attic, except along the walls where the shadows remained. The space was overwhelming. She didn't know where to start. And even though the urge was strong to go through Judy's boxes, she had to do some work up here. Her mother would get suspicious if she descended down to the first floor without any full trash bags. And if she ever suspected Debbie was going through her sister's personal effects, Darlene Melvin would surely go into orbit. She'd been known to explode over less.

It didn't take long for Deb to fill two industrial-sized black trash bags. She hauled them downstairs to the second floor and left them at the top of the landing. She listened briefly for any noise downstairs, aside from the blaring television.

"You all right, Mom?" she called.

The television was muted.

"What?"

"Are you all right? Do you need anything?" Debbie asked.

"No."

"All right."

She climbed back up to the attic and pulled out another one of the boxes of Judy's belongings closer to the light. She peeled away the yellowed Scotch tape and opened the box, relieved to see that the dust of accumulating years had not breached it.

The solemnity of the moment hit her as she surveyed the personal items of her dead aunt, causing her to pause. Stuffed animals, now musty with age, were at the top of the box. There was a small pink teddy bear, a giraffe, and a pale blue rabbit with floppy ears. Carefully, she pulled them out to get at what was buried at the bottom of the box. There were several notebooks with black-and-white marbling on the covers. She pulled one out and leafed through it. They were notes from a history class. The slanted writing was small and feminine, nothing at all like her mother's boxy scrawl. She flipped through the pages, seeing it was full. The next notebook contained English notes. After that, it was a math notebook. Carefully, she leafed through each page, not to see what her aunt had learned in her last year at McKinley high school but to look at all the doodles that had been scribbled in the margins. There were flowers, hearts, dogs and cats, and initials with a heart around them. *J.M.*, her aunt's initials, with the letters *B.D.* Debbie found herself smiling at the thought of her aunt's crush and wondered who it could be. Had he ever known or suspected, or had that secret died with her? As the pages went on, the hearts had arrows through them, until finally they were drawn as two perfect halves. Debbie sat back on her haunches and sighed. A young girl with dreams. But the end of the road came sooner than she or anyone could have expected. Beneath the notebooks, there were textbooks: history, math, and English. Carefully, she put everything back into the box and closed it up, making a note to pick up some packing tape to secure any box she opened.

It was then that she heard her mother calling her.

"Debbie!"

Startled, she dropped what she was doing and ran down two flights of stairs. Her mother stood in front of her recliner, holding on to one crutch, the other on the floor. Debbie ran to it, picked it up, and handed it to her.

"I've been calling you. Didn't you hear me?" Darlene said sourly.

"I'm sorry, Mom, I didn't," Debbie said.

Her mother set off for the bathroom on her crutches, and Debbie followed her.

Halfway to the bathroom, her mother stopped and said over her shoulder: "I don't need an escort. Stop hovering."

"I only want to make sure you don't fall."

"What are you going to do? If I start falling, I'm going down whether you're here or not," Darlene said. "And if you're in my way, you're going down with me."

"All right," Debbie conceded. She glanced at the clock on the wall. "I suppose it's time for lunch."

"I'm not hungry," her mother said, and she closed the bathroom door behind her.

Through the closed door, Debbie said, "Mom, you've got to eat something."

"Not now," her mother said sharply.

Debbie debated further arguing with her and decided it wasn't a good idea.

"Are you standing outside the door?" her mother asked.

"Just going away."

Darlene mumbled something, but Debbie couldn't make it out. She went to the kitchen and dried the dishes that had been left in the draining rack and put them away. Once her mother was settled back into her recliner, Debbie placed two pillows beneath her casted leg to elevate it.

"Pull them down a little bit," her mother said, wincing. "They're too far up."

Once her mother was comfortable, Debbie sat in her father's vacant recliner next to her.

"Mom, can I ask you a question?"

"I don't think I could stop you if I tried," Darlene said. She pulled a cigarette out of her cigarette case and lit it. She took a long drag and closed her eyes and leaned back.

"Why did you marry Dad?"

Her mother shrugged, cigarette poised in her hand. "I don't know. It seemed like a good idea at the time."

"Did you love him?"

Another shrug. "I don't know. I suppose I did. Once."

"What is it about Dad that bothers you so much?"

Her mother didn't hesitate. "Everything." She shifted in her chair and attended to her cigarette, flicking off the ash into the glass ashtray next to her. Waving her daughter off, she said, "That's enough, Debbie. You always were nosy. I want to watch my show." She unmuted the television, and the volume practically blasted Debbie out of her chair.

Deb stood and said, "Back to work."

"You weren't asked to do that. You take on too much work," her mother griped.

Debbie didn't bother with a response. She headed back up the stairs and brought down the two full garbage bags, carried them outside, and stuffed them into the wheelie bin. Next, she carried down some broken furniture.

On the first pass, Darlene asked, "Where are you going to put all that?"

"I'll have to put it in the garage for now. I'll call the town and see when the bulk pickup is." Debbie paused. "Did you want any of this?"

"No, throw it all out," her mother said with a frown.

Deb grabbed the key for the garage and carried out two broken chairs, one in each hand. After she unlocked the garage, she stepped inside and found the light. Her heart sank. It was another version of the attic. Packed with boxes and junk and a car that no longer had license plates or tires. She decided it was not hers to deal with right now. All she had to do was concentrate on the attic.

She ran back up the stairs to get the next load, but changed her mind and instead decided to haul all the boxes marked *Judy* down to her old bedroom. Her mother wasn't going up the stairs anytime soon, so they'd be fine there. It was preferable to sift through her late aunt's belongings in her old room than up in the damp, dusty attic.

This room was no different from the others in the house, with piles on the bed and every available space on the small dresser. She deigned this room *Judy Central* and one by one, carried the boxes down from the attic, starting with the one full of albums as it was the heaviest. She ended up dragging it down the staircase, step by step. She stacked the boxes in the corner.

Every muscle in her body ached; she'd done enough. It was time to go home.

Her mother was asleep in the chair, snoring loudly. Debbie heard the kitchen door open and suspected it was her father, but was surprised to see her brother.

Whispering, she said, "Mom's sleeping."

"That's all right," Darren said. "I'll hang around until she wakes up."

"Who's there?" demanded Darlene, now awake.

Debbie and Darren went into the parlor, where their mother was using the remote to change the television channel.

"Hey, Mom, thought I'd stop by and see how you're doing," Darren said.

"Well, my leg is still broken if that answers your question," was Darlene's reply.

"How's it going with your nurse?" he asked, indicating Debbie with a nod.

"She'll do." Coming from their mother, it was high praise.

Debbie took that as her cue to exit.

Chapter Forty

As Debbie walked out of the house into the damp and frosty night air, she ran into her father, who carried a large plastic bag with two Styrofoam containers.

"Hey, Dad."

"How's your mother?" he asked.

"Good, she's had a good day," she replied. "What've you got there?"

"Dinner. The special at the bar was pork and sauerkraut and mashed potatoes. It's your mother's favorite."

"That's nice."

"I'm sorry, Debbie, I didn't get you one. I can go back and get another dinner," he said, trying to shove the bag into her hands.

"No, Dad, that's all right. I've got plans." She didn't need her father to go back to the bar. Although he never seemed to need an excuse.

"All right, honey," he said. "I don't know if your mother has said anything, but thanks for all your help."

"No problem, Dad."

He looked toward the house. "She's tough, and there aren't many people who'd put up with her."

"You just have to know how to handle her."

"Something I've never learned," he said with a sigh.

"I'll try to stop by tomorrow night after work," she said.

He nodded and walked slowly into the house.

As soon as Debbie arrived home, Oscar and Bella came at a run toward her. She patted them vigorously, and there was joyous barking. Even the cats came out to investigate and add loud meows to the cacophony.

"I've missed you all too! Very much." She refilled the water bowls and set out dog and cat food for their dinner amidst the loud meows from the cats, who were protesting that she was fifteen minutes late with their meals. Once the dogs settled down, she let them out so they could do their business and went to run a bath. Every muscle and joint ached. She was also hungry. She'd had a sandwich earlier at her mother's, but that had been hours ago. But first, she wanted to soak in the bath. As the water ran, she went around and gathered dirty laundry and towels and threw them in the wash.

When the tub was full, steam rising off the top of it, she turned off the taps. She went to the back door and called the dogs, both of whom came running. Inside, they scrambled to their bowls, nails clicking on the linoleum.

In the bathroom, she disrobed, letting her clothes fall into a pile on the floor. She stepped into the bath and almost cried with joy at the relief a tubful of hot water brought. She left the door ajar because if she didn't, her pets would be on the outside of it, barking and meowing, begging to come in. One of the cats squeezed through the narrow opening, walked in, tail high in the air, and looked around. Satisfied, she soon exited. Deb leaned against the back of the tub and closed her eyes. The hot water soothed her sore muscles.

She must have dozed off, because when she opened her eyes, the water had gone cold. She stepped out, dried off, and threw on a nightgown and her pink terrycloth bathrobe. She shuffled to the kitchen, her stomach now growling, in search of something to eat.

She stared at the inside of her refrigerator, hoping something would magically appear. As she was thinking she might have a bagel and cream cheese, her phone rang.

She smiled when Jim's name flashed across the screen.

"Hi," she said, leaning against the kitchen counter, the bagel forgotten.

"How's it going, Debbie? How's your Mom?"

"She's coming along." She'd spare him the spiky, gory details.

"Look, I know it's last minute, but I've made beef bourguignon and I've got a ton of it. Would you like me to bring some over?"

Her stomach growled in response. "I'd love some, Jim. But I'm already in my pajamas."

"I don't mind," he said easily.

"Are you sure you don't mind?"

"Not at all. I'll be there in ten minutes."

While she waited, she quickly cleaned up the place, stacking magazines on the coffee table, and gave Oscar and Bella a short lecture on how they should behave themselves. They listened intently, their faces open and their tails wagging. She didn't think she got through, though.

When the doorbell rang, the dogs ran at great speed toward the door, barking. She opened it only an inch to keep them from escaping.

"You do like dogs, don't you, Jim?" she asked, hopeful. Whatever he had in the dutch oven in his hands smelled glorious.

"Sure," he said.

To both dogs, she said, "Down." They listened, sat, and looked at the new arrival with hope and expectation.

Jim walked in and asked, "Where should I put this?"

"Follow me," she said. Now she was sorry she hadn't got dressed. Although she lacked energy, she should have made the effort, she decided. Jim followed her to her kitchen and set the ceramic dutch oven on the stove.

"It smells wonderful, I'm so grateful for this," she said honestly. "And I'm super hungry."

"Good. Hang on, I've got a bottle of wine in the car. I'll be right back." And he was out the door.

She removed the lid and peered in at the rich, hearty stew, inhaling the scent. She took two deep plates out of the cupboard, grabbed some silverware, and set the table. With nothing else to use as napkins, she tore two sheets of paper towel off the roll and set them next to their plates. Finally, she pulled two wine glasses off the rack.

When Jim returned, the dogs rushed him, barking.

"Still me," he told them.

"Down!" Debbie scolded.

Jim set down the bottle and Debbie handed him a corkscrew. He opened the wine and set it aside. "We'll let that breathe for a few minutes." He removed his coat, and she noticed he was wearing pajama pants and a T-shirt. She laughed.

Jim looked at his own apparel and said, "I thought, why not? We should wear comfortable clothing while eating comfort food."

She encouraged him to take a seat at the table, then retrieved a ladle from the utensil drawer and began doling out generous scoopfuls of the beef bourguignon. She couldn't wait to get at it. She wished she had a loaf of french bread to go with it.

She set the plates on the table and sat, pulling her chair in closer. She eagerly took the first bite and savored it, closing her eyes. "This is wonderful," she announced.

"Glad you think so," he said, starting his meal. After a few minutes, he poured the wine.

The cats disappeared, and the dogs eventually settled down in the corner, lifting their heads every once in a while to see if anything was coming their way from the kitchen table.

Jim looked at Debbie. "So how was your day, dear?"

She was glad she didn't have a mouthful of food because she would have spit it out when she burst out laughing. "It went all right. Mom can be spiky at times," she said.

He nodded. "I see. Does she need a lot of help?"

"Not really, but it makes me feel better to be there in case she needs anything and to make sure she doesn't fall. I've started doing a big clean in the attic, and I've been running up and down the stairs, bringing down stuff for the trash."

"Do you need some help?" he asked.

Debbie shook her head. "No, thanks. I'm almost finished anyway." It was a small fib but the question wasn't whether she needed his help. The question was, did she want Jim to meet her mother? She didn't think so. He was a nice person; why do that to him? No sense in scaring him away just yet. Especially since she really enjoyed his company and as a bonus, he was a great cook.

Jim poured Debbie a second glass of wine but refused one for himself as he still had to drive home. She cleared the plates and announced, "That was delicious."

"I guess I better head off."

She didn't want him to leave. He was so nice and pleasant, the antithesis of her mother. Wasn't life all about balance? "My plan was to curl up on the couch and watch an old movie, nothing special," she said. An invitation lingered in the air. She added tentatively, "You're welcome to join me."

"You're sure you don't mind? I know you're tired."

She narrowed her eyes at him and teased, "You don't expect me to entertain you, do you? I can just chill?"

He laughed. "Of course. I'd be doing the same thing if I was going home."

"Go on then, make yourself comfortable. I've already got a movie picked out for tonight. I'll load the dishwasher and be right in."

"Let me help you," he offered.

She held her hand up. "Nope. You cooked this wonderful meal. I'll do the cleanup. You go on and relax."

With a grin, he said, "Okay, boss."

It wasn't long before she joined him in the living room. She'd chosen *Jezebel* with Bette Davis and Henry Fonda. But within five minutes, she was fast asleep. When she woke the following morning, the television was off and she was covered with a blanket. Jim was gone. Smiling, she sat up, stretched, and let out a big yawn. The dogs and cats appeared, looking to go out and be fed.

There was a note on the kitchen table: *Great movie. Never seen it before. I'll tell you about it later.*

She laughed out loud and tucked the note away for safekeeping.

CHAPTER FORTY-ONE

Debbie systematically made her way through the rest of the attic. It amazed her, the condition of some of the items that were saved: small appliances with frayed electrical cords, chipped and cracked plates, and old clothes that either no longer fit or were never going to be worn again. They saved *everything*.

She divided her time between cleaning out the attic and searching through the boxes that contained her aunt's belongings. It had been years since she'd spent time in her old bedroom. It was as she'd left it, decorated in all things orange: an orange chenille bedspread, an orange bean bag chair in the corner, and orange-and-yellow floral curtains on the window. Her mother would never bother with an update of a room that was no longer used. Why spend money on that when you could use it to buy junk from late-night infomercials? The room smelled sour and despite the cold weather, Debbie went over to the window and opened it up a crack.

She looked around. Posters of her favorite boy bands and television shows covered the walls. There was a single closet with a hardwood door. A gold rug covered the floor, threadbare in the traffic pattern areas in the center of the room, the front of the dresser, and the side of the bed. She'd never had a desk and used to do her homework kneeling on the floor by her bed with her books spread out before her.

In a far corner of the attic, there'd been a record player inside a cream case, and she'd carried that down. After a scrub with some hot soapy water, it looked almost as good as new. And to her delight, it still worked. She pulled out the first album she'd found in the box, *Runnin' Out of Fools*, placed it on the turntable, and lowered the needle onto the vinyl record.

She decided that one side of the album would be how much time she would allocate to sifting through her aunt's belongings. Anything longer than that and her mother would surely get suspicious. As much as she wanted to get lost in it, she couldn't spend hours up here.

She pushed the box of albums aside, thinking she'd go through them one at a time. The next box she opened was full of clothes. Sorting through them was like walking through a time machine. Other than the slight smell of must, they were in perfect condition. She pulled the items out one by one. First, there was a pair of well-worn rust-colored Levi's corduroys. Then there were three pairs of bell-bottom jeans. She smiled when she pulled out a couple of tie-dyed T-shirts. Next were two polyester blouses with bell sleeves, one pale pink and the other baby blue. There were nightgowns with quilted bodices with tiny pink flowers on them. There was one cowl-neck sweater the color of cream. There was a plaid skirt with a large safety pin on it. And last, there were six pairs of days-of-the-week underwear, but Saturday was missing.

Debbie sat with her back against the dresser and stretched out. She was overwhelmed with sadness at her aunt's paltry clothing history. Was this it? Had they merely saved the favorites? Or was this everything?

In her hand was an article of clothing: a plaid shirt with a ribbon around the collar, the one she recognized from the yearbook photo in the newspaper. She held it to her face and sniffed it. Underneath the scent of staleness and must was the faint scent of *Sweet Honesty*. The only reason she recognized it was because there'd been a bottle of it on her mother's dresser for years.

The needle skipped, the sound of static interrupting her thoughts. She stood, removed the album, and put it back in its sleeve. Carefully, she folded every article of clothing and returned them to the box, closing it up.

She went back to the attic, worked for another half hour, and then made her way downstairs to see if her mother wanted lunch.

A week later, Debbie was almost finished cleaning out the attic. And she was also mostly finished with going through her aunt's things. She'd found some pictures of Judy, who had the trademark red hair of the family, and she set aside two photos, both Polaroids with white borders. The first had the date *Dec 1974* stamped in black letters. It showed Judy standing in front of a Christmas tree, holding up a lime green skateboard and wearing a broad smile. The second photo, dated *July 1975*, showed Judy sitting next to Darlene on a floral velour couch. They sat shoulder to shoulder, smiles wide, faces bright. Darlene wore a halter top and cutoff jeans. Judy wore a short-sleeved T-shirt with some TV show on it that Debbie couldn't make out, and a pair of blue shorts with white piping. Debbie stared at it. Her mother was unrecognizable. She appeared to be an altogether different person: youthful, full of joy, and with an open expression. She tucked the photos into her pocket. She'd get them framed. It would make a nice Christmas gift for her mother.

Another important discovery was Judy's diary. Debbie had been torn about reading it. Was it an invasion of privacy if the person was dead? She hoped not. A clearer picture of her aunt was beginning to emerge. She had hopes and dreams, she disagreed with her parents, she looked up to her sister, and she had a crush on a boy at school. All normal things that ceased to exist on August 9, 1975.

Judy didn't write in her diary every day. After one two-week period of nothing, she had written, *I'm so boring, I have nothing to report.*

In the weeks leading up to her death, she'd been writing about how she'd heard about a disco over in Cheever. All her friends were going, and she wanted to go too. Her parents had forbidden it, but there was a Plan B:

I asked Darlene if she'd take me to that disco up in Cheever. She said she'd think about it!

And then the next day, she wrote, *Darlene told me to stop pestering her about the disco. She doesn't like disco. She'd rather go to a concert.*

Enthralled, Debbie read on.

The last entry was dated August 7, 1975. *Tomorrow night is the night! Darlene said she would take me to Flashes! Yay, sis! I can't wait. I already have my outfit picked out.*

There were only blank pages after that.

The door to the bedroom opened, and there was a tick of a second before Darlene's voice boomed, "What are you doing?"

Debbie jumped up from her position on the floor, dropping the diary. Quickly, she turned off the record player, leaving the album as is. She turned to face her mother, whose face was the color of scarlet.

"Who gave you permission to go through Judy's things?"

Debbie felt like she was eight years old and had been caught trying on her mother's nail polish. For a moment she forgot about being caught and said, "What are you doing upstairs? You're not supposed to be using the stairs yet."

"I wanted to see how you were coming on with the attic, but it seems you were only using it as an excuse to snoop!" She leaned against the doorframe for support.

Debbie went to protest, but her mother was on a tear. "All this time, I thought you were breaking your back cleaning out that dirty old attic and you're in your room, trawling through my sister's things and sticking your nose where it doesn't belong!"

Darlene was enraged. Her eyes were wide, and a vein Debbie had never seen before bulged in her forehead. "Pack everything up and put it back where it belongs. And then get out of my house."

She turned on her boot and limped out of the bedroom, leaving the door wide open. Debbie followed her.

Darlene waved her off. "Get away from me, Debbie."

"Mom, you're upset, and I don't want you to fall down the stairs. You don't need another broken bone."

"I don't need a lot of things, but here I am," her mother snapped.

With Debbie right behind her, despite her protests, Darlene managed to get down the stairs, one step at a time, despite the cumbersome and clunky boot. When she made it to the bottom, she headed for her recliner. Once she sat, she reached for her pack of cigarettes, her hands shaking.

"Put up the recliner, Mom, you need to elevate your leg," Debbie told her.

With a cigarette dangling from her lips and the lighter in her hand, her mother said, "I don't feel like putting it up right now. And I'll remind you that I'm still your mother."

She kept flicking the lighter, trying to get it to light. There was a series of clicks but no flame. She muttered expletives beneath her breath.

"Here, let me help you," Debbie said.

Darlene swatted her hand away. "I don't need your help."

With a giant sigh, Debbie sat down in the other recliner, the one that was rarely, if ever, used by her father.

"Mom, I'm sorry I went through those things. I wanted to know more about her."

"Why didn't you ask me?" Darlene demanded, taking a succession of long drags off her cigarette.

"I did ask you. You said you didn't want to talk about it."

Darlene went off on a rant. "You had no right whatsoever poking your nose around in those boxes. You didn't even have the right to open them. But you do whatever you want, never thinking how it might affect other people."

"That's kind of harsh," Debbie countered.

"Sometimes the truth is harsh!"

In the middle of this rant, Jerry appeared in the doorway, realized he'd landed in the middle of a tornado, muttered "Oh boy," and turned and walked back out the door.

"Why can't you tell me what happened? It was over fifty years ago," Debbie pointed out.

"Wake up. Sometimes you carry things around with you forever, so fifty years is nothing."

"Maybe you need to talk about it," Debbie said quietly.

"Pfft." Darlene stubbed out her cigarette aggressively and lit another one. "Those boxes haven't been opened since I packed all her stuff away."

"Maybe it was time."

"Do you have any idea what it was like to walk into that room and see her things lying out? To see those rust corduroys that she *lived* in, lying out?" When Debbie didn't answer, Darlene demanded, "Do you?"

Debbie didn't take her eyes off her mother. "No, I don't. I'm sorry."

"It was fresh and raw again. Like it was yesterday. Like Judy was killed yesterday. Like the last fifty years never happened, never existed." Her mother snapped her fingers and said, "Poof!"

"What happened?"

"You know what happened!" her mother yelled. "Judy was killed in a hit-and-run and left on the side of the highway like some poor animal."

"No, Mom, that's not what I mean," Debbie said.

Her mother looked at her, confused.

"I mean, what happened to *you*?"

Tragedy was never only about the victim, but also the people left behind to suffer it, to live through it, to try and move past it.

In a cold voice, her mother said, "I told you to get out of my house."

Debbie felt as if she'd been slapped. Without a word, she picked up her purse. As she was walking out of the house, Dawn was walking in. She hadn't seen her sister since the infamous brunch.

"She's all yours. You can take care of her now," Debbie said angrily. She didn't wait for her sister's reply. Instead, she rushed to her car, wanting to get away as fast as she could. Because if there was one thing she'd learned from her family it was this: she didn't stay where she wasn't welcome.

Chapter Forty-Two

Now that she didn't have to spend all her spare time at her mother's house, Debbie threw herself into her job at the shelter. She'd been distracted, but now it was time to roll up her sleeves and get back to work. By keeping busy, she could avoid dwelling on her mother and the fact that she had wounded her. Wounded people wounded other people. She created a project for herself: find a home for Quint, who'd been at the shelter for more than two years now, and for Spotty, who continued to bark at the wall and during Barry Manilow songs and who, by the looks of it, was in danger of turning into a long-term resident like Quint. One of the volunteers, a photographer, offered to take a professional photo of each of them. Quint, a golden retriever, was kitted out in a navy blue scarf, which Debbie thought made him look sharp. For Spotty, she'd put a dapper bow tie around his neck. One of the staff at *The Lavender Bay Chronicles*, who'd adopted a puppy from the shelter five years ago and had returned for a cat the previous year, helped her write copy for an article. Together they came up with the idea that each week there'd be a column highlighting a cat or dog that needed a home. After leaving the newspaper's offices, Debbie felt better.

On her lunch hour, she went home and picked up the dogs and headed to the beach, where she'd agreed to meet Jim.

She loved the beach, no matter the weather. Currently, it was damp and misty. A slight fog lay over the lake, and Canada was invisible from this vantage point. The lake looked turbulent: dark, with roiling waves and foamy whitecaps. There were only a handful of people around.

She'd bundled up in her heavy lavender coat. On her head was a cream-colored knit cap with a matching pom-pom. She double-checked her coat pockets for poop bags in one and two tennis balls in the other.

As she clipped the leads to the dogs, Jim pulled in next to her. He was similarly dressed in a North Face jacket.

"Hey," he said, and surprised her by leaning in and kissing her cheek. "How are you?"

That kiss, though simple and tender, made her feel like a lovesick teenager. She could barely suppress her smile. "I'm fine. You?"

He grinned. "Better now that I've seen you."

She lowered her head to hide her blush. Jim leaned over and petted the dogs. They walked down the concrete ramp to the beach, and the damp air settled in around them.

She removed the dogs' leads, and Jim offered to carry them for her. She tossed the tennis balls, and both dogs took off at a run to retrieve them. They returned, dropped them at her feet, and she tossed them again, repeating the process as they walked the length of the beach.

In the distance, she spotted Angie's sister Nadine and her dog, Herman. She threw up her hand in a wave, as did Jim. Nadine responded in kind.

"How's your mom doing?" Jim asked Debbie.

"She's coming along. She's mad at me so I'll leave her be for a while," she said. Hurriedly, she explained, "It's my fault. I was snooping around where I shouldn't have been."

"She guards her privacy."

Debbie nodded. "Mom explodes, and it's best to stay away from her for a while until she cools down. It'll blow over." She tried to exude a confidence she didn't feel. She said again, "It was my fault. She had every right to be angry."

Next to them, waves rolled in with a thunderous roar.

"Will I get to meet her sometime?" he asked.

Debbie's eyes widened and she felt something akin to alarm, and then terror. "Oh God, no!"

It was almost impossible not to see the stricken look on Jim's face. He stared at the ground in front of him. Words tumbled out of her mouth. "Oh, Jim, no, I don't mean it like that. My family is . . . er . . . challenging. My mother is tough. There's no other way to put it. And I'd be so afraid . . ."

"Afraid of what?"

She couldn't look at him. She coughed and cleared her throat and went for honesty. "I'd be afraid that once you met her, you wouldn't want to see me again."

Jim stopped walking and stood there on the damp sand. It forced her to stop walking too, and it also forced her to look at him.

He frowned and said, "How could you think that?"

"Because I know my mother." She wanted to add, *and she'd ruin a free lunch.*

He dropped the leads, took a step toward her, and took both her hands in his. "Debbie, I can handle it. No matter what. A difficult mother isn't a dealbreaker."

"It isn't?"

He laughed and shook his head. "No, of course not. Why should it be? I like you too much to let someone else come between us."

"You do?"

He nodded. They walked on and he held her hand in his.

"So, I've been thinking ...." And his voice trailed off.

"Thinking is good," she teased. "More people should try it."

"Is it time to be boyfriend and girlfriend?" He waggled his eyebrows and grinned.

She narrowed her eyes at him and said in mock offense, "You just want to meet my mother."

A shout of laughter escaped him and pulled her hand to his mouth and kissed it. "You're really great, Deb."

A fine mist lay on her face. Despite the cold, she felt invigorated. And at that moment, happy. They picked up their stride, soon deciding it was time to turn around and head back to work. The dogs had run ahead, and she whistled loudly for them. Both stopped what they were doing and stared at her. She waved them to come on, and they took off in her direction. She and Jim walked back toward their cars, making plans for the weekend and where they might go hiking to see the fall colors.

They'd just reached the parking lot when they ran into Edna Knickerbocker and her friend and next-door neighbor, Hal. They were similarly bundled up in heavy coats, gloves, and hats.

Edna waved. "Hello there, Debbie! Hello, Jim!"

"Hi!" Jim said.

"We haven't seen you here in a while, young lady," Hal said.

"I've been busy with my mother," Debbie explained.

Beside Hal, Edna grinned. "And Jim, I've never seen you on the beach before."

With a nod toward Debbie, he said, "You can thank Deb for that."

The dogs sat in front of them, whining and begging for attention. Edna and Hal spoke to Oscar and Bella and petted them, and the dogs settled down.

"How is your mother, Debbie?" Edna asked.

"She's fine." It was as close to the truth as she was going to get as far as her mother was concerned. Deb felt her mother had reached her optimal level in life. It was as far as she was going to go.

"That's good to hear. She must hate having a broken leg," Hal said.

Debbie nodded in agreement. As Edna and Hal continued to fool with Oscar and Bella, a thought occurred to her, and she momentarily forgot about her mother. "Have either of you thought about opening up your home to a dog or a cat?"

Edna and Hal looked at her and then each other, and burst out laughing.

"I've never had either," Edna admitted. "Not even growing up. My mother didn't want any animals in the house."

"I always had a dog when my kids were growing up but once they moved out, I never had another pet. I didn't want to be tied down. I wanted to travel," Hal said.

"But we never leave Lavender Bay," Edna said.

"That's because we have everything here that we need," Hal said.

"That's true."

"You might want to consider adopting a dog," Debbie said. Granted, they were elderly, but they were in pretty good shape. It seemed that they'd always been around and always would be.

Beside her, Jim snorted.

She looked at him coyly. "What?"

He shook his head, still smiling. "Nothing."

"To be honest, I never gave it any thought," Edna said truthfully.

"We have some lovely dogs who are in need of a good home," Debbie said sweetly.

Edna tilted her head slightly and narrowed her eyes at Debbie. "Oh my, you are a dangerous young lady. I've heard that you put a spell over people and then they end up with dogs and cats they didn't even know they wanted."

Debbie laughed. "I don't think I'm as bad as that."

"Be careful here, guys, this is her windup. Ask me, I know," Jim told them. "I'm now the proud owner of a cat."

Edna hooted. "It must be love."

"Must be," Jim said.

Debbie looked at him and smiled.

Hal piped in, "I think you *are* as bad as that, because now Edna and I are going to be thinking about adopting a dog."

"Okay, think about it. You know where I am. It was good seeing you both." Deb called the dogs, who'd wandered off, and waved goodbye. As she walked away, she heard snippets of Edna and Hal's conversation.

"Do you think we're too old to get a dog?" Edna asked.

"What do I always tell you, Edna? We're only as old as we feel."

"Well, I feel like I'm fifty-nine."

"There you go . . ."

Smiling, Debbie walked hand in hand with Jim to their cars with the dogs following her, hoping she'd see Edna and Hal someday at the shelter.

Chapter Forty-Three

A few days later, Debbie opened her door and was surprised to see her father standing there. "Dad? What are you doing here?" Behind him, snow fell slowly and gently. The first snowfall of the season.

"May I come in?"

"Of course."

She tried to remember the last time her father had visited her at home, but it failed to come to mind. "Watch the steps, Dad."

"Will do."

Jerry Melvin stepped into the house and the dogs came at him full tilt, which caused him to jump back, eyes widening.

Debbie halted them mid-run. "Down."

Immediately, they stopped and sat in place.

"Hey, that's pretty good," Jerry said. "I'll tell you, if that big one got to me, I was going down and if I go down, I'm not getting back up."

"They like company," Debbie explained. "Would you like a cup of coffee or tea?"

"Coffee's fine," he said, following her into the kitchen. "You've got a real nice place here, Debbie."

"Thanks, Dad. You should come by more often."

"I don't like to bother you guys, you've got your own life."

"You're not bothering me." She wouldn't speak on behalf of Dawn or Darren. She had no idea what they thought about anything. She went about making coffee and then joined him at the table, waiting until it was ready. "Why don't you take your coat off."

"Sure," he said. He struggled to get it off, and Debbie assisted him. "Everything's difficult. Don't get old, Debbie. There's no future in it."

His advanced years played out on his face. It was a series of jowls, cragginess, bumps, and spots, and topping his head was hair that was sparse and patchy at best, as if not every strand had gotten the message that they were leaving town.

She smiled. "Noted."

Oscar, the bigger of the two dogs, walked through the kitchen, eyeing Jerry.

"Go lay down," Debbie told him.

The coffeemaker beeped, and she stood and prepared two mugs of coffee. "How do you take it?" she asked.

"With a little half-and-half. I'm watching my choles-terol."

She handed him his mug, and he took a sip. "That's nice coffee."

She nodded, wondering about the purpose of his visit. She knew there was one; he hadn't simply shown up for coffee and conversation. Directness was probably best. "Dad, do you have something to say?"

"Actually, I do," he said, staring into the coffee cup in front of him. "It's about your mother."

Debbie snorted. "Darlene Melvin. Mother of the year."

He held up a hand. "Now wait a minute there, young lady. There's no need for sarcasm. That kind of sarcasm is usually covering up some kind of hurt. She told me that she blew up at you."

She was surprised at his insight; her father wasn't nor-mally noted for his self-awareness.

"She actually told you?" This surprised Debbie more than anything. "I didn't think Mom talked to you about anything at all."

He laughed. "Only when the sun, stars, and moon are in perfect alignment."

"Gee, you sure give her a lot of latitude."

"It's doable when you know the reason she is the way she is."

"Why didn't she ever go to therapy?"

"This is your mother we're talking about."

Debbie drew in a deep breath. Her family was never going to change.

"Now, you haven't been over in a week," he said.

"Dad, I'm forty-one years old. I'm not eight again. I'm not going to put up with her yelling at me like that. Or kicking me out of her house. Not anymore."

"I understand all that. It's why I stay out of her way."

"And that's not right."

"Probably not, but that doesn't need to be discussed right now."

Debbie thought it should be talked about at some point.

"I think she misses you," he said.

She couldn't hide her shock. Her father caught it, and he started laughing. "She does," he insisted.

She smirked. "How can you tell?"

"Remember, I've been married to your mother for almost fifty years. I know her. And I know what's bothering her. She misses you, I'm telling you. Do you think she would have told me about blowing up at you if it didn't bother her?"

Debbie didn't know what to say to that. There was some logic there, she supposed.

He continued. "When she broke her leg, you started coming around more often and she got used to it. She liked it."

Debbie doubted all of this.

"Okay, smarty pants," he said. "When you were coming over, did she ever ask you to leave? Tell you to go home? Did she ever give you a hard time about being there?"

"Actually, she did. The last time I was there. She told me to get out of her house."

"In the heat of the moment, your mother says a lot of mean things. She blows up, but then she cools down. But I bet if you showed up, she wouldn't kick you out," Jerry told her.

"How can you be so sure?" Debbie hadn't spoken to her mother in over a week.

Jerry smiled. "Because she lets me come home every day, doesn't she?"

Debbie couldn't help that she laughed.

Relieved, Jerry said, "That's the spirit, kiddo. Chin up." And then he heaved a big sigh of relief. "I think I need a drink." He finished the rest of his coffee and stood up. "That's that then. I've got to go."

Debbie held out his coat for him and helped him get into it.

As she walked him out, he said, "Thanks for the coffee."

"Any time, Dad. And don't be such a stranger."

"I might surprise you sometime and stop over again," he said with a laugh.

"I hope you do," she said, and she meant it.

She closed the door behind him. Now what to do about her mother.

After work the following day and before she was to go to dinner at Jim's, Debbie didn't go see her mother. She went and saw the woman she considered her second mother, Louise Cook. She was relieved to see the lights on at the Cook household on Heather Lane. Her hope was that Louise was alone, because she wanted to talk to her privately.

As she stood on the porch in the darkness, she hesitated. It had been a while since she'd sought out Louise's advice. When she was a teenager, she asked Louise things she didn't feel comfortable asking her own mother, which was just about everything. And after she graduated from college and after Louise's husband, Martin, had passed away, she'd dropped in to see how she was doing. But aside from coffee mornings, it had to have been at least ten years since she last stopped unannounced.

She rang the bell and heard the muted corresponding chime inside the house and then the approaching footsteps. The porch light went on, the door opened, and Louise stood there and broke into a smile at the sight of Debbie.

"This is a pleasant surprise. Come in, Debbie."

"I'm not interrupting, am I?"

"Of course not! Peter and I were only watching television."

As Debbie walked in, she noticed the large-screen television had been paused, the frame frozen. On the back of the sofa, the cat, Peter, sat up and regarded her with his one eye, looking a bit judgy at the interruption.

"Come on back to the kitchen," Louise said. "I'll make some tea. Or would you prefer coffee?"

"Tea's fine," she said, removing her hat and scarf as she followed Louise. The house was comfortably warm and smelled of baked cake.

There was only the light above the stove, and it was so quiet it was surreal. She was so used to all the noise and bustling activity of the Sunday coffee mornings that it took her a moment to get used to it.

"Sit down, honey," Louise said as she put the kettle on and pulled down mugs.

Debbie removed her coat and hung it on the back of the chair. She laid her hat and scarf on the seat. She fluffed up her hair and sat, feeling cozy in this kitchen and with this woman.

Louise carried a box of cookies over to the table. "I don't have any fresh baked goods, but I do have these."

She showed Debbie the green box, Salerno Santa's Favorites, an anise-flavored Christmas cookie.

"I used to love those, and I haven't had them in years," Debbie said. "I didn't know they still made them."

"They're only out at Christmastime." Even though Thanksgiving hadn't even passed, retailers and brands wasted no time in getting their holiday wares out there.

The kettle whistled, and Louise made two cups of tea and carried them over. She then set a jug of milk and a bowl of sugar on the table. Debbie fixed her tea the way she liked it.

Now that she was here, Debbie felt foolish for bothering Louise. She couldn't keep running to Angie's mother every time she felt overwhelmed.

Louise held her mug with her two hands and sipped from it. "How's your mother?"

Debbie stared into her mug of tea. "The usual. Prickly. Angry. But at least her leg is healing."

"It's hard to be a caregiver to someone who is . . . a little difficult," Louise said diplomatically.

Debbie sighed. And the words poured out of her. She told her how her mother raged at her for looking through Judy's things and then threw her out of her house.

"Your mother is a private person," Louise said when she was finished.

"I know she is, but she acts like I was committing a prison-worthy offense."

"She is who she is."

"Even now, speaking about her to you, I have this feeling that I'm being disloyal," Debbie confessed.

Louise smiled. "That's because you're a good person and a good daughter."

"My mother doesn't think so."

"Although your mother may not show it or say it, I'm sure she thinks you're a good daughter," Louise said. "No matter how difficult she may be, as your mother, she must see that you're a good person. I wouldn't believe anything else about her."

Debbie finally voiced what she'd been thinking since the second grade, when she first met Angie and then the rest of the Cook family. "I always wish that my family could be more like yours. That my mother was more like you." Now the tears came, not because of this impossible hope and expectation but because of the overwhelming guilt at saying this out loud and the sense that she had betrayed her mother.

Louise reached across the table for Debbie's hands and gave them a gentle squeeze. "Don't feel bad for how you feel. And you're always a member of our family. You know that."

"You've all been so good to me over the years." The Cooks had been her refuge. She picked up her mug of now lukewarm tea and sipped at it. "I know my mother never recovered from her sister's death, and it certainly explains a lot about her."

"I'm sure it does. Gail and I were lucky. We had a narrow escape, and it brought us closer. But your aunt wasn't so lucky, and it affected the rest of your mother's life."

Debbie was finally able to voice the awful thought. "Do you think the creep that tried to run you and Gail down might have hit Aunt Judy and killed her?"

Louise shrugged. "At the time, Gail and I wondered about that. He was the first person who came to mind when we realized someone had died on the highway."

"But he never was caught," Deb said.

Louise shook her head. "I've given that some thought too. It was as if he simply fell off the face of the earth. There are three possibilities: he died, he went to prison for something else, or he moved away."

Debbie sighed. They would probably never know who killed Judy. And she'd never mention this possibility to her mother. Despite Darlene's toughness, she didn't think she would be able to handle this news.

"It's so hard to be close to her. She keeps everyone at arm's length," Debbie complained.

Louise didn't say anything at first but then she said, "I'm going to give you some unsolicited advice, honey."

Debbie waited.

"Meet your mother where she's at. Accept her where she's at."

Debbie knew she must look as confused as she felt.

"What I mean is, you have an ideal in your head about how your mother should be." Louise shook her head. "And she can't be that ideal. That's what's stressing you out and has been stressing you out your whole life. Instead, accept her as she is, where she is."

"Don't change her?" Debbie asked. "Lower my expectations."

Louise nodded. "Yes. That is a form of love: accepting someone just as they are, flaws and all, and not expecting any change. If you can do that, you might find some peace."

Debbie took a deep breath as she digested this. She might not be keen on Louise's advice, but she knew the other woman was right. If she could take it on board, it might save her some future grief.

They had one more cup of tea and spoke of generalities, and Louise told her how happy she was to hear that she was dating Jim Sloane, and she hoped to see them at Christmas. Debbie would like that as well. She always managed to spend some part of Christmas Day with the Cooks and Campbells.

When Louise walked her to the front door, Debbie turned and threw her arms around her and hugged her tight. "Thank you so much."

"Anytime, honey. I'm glad you stopped."

She put on her hat, scarf, and coat and headed out, feeling better than when she arrived.

CHAPTER FORTY-FOUR

Three days after her father's visit, Debbie stopped at her mother's house on her way home from work. As soon as she entered the house, she heard raised voices. She closed her eyes and sighed. Back to the battlefield. She hadn't thought it would be so soon. The shouting stopped, and Dawn stormed into the kitchen and brushed past her, her face full of fury.

"You can have her. She's so unappreciative of anything you do for her," Dawn said. "So ungrateful."

"I can hear you, Dawn!" their mother shouted from the other room.

"I see a nursing home in your future, Mom!" Dawn yelled back.

Debbie put a hand on her arm. "Go home, Dawn. I'll take over from here."

Her sister continued her rant about their ungrateful mother as she rushed out the door and slammed it behind her.

Debbie took a deep breath and walked into the living room. Her mother was in her recliner with her feet up, the cast having been removed.

"Hi, Mom."

"Hi, Debbie," her mother said. She had her arms folded across her chest. The ashtray next to her was full of cigarette butts.

Debbie sat in the other recliner. "What's going on?"

"Your sister, that's what's going on. Look what she's trying to get me to drink." She pointed to the can of Diet Pepsi beside her. "I've never drunk diet pop in my entire life. I'm a Pepsi girl."

"Maybe she picked up the wrong thing," Debbie said, trying to still the turbulent waters.

"No, she didn't. She said I'm drinking too much pop, it's loaded with sugar, and I need to switch to the diet version." She looked at the can with anger. "That's worse. It's loaded with artificial sweetener. I'm not touching that stuff."

"Mom, it's all right," Debbie said softly. "I'll go up to the store right now and get you regular Pepsi. Now, in fairness, Dawn was only trying to look out for you. She was doing what she thought was best."

Her mother scowled and poked herself in the chest. "I know what's best for me."

"I'll be right back." Debbie left, went to the store, and returned with a two-liter bottle of Pepsi. Before she put it in the fridge, she showed her mother. "See? Do you want a glass?"

"Yeah, I do."

"It's not cold. Do you want ice?"

"One cube," her mother said.

She got her mother's drink and sat down again, determined to spend some time with Darlene and *accept her where she was at*. Her mother never mentioned that she hadn't seen her in over a week. Never said a word about how she kicked her out of the house the last time she'd seen her. Debbie supposed they were going to pretend it never happened. And forget about an apology—her mother was never one to offer any of those. Again, she reminded herself of Louise's advice.

"I've got something for you, Mom." She lifted her purse from the floor and pulled out the framed photo and handed it to her mother. It was supposed to be a Christmas gift, but Debbie couldn't wait and now thought of it more like a peace offering.

Eyebrows furrowed, Darlene took it and held it in her hands, staring at the photo of her and her sister, taken a month before Judy was killed. Her mother betrayed no emotion on her face; she simply stared at the photo and then placed it on the table beside her, face down.

Debbie shrank back in the recliner, thinking that at least she hadn't exploded.

Darlene reached for her cigarette case, pulled one out, lit it with her lighter, and took several long drags.

"I always looked out for her," she said. "Judy wasn't tough like me. She was a sweet kid. I was protective of her. I had to be. And for some God-forsaken reason that I never understood, she loved me and looked up to me. I couldn't get rid of her. She always wanted to be with me, followed me everywhere from the time she could walk." Tears filled her eyes.

Debbie settled in, deciding not to say anything, afraid that if she spoke, it would break the spell and her mother would shut down.

Darlene picked up the glass and took a few sips of the Pepsi. The cigarette was poised between her second and third fingers, a thin blue stream of smoke trailing up toward the ceiling. "I was supposed to take her to the disco that night. There was one up in Cheever. Flashes was the name of it. I was going to drive her. But I bailed at the last minute. The Rolling Stones were playing up in Buffalo at Rich Stadium, a friend had an extra ticket, and I told Judy I'd take her the following weekend, never thinking she'd go off to Cheever by herself. I told her this concert was a once-in-a-lifetime event. That I'd probably never have the chance to see the Stones in concert again."

"But Mom, you weren't to know . . ."

"No, but I should have kept my word. When she died, she died disappointed in me. I had let her down. She must have hitchhiked up there and then tried to get home the same way. And because of me, she died alone on the side of the road."

With that, Darlene broke down in great, hulking sobs that caused her body to shake from head to toe. Debbie watched, helpless, unsure of what to do or even what to say.

When the crying appeared to subside, Darlene gave a sniff and looked away, embarrassed by her show of emotion.

"Mom, what do you think Judy would say to you if she could see you today?"

Her mother nodded her head up and down and took a puff of her cigarette. "I'll tell you what she would say, she'd say, 'Thanks a lot, sis!' That's what she would say." This brought on another round of crying.

Debbie felt sorry for her.

"This is why I didn't want to talk about it," Darlene said. "I knew if I started talking about it, I'd start crying, lose control of my emotions." She shook her head in disgust.

"There's no shame in crying."

Her mother's head snapped up. "There is for me."

Debbie didn't say anything else and finally, Darlene spoke. "I haven't talked about that night in fifty years. And it will be another fifty before I talk about again."

And with that, the subject was closed.

Debbie sighed, not sure how to help her mother. Maybe she had never properly grieved for her younger sister. Maybe as far as her stages of grief were concerned, her mother was still stuck in 1975. And maybe they'd all been stuck because of it.

There was no more mention of Judy. Her mother had said all she wanted to, and Debbie didn't ask a single question, knowing the topic was closed. Her father came home, and Debbie pulled out three frozen pot pies and cooked them in the oven. When they were finished eating and she had cleaned up, her mother had gone quiet, and Debbie took it as her cue to leave.

"I think I'll go back out," Jerry said.

"It's dark out, Dad," Debbie said. "Wait until tomorrow."

"Just for one more."

She was surprised her mother didn't add to the conversation; she usually had some comment to make. But Debbie suspected her earlier outburst had sapped her of all her energy. Against her better judgement, she drove her father over to the Dog Days Bar on her way home.

It had snowed plenty, and she was afraid he might slip and fall. Instead of dropping him off, she accompanied him inside. The place hadn't changed much in all the years since it opened. It was as she remembered from childhood, when her mother used to send her across the street to tell her father it was time to come home for dinner. It was dim inside, the only lights over the bar proper, the rest of the room in shadows. There was only one more customer at the other end of the bar. As they walked by, Jerry patted the other man, of indeterminate age, on his back, saying, "How's it going, Stan?"

The man, who was hunched over his beer bottle, mumbled something incoherent.

"That's what I thought," Jerry said.

They went to the other end of the bar. Her father's preferred seat was the last one at the far end, against the wall. That way he could sit sideways and watch all the goings-on, of which Debbie was sure there were plenty.

Her father ordered a bottle of Genny beer, and Debbie went for a glass of Pepsi. She didn't know how he tolerated all that alcohol. By this point in his life, he must be pickled. But he tooled along and would probably outlive them all. It must be a great preservative.

"Dad, can I ask you a question?" She traced her finger along the cool condensation covering the bar glass.

"Sure, kiddo, ask me anything." He took a slug of Genny as if to fortify himself.

Debbie rested her head against her hand. "How did you and Mom ever get together and get married?"

"I'm sure a lot of people would like to know that," he said. He turned the beer bottle on the top of the bar slowly round and round. With a laugh, he added, "Including myself."

"Did you love each other?"

Jerry seemed shocked by the question. "Of course we did. What do you take us for?" He paused and took another sip of his beer. "Even when your mother was younger, she never did anything she didn't want to do."

Debbie knew that truth about her mother all too well.

"There's such an age difference between you and Mom," she said.

"There is. I knew the MacNamara family. I worked with your grandfather. He was a nice man and a good boss. When Judy was killed, it destroyed him." He paused, drew in a deep breath as if steeling himself, as if talking about it, even after all this time, still caused him pain. "It destroyed all of them." He went silent. Debbie waited, allowing him to gather his thoughts.

"After Judy died, I used to stop over to make sure they were all right. To see if they needed anything." Her father in the role of caregiver was foreign to her. "Sometimes it was simply a matter of sitting at the kitchen table with them, drinking a beer and keeping them company in that awful silence. No one knew what to say to them.

No one. What do you say when something like that happens?"

Jerry paused, seemed reflective. His gaze suggested he was elsewhere.

"Your mother was there sometimes. Now, I'd met Darlene and Judy a couple of times. They'd sometimes stop at work and drop something off for Lenny. They were nice girls. They were a nice family. But Darlene was tough. Tougher. Whereas you felt protective of Judy, Darlene needed no protecting. In fact, you knew she'd protect you." He chuckled.

Debbie soaked in all this information about her mother and her family like a sponge.

Jerry continued. "One evening, I'd stopped after work and they were all quiet. The air was tense. Darlene came up to me and asked if I would take her for a drive. I was surprised and I hesitated. After all, I was fifteen years older than her. But she said she needed to get out of the house. I understood. Well, maybe I didn't, but I wanted to help.

"When we got into the car, all your mother said was 'Keep driving until I tell you to turn around and bring me home.' So, I did just that. I gassed up before we got on the highway and drove north, all the way up to Buffalo and then beyond that to Niagara Falls. It was a warm evening, and we drove with all the windows down. When we reached the sign for the Niagara Falls city limits, your mother said, 'Turn around, I'm ready to go home.' I asked her if she wanted to see the falls. She didn't. So, I did a U-turn right in the middle of the road and headed back to Lavender Bay."

He stopped and grimaced, coughed to clear his throat. "When I dropped her off, she said 'Thanks.' And got out of the car. She hardly spoke during the entire ride. Just looked out the window." He shook his head and coughed again.

Debbie stared at him, rapt.

"Anyway, when I returned the following night, she was waiting for me. Said nothing, just got into the car. And we drove every evening for months, until the snow fell. Darlene never said much. But for whatever reason, she felt safe with me. Me? Can you believe it?" He laughed in disbelief. "I was no upstanding character of Lavender Bay." He turned and looked at her and said, "Did you know I used to go out with Edith Bermingham when we were young?"

Jarred by this most unlikely of tangents, Debbie said, "No, I didn't." She couldn't even begin to picture that, and would definitely be quizzing him about it at a later date, but for now she needed him to get back on track. "What happened then?" she asked.

"I fell in love with your mother. She reminded me of a wounded bird. A bird who recovers but is never the same, and it makes you love it even more. Your mother exists in this life, but that's about it."

"Do you think she loved you?" Debbie realized it might be a painful question but was curious.

"When we married, she told me she loved me and you know your mother, it takes her a lot to say something like that. But whether she confused gratitude with love, I don't know."

Debbie smiled at her father. "When did you gather so much insight? And wisdom?"

Jerry burst out laughing. "What do you think I'm doing over here? Drinking? No, I'm thinking. All the time. All day long."

"Don't do too much of that, Dad, it's not good for you," she teased gently.

"Now, I must use the bathroom. My bladder and prostate aren't what they used to be." Carefully, he slipped off the stool and walked slowly to the men's room.

The bartender, a man about Debbie's age, approached her. "Another Pepsi?"

"Sure," she said. "And maybe another bottle of beer for my dad." Even though his current one was only half finished.

"Jerry never has more than one beer when he comes in here," he told her.

Her mouth dropped open. She finally managed to get out, "Really?"

"Yeah. When he turned eighty, he said he was turning over a new leaf." The bartender laughed at the memory of it. He set a glass of Pepsi down in front of Debbie.

"Does he drink anything at all?"

"Sure, he nurses a club soda for the entire time he's here."

What did it say about her as a daughter that she didn't know this pertinent fact about her father? Not much, that's what it said.

CHAPTER FORTY-FIVE

It was a snowy day in the weeks leading up to Christmas when Edna and Hal walked into the rescue. Debbie was unable to contain her surprise. Or her hopeful expectations. The rescue wasn't a place one came to browse. Usually, someone left with a cat or a dog.

The two of them looked around the place.

"I've never been in here before," Edna said. She wore a parka and a brown knit hat with a pom-pom on top of it.

"Me neither," Hal replied.

"It's so bright, and I love the colors," Edna said.

"Yep. And it doesn't smell too bad."

Edna scrunched up her nose. "You're right, it doesn't."

Debbie walked over to greet them. "I'm so happy to see you here."

"We're only here to take a look," Edna said. "We make no promises."

"Understood."

"And Edith might stop in. She's thinking of getting a cat," Edna told her.

"That would be great. We have quite a few up for adoption. Let her know that the kittens go quick at Christmastime, but we do have some older cats."

"I think she'd prefer an older cat."

"Let me give you a tour of the place," Debbie said. She led the two of them around, showing them the rooms and the state-of-the-art equipment.

"It's so clean," Edna noted.

"We try."

As she led them to the kennels, she explained the adoption process to them. As soon as she opened the doors to the kennels, the volume increased as all the dogs vied for attention.

"Oh my goodness, look at them," Edna said. She placed her hand on her heart. "The poor things."

"You'd want to take them all," Hal added.

"You sure would."

That was a universal feeling among people who loved animals, Debbie thought. Even though Edna had never had a pet, maybe she was an animal lover at heart and had never realized it. Sometimes, life worked out in beautiful ways.

They went from kennel to kennel, looking at each dog and studying the accompanying bio.

Hal stopped at Quint's kennel. Unlike the other dogs, who stood at the doors of their kennels barking for attention, Quint remained in the corner, curled up, and watched them with disinterest.

Hal frowned. "What's wrong with him? Is he sick?"

Debbie grimaced. "No, there's nothing physically wrong with him. I think he's given up on adoption. He's our longest resident. He's been here two years."

"Two years!" Edna said, aghast.

"That's awful," Hal added. "He's a good-looking dog."

"He is. He has a sweet temperament, but no one seems to want him." It broke Debbie's heart.

"That's criminal," Hal said.

They lingered for a bit at Quint's kennel before moving on to Spotty next-door.

Edna peered down her nose through her glasses and read the bio.

"It says here that Spotty is 'loaded with personality.' I like that."

Debbie decided full disclosure was required. "Um, just so you're aware, Spotty has some weird habits."

"I'm a little weird myself, so that's all right." Edna bent down and reached out to pet Spotty through the door. The dog wagged his tail. "Hello, pooch."

"Hold on, Edna, what kind of weird habits?" Hal asked.

"He barks at different things for no reason," Debbie said.

Edna frowned. "Don't all dogs bark?"

"Spotty barks at unusual things. Like the wall. And he barks along with Barry Manilow."

"That's all right. But does he like Johnny Mathis?" Edna asked.

Debbie shrugged and smiled.

As Edna fussed over Spotty, Hal returned to Quint and knelt down. "Come here, boy." It took several attempts but eventually, Quint stood and slowly walked over, his head lowered and his tail wagging tentatively.

"What's going on here, boy?" Hal asked, and he reached in and petted him. Quint nuzzled his hand. Hal looked up at Debbie and said, "There's nothing wrong with this dog." His tone was one of outrage.

"I know, Hal, I can't explain it either."

Edna looked over at Quint. "I can't adopt two dogs, Hal. That would be impossible."

"You take Spotty, and I'll take Quint," he suggested.

Edna clapped her hands and crowed, "That's perfect!"

The dogs were gathered up, folders containing pertinent information were handed to Edna and Hal, and as they walked out of the building with Spotty and Quint, Debbie called out after them, "Merry Christmas!"

"And to you as well," Hal said.

"Ta-ta," Edna said. As the door closed behind them, Edna looked down at Spotty and said, "Now let's go home and put on some Johnny Mathis."

Chapter Forty-Six

With ambivalence, Debbie carefully drove over to her parents' home for Christmas dinner. The holiday meal was always served at one sharp, so she left her house at twelve thirty to get there a few minutes early. It wasn't as if her mother would need any help. The menu always consisted of the same thing: chicken pot pies and either a Sara Lee cheesecake or a Pepperidge Farm cake. If her mother was in a good mood, she'd trot out that tired line about how a chicken pot pie was a turkey dinner all rolled into one.

She loved how quiet the roads were. It was always like this on Christmas Day. She'd gone earlier to the shelter to check in on the animals, feed them, and walk the dogs. There'd been a foot of fresh snow that forced her to drive slower than normal. Ahead of her, a lone plow, lights flashing, drove along one side of the road, its six-foot blade pushing snow off the road and dumping it along the curbs.

There were lights on in the front window of the house on Clover Drive. She parked in the driveway behind Darren's truck. There was no sign of Dawn's car. She sat there for a moment, staring at the clock on the dashboard and doing some quick math in her head, trying to figure out exactly how long she'd have to stay before she could head over to the Cook's house without appearing to be rude. Finally, she sighed, gave up, and stepped out onto the snowy driveway. The snow was light and fluffy and dispersed like powder as she trekked to the side door, her hands full of bags of gifts and a couple of desserts she'd brought.

When she opened the side door, she was hit with heat and the smell of something wonderful. The pot pies must be ready, she mused.

Darren appeared and said, "Do you need a hand?"

She nodded and handed him the red velvet cake she'd bought from Coffee Girl. "Merry Christmas."

"Merry Christmas." He relieved her of the bakery box and one bag of gifts. He peered into the bag and said, "Are these all for me?"

"Ha-ha."

She stepped into the kitchen and her mouth fell open. The electric roaster she'd dragged down from the attic had been pulled out of its corner and stood next to the counter, its cloth cord trailing across the countertop to the socket.

Her mother stood at the stove, pouring a bag of frozen peas into boiling water and reaching for a bag of frozen corn to pour into another pot.

On the counter next to the stove were two boxes: one of Stove Top stuffing and one of instant mashed potatoes.

"Merry Christmas, Mom," Debbie said.

Without turning around, Darlene said, "Merry Christmas, Debbie."

Jerry sat at the kitchen table, watching Darlene. Debbie leaned over and kissed his forehead. "Merry Christmas, Dad."

"Merry Christmas, honey."

She turned back to her mother, who was reading the instructions on the box of stuffing. "Mom, what's going on?"

"Huh?" Darlene poured the contents of the box into a large Pyrex bowl and measured out some butter and hot water, adding them to the bowl.

"Are you cooking?"

Darlene paused, one hand on her hip. "Now, Debbie, I consider you a reasonably intelligent woman. Isn't it obvious what I'm doing?"

"Yes, but—"

Her mother waved her away and put the stuffing bowl in the microwave, then checked the vegetables cooking away on the stove. "I decided this year I wanted to do a turkey for Christmas, but then I changed my mind and decided on roast chicken. I've cooked two and that should be plenty."

"I love roast chicken," Debbie said. *Who didn't?*

Her mother put a hand up. "Now, it's been a long time since I've cooked a roast, so I make no promises."

Darren snorted. "I'll say."

Darlene shot him a withering glare, and he shrank in his seat and muttered, "I'm sure it will be fine."

"Can I do anything to help?" Debbie asked, touched by the effort her mother was making, not wanting to examine too closely whether it was a positive sign or simply a random impulse. Being Christmas Day, she opted to think it was the former.

"I've got everything under control," Darlene said, "but I suppose we should eat at the dining room table."

There was stunned silence all around, but Darlene took no notice.

"Do you want me to clear the table off? Set it?" Debbie asked, hopeful.

"Yeah, that would be good." With a scowl, Darlene looked at her husband and son. "And these two clowns can help. Darren, put your phone down for a little bit and give us a hand."

Reluctantly, he laid his phone on the table and stood. "Come on, Dad."

"And be careful, don't break anything," Darlene called after them.

With their help, Debbie managed to clean off the dining room table and chairs, piling the stuff against a far wall so nothing would be broken. She found a tablecloth in the bottom drawer of the china cabinet and shook it out and laid it over the table, going around it to make sure it was even.

She gathered silverware and plates from the kitchen. The door opened and Dawn stepped in. Her cheeks were flushed red with cold, and her nose was running.

"Merry Christmas," she said flatly.

"Merry Christmas," they all responded in unison.

"Where are the kids?" Debbie asked.

Dawn pulled off her hat, gloves, and coat. "They'll be here shortly. They're only just getting out of bed."

"Dawn, help me get this roast out," Darlene said.

"What's this?" Dawn asked. "No chicken pot pies this year?" She stepped closer to Darlene and waited for further instructions.

"I thought we'd give it a break for a year."

"I kind of like chicken pot pies," Dawn said.

"There's always someone who's going to be unhappy," Darlene huffed. "Now hold that platter while I take the chicken out."

Dawn lifted up the platter and went to reply to her mother's comment, but Debbie cut her off. "Mom, do you want me to start carrying these bowls into the dining room?" On the counter were four serving bowls with mashed potatoes, stuffing, corn, and peas.

"Yes."

She carried the bowls in two at a time. Darren, on his own initiative, filled glasses with water from the kitchen tap and set them down at the place settings on the table. In the kitchen, Dawn argued with Darlene. It finally went quiet. Maybe they remembered it was Christmas Day. Jerry came in and sat at the head of the table. Debbie took the chair in front of the window, and Darren sat next to her.

Darlene carried in the platter of roast chicken, already carved up, and set it in the middle of the table. Dawn followed, wearing a sour expression, and took a seat across from Debbie. The door opened and Dawn's two kids walked in.

"Nothing like waiting until the last minute, kids," Darlene said to them, her hands on her hips.

"Sorry, Grandma," they muttered.

"Come on then, sit down, we're ready to eat," she said, taking her seat at the foot of the table.

The kids took a seat on either side of their mother.

"Debbie, would you start passing everything around?" Darlene instructed.

They ate dinner with minimal conversation and at the end of it, when the red velvet cake was brought out and had been consumed, Debbie looked around the table, thinking, *This is my family.* She didn't feel the usual disappointment that went along with that thought. Her niece and nephew across from her were engaged with Jerry, who was joking around with them. At the other end of the table, Darlene smoked her second cigarette and seemed almost relieved that the dinner was nearly over. And next to her, Darren had his hands folded in front of him on the table. He hadn't looked at his phone once during the meal. The miracle of Christmas.

It was usually about this time that she started making excuses so she could leave and head over to the Cooks'. But for whatever reason, she lingered. In fact, she stood and announced she was going to make coffee and asked if anyone wanted one.

"No coffee for me, but I'll take a glass of Pepsi," Darlene said.

When Deb returned with a pot of coffee and her niece brought in cups and spoons, Darlene was passing around Christmas envelopes with cash in them. She hadn't bought actual gifts since her children believed in Santa Claus. As for Jerry, she'd never give him cash, but she did give him gift cards for the gas station.

Debbie sipped her coffee and thought about the Cooks; she supposed she should think about heading over there. Later that evening, she was going to Jim's, and they would be spending their first Christmas together. She'd been looking forward to that more than anything.

She looked around the table, thinking Louise was right. There was peace in meeting her family where they were at. Smiling, she picked up the carafe and poured herself a second cup of coffee.

CHAPTER FORTY-SEVEN

Darlene made her way down the driveway and got into the passenger side of Debbie's car. She'd called her the day before, asking her if she wanted to go out to breakfast. Once Debbie recovered from her shock at the invite, she said yes and told her mother she'd pick her up.

"It's so cold this morning," Darlene said. "I didn't want to get out of bed."

"Do you want to cancel?" Debbie asked.

Her mother shook her head. "Nope. Come on. Let's get this over with."

Nice.

"Wait a minute," Darlene said, looking inside her purse. "I don't have my wallet."

"You don't need it."

"I never leave the house without my wallet," Darlene said firmly. Debbie knew there'd be no going anywhere until she got the wallet.

"Where is it? I'll run in for it." She put the car in park, turned it off, and undid her seat belt.

"It's in my nightstand next to my bed."

"Why isn't it in your purse?"

"Because I always take it to bed with me."

"Why?" Debbie realized she wasn't the only one in her family with strange habits.

"Because early on in our marriage, your father used to take money out of my wallet to go to the bar."

Debbie winced. She ran into the house, up the stairs, and past the closed door of her father's bedroom. She could hear him snoring loudly behind it.

In her mother's room, she made her way around the bed to the nightstand and opened the drawer to retrieve the wallet. It was then that she noticed it: On the nightstand, next to the bed, was the framed photo of Darlene and Judy she'd given her before Christmas. Her mother hadn't thrown the photo out after all.

Back in the car, Debbie went through her routine. She pulled the seat belt over three times, back and forth, counting under her breath before locking it in. Buckled in, she reached up for the rearview mirror but did not adjust it. She double-checked that her phone was in the center console, face up. She looked in her side-view mirrors and then in her rearview mirror before pressing the keyless ignition button.

"What was that?" her mother asked.

"Huh?"

"The thing with the seat belt and the mirror."

"That's nothing, it's just my routine."

Her mother nodded and made no comment.

As Debbie drove down Main Street toward the diner at the other end, her mother passed comment on everything she saw.

"Would you look at that? Wearing shorts in this kind of weather," Darlene said. "What's wrong with him?"

Debbie glanced in the direction of her mother's gaze. The offender was a young guy, probably eighteen or twenty, and he wore a pair of shorts with sneakers and a winter coat. "He's young, he can handle it."

"He's stupid is what he is," Darlene muttered.

There was blissful silence for about two minutes. "Look at how they parked that car in front of Prime Vintage. It's almost out in the middle of the street. They probably had to take a taxi to get to the curb."

"Mom, are you going to be grumpy all morning?" Debbie asked, slightly regretting the idea of going to breakfast.

Without missing a beat, Darlene replied, "Probably. And all afternoon and evening."

Debbie smiled to herself. This was her mother. It was as good as it was going to get. She drove into the parking lot of the diner, coming to a stop near the front door.

"I'll drop you off here and park the car."

"I'll get us a booth," Darlene told her. She grabbed her purse and navigated the salted pathway to the entrance of the restaurant. Once she was inside, Debbie pulled away and went to park the car.

As soon as Deb stepped into the diner, she was greeted with the aromas of bacon and freshly brewed coffee. Her stomach responded appropriately. The Christmas decorations had all been taken down and the place looked bare. It was time to get back to normal. Although she'd had a great Christmas with Jim and was beginning to see what all the fuss was about.

Her mother waved from the back of the restaurant. Debbie walked past a long row of booths until she arrived at the last one, where Darlene was already scanning the menu.

Debbie slid into the booth, pushing her purse into the corner. She didn't take her coat off yet. It was cold outside.

The waitress didn't stop as she sailed by, asking, "Coffee to start?"

Debbie nodded. "Please."

"Pepsi for me," Darlene said.

"Anything look good?" Debbie asked, picking up the menu and glancing at the breakfast items.

"Everything looks good," her mother said. She looked up briefly. "I can't remember the last time I went out for breakfast. I used to love it. When I was young, Mom,

Dad, Judy, and I went out to eat every Sunday after church."

This surprised Debbie. She couldn't ever remember her mother going to church. For anything. Although she attended wakes, she rarely went to funerals, if at all.

"Do you think you'll start going to church now?" she teased.

"Calm down, Debbie, you're getting ahead of yourself," her mother said.

"Was that an attempt at humor?"

Darlene appeared thoughtful for a moment. "It might have been." She snapped her menu shut when the server appeared, a woman in her sixties with hair dyed an unnatural shade of red, whose name tag said *Ruby*. Once they placed their orders, Debbie attended her coffee, spooning sugar from a glass jar and opening creamers and pouring them into her cup. Her mother peeled the paper wrapper away from the straw and stuck into her glass of pop.

Suddenly it went quiet between them, and anxiety filled Debbie. She couldn't think of anything to talk about. She shifted in the booth seat and removed her coat if only for something to do. Her mother folded her hands in front of her.

Darlene came to the rescue. "It's a shame they don't let you smoke in restaurants anymore. I could really go for a cigarette."

It spurred Debbie to ask, "Have you ever thought of quitting?"

Her mother half shrugged. "I'm too old to quit. I've been smoking for over fifty years. I suppose the damage is done at this point."

"It's never too late."

"It is for me. I like smoking. I know that isn't the proper thing to say, but I do. It relaxes me."

Debbie didn't know what to say to that.

"Are you taking your inhalers?" she asked.

"When I remember."

"Do they help?"

"I don't think so."

"Dad didn't want to join us this morning?"

Darlene looked at her daughter. "Your father? You know your father, he's not a morning person. By the time he gets up, it's time for lunch."

That was true.

Ruby appeared with their breakfast and set their plates down. Debbie had ordered the Eggs Benedict, and Darlene had chosen two eggs sunny-side up, rye toast, hash browns, and bacon.

"More coffee?"

"Yes, please," Debbie said with a nod. She picked up her fork and dug in.

Her mother went quiet as she tackled her breakfast. It was good to see her attack it with gusto; it meant she had an interest in something. The silence was neither awkward nor unpleasant. More like companionable.

Debbie was halfway through her meal when she spoke up. She took a giant leap.

"Mom, I'm seeing someone, and I really like him. Would you like to meet him?"

Her mother looked at her sharply. "Aren't you afraid I'll embarrass you?"

Debbie smiled. She thought of Jim, who was so kind and who was quite smitten with her, at least according to reports. She didn't think her mother could embarrass her in front of him. Boldly, she said, "Do your best."

And with that, Darlene burst out laughing. "Challenge accepted."

Now they both laughed. Once they finished their breakfast, they pushed their plates aside, and Ruby cleared them away and topped off Deb's coffee cup and brought out another Pepsi for Darlene. They were in no hurry to leave. Darlene spoke about her physical therapy, which she was continuing, complaining about the therapist and the exercises. Debbie realized she wouldn't be her mother if she didn't complain.

As they lingered over their beverages, Darlene opened her purse, took out a small box, and slid it over the table toward Debbie. She cleared her throat and said, "That's for you."

Carefully, Debbie opened it. It was a small round amethyst on a gold chain. Her eyes widened. "Mom, it's lovely."

"That was Judy's." Darlene coughed again. "My parents gave her that for her eighteenth birthday. She didn't wear it for very long. I know amethyst isn't your birthstone, but you always seem to be wearing different shades of purple."

"Thank you," Debbie said quietly. She unclasped it and put it around her neck.

"Anyway, I wanted you to have it."

Debbie was touched by the gesture and didn't think she could talk about it without crying. And knowing that her mother didn't do tears, she asked Ruby for the bill.

Finally, they made their way out of the restaurant. When Debbie pulled in to the driveway at the house on Clover Drive, her mother hesitated as if she wanted to say something.

"Are you all right, Mom?"

"Did you want to go to breakfast again next Sunday?" Darlene asked, her expression hopeful. "Or do you have plans?"

Debbie thought of the weekly coffee mornings at the Cooks', but it was a fleeting thought. She was surprised to realize she would rather go to breakfast with her grumpy mother. She shook her head. "No, I don't have any plans."

Her mother smiled, which was nothing short of miraculous, because she so rarely did it. "That's great. I love going out to breakfast."

"Okay, Mom."

Darlene got out of the car and made her way inside. Debbie waited. Her mother did not invite her in, and she did not ask. They'd just spent a good part of the morning together. Small doses. One little step at a time. She supposed she should invite Dawn or Darren to join them. But not right now. For now, she wanted her mother to herself.

ALSO BY MICHELE BROUDER

The Lavender Bay Chronicles
The Inn at Lavender Bay
Lost and Found in Lavender Bay
Second Chances in Lavender Bay
New Beginnings in Lavender Bay
Looking Back in Lavender Bay
Sisters and Friends in Lavender Bay
Hideaway Bay
Coming Home to Hideaway Bay
Meet Me at Sunrise
Moonlight and Promises
When We Were Young
One Last Thing Before I Go
The Chocolatier of Hideaway Bay
Now and Forever
Escape to Ireland
A Match Made in Ireland
Her Fake Irish Husband

Her Irish Inheritance
A Match for the Matchmaker
Home, Sweet Irish Home
An Irish Christmas
The Happy Holidays
A Whyte Christmas
This Christmas
A Wish for Christmas
One Kiss for Christmas
A Wedding for Christmas
Audiobooks
Coming Home to Hideaway Bay
Meet Me at Sunrise

All books available in ebook, paperback, and large print paperback. Audiobooks coming soon.